Daughter OF THE GAME

TO UNDERSTAND THE ENDING, YOU MUST KNOW THE BEGINNING.

Prequel: IN THE SHADOWS

Guaranteed Paper Publishing, Inc.
12138 Central Avenue
Suite #542
Mitchellville, MD 20721

Daughter of the Game Prequel: In the Shadows

Library of Congress Control Number: 1-1598183221
ISBN-10: 0979177537
ISBN-13: 978-0-9791775-3-8

The text of this book is set in Garamond and Garamond BE SwashItalic.

Printed in the United States of America.

www.guaranteedpaperpublishing.com

Typography by: Miss Queen

Edited by: Michelle James

Substantive Editing by: Ms. Ayala

First Edition

Also by KAI:

DAUGHTER OF THE GAME

DAUGHTER OF THE GAME II:
SECRET KEEPER

DAUGHTER OF THE GAME III:
BURNING WATERS

THE LOUDEST SILENCE

~Yea, though I walk through the valley of the shadow of death, I will fear no evil: for thou art with me; thy rod and thy staff they comfort me.
Psalm 23:4

To D.J.,
For always being here, my protector and true friend.

To my father, Lawrence G. Wilson

I am always your little girl; in equal parts enamored, intrigued and overwhelmed by your life and your legacy. You remain the most brilliant, complicated person that I know—my reach of understanding always just a little too short, my learned knowledge always a little too bland.

You bestowed upon me a heritage. Memories. Entitlement. A family line tracing back to the Virginia plantation, an African American Hebrew lineage, an American story that makes so many pale in comparison.

Thank you for pouring your knowledge into me, spoon feeding it with love and reality, letting it sink down into my roots and create an unshakable foundation. My lessons were learned the hard way; for this I am grateful. They make me exactly who I am today.

You claimed me Life and named me Adorable. I wear my name like the shield you intended it to be. So appreciative that you took the time to define me, denote me special, assign me unique. As only a father can do.

They wonder from where my strength comes—it has always flowed directly from you.

Love Forever,

Aisha KAI

To my many uncles, all of whom poured into me love of family and life

Daughter of the Game

TO UNDERSTAND THE ENDING, YOU MUST KNOW THE BEGINNING.

Prequel: IN THE SHADOWS

~I'm learning that self-love is recognizing the truth and accepting it, because every person's truth is uniquely their own.

It is not up to me to judge another's truth, but, rather, to define my own truth and live by it.

If we have love for one another but our personal truths conflict, and we cannot change and remain true to ourselves, then we were never meant to be together.

We are responsible for our own choices: what we do to others and what we allow others to do to us. Pretending ignorance is unacceptable. We are solely liable for our own truth.

I must love myself enough to live by my personal truth because, ultimately, I can only answer for me.

KAI

DAUGHTER OF THE GAME PREQUEL

In The Shadows

KAI

Guaranteed Paper Publishing, Inc.
12138 Central Ave. Suite 542
Mitchellville, MD 20721

www.guaranteedpaperpublishing.com

Toxic Love

How do you stop love's rollercoaster, when there are no brakes?
How do you get off, when he won't slow down?
Steady accelerating with each loop and every dive
Spinning and shaking, twisting and turning
Transforming the thrill into a continuous nightmare
Repeating the same pattern over and over and over
Each time more exaggerated and delirious
Each time more dangerous than before
Excitement turns to dread
Adrenaline rush turns to fear
You finally realize that he can't stop
Won't ever stop
Making you sick, dizzy, nauseous
Something once so intriguing
Is now nothing more than a death trap
How do you escape?
There is no safe way out, nothing to save you
When you're finally thrown, or your heart finally gives out
When the spin finally snaps your neck, or your sanity finally breaks
Because on his ride, your death is inevitable
Accept that there is no safe escape
You have only one option
When love's rollercoaster is at its lowest point
Tuck in your chin, close your eyes, pray
Jump
And hope you survive the fall

Monique:
Trying hard to reach out
But when I tried to speak out
Felt like no one could hear me
Wanted to belong here
But something felt so wrong here
So I prayed I could break away…

~**Break Away**, *Kelly Clarkson*

Armand:
I got 99 problems, but a bitch ain't one
If you having girl problems,
I feel bad for you, son,
I got 99 problems, but a bitch ain't one.
Hit me.
~ **99 Problems,** *Jay-Z*

Insanity: Doing the same thing over and over, expecting different results.

Nothing about the game is new. Nothing about the life is new.
From generation to generation, it's all the same.
Just different players, making the same moves, expecting different results.
Insanity.

Dare to choose new path.

Daughter of the GAME

TO UNDERSTAND THE ENDING, YOU MUST KNOW THE BEGINNING.

Prequel: IN THE SHADOWS

~Whatever affects one directly, affects all indirectly. For some strange reason, I can never be what I ought to be until you are what you ought to be. And you can never be what you ought to be until I am what I ought to be—this is the interrelated structure of reality.
Dr. Martin Luther King, Jr.

TW2 - ***and so it begins:***

WE ARE THE WATERS.

YOU ARE MINE.

I AM YOURS.

AND WE ARE EACH OTHER.

FOREVER.

.

~ Prequel – In the Shadows ~

CHAPTER ONE

The Lesson

Monique, age 4
Michelle, age 6

Monique played with the frill edges of her mother's blouse, listening to the beat of her mother's heart as she sat in her lap with her head against Miriam's shoulder. Michelle sat next to them, eating a pickle, laid out on Uncle Jimmy's leather futon, her tiny legs kicking the pillows up and down. Adults were all around them playing card games in each room…folks shouting, laughing and cussing each other out.

Monique put her thumb in her mouth. She and Michelle had finally tired themselves out. They had bounced around all night—eating, playing and weaving in and out of grown folks. Her Uncle Jimmy pulled her hand away from her face as he passed, making his way back to his seat at the table.

"Who are you?" Uncle Jimmy said, pointing at Monique as he sat opposite them at a table full of men.

Pete was on his right hand side, Monty on the left. Marshall, Pete's best friend was on the other side. They were playing another game of spades. Someone was going to be fighting before it was over.

"Oh boy, Uncle Jimmy is about to start his Waters' family lesson." Miriam laughed and sat Monique on the futon next to her sister. "Anybody want another beer? Where did Lela go?" she said to no one in particular, wandering out of the room.

"You heard me, Mo Mo?"

"Uh huh," Monique nodded, her eyes big and focused on Uncle Jimmy.

All the men in her family were huge to her, with deep voices and wide hands. She had no idea why Uncle Jimmy had decided to focus on her. Again. He was always teaching her some lesson.

"I said, who are you?" His wild hair seemed to stand straight out.

"I am a Waters," Monique answered by rote memory, pushing Michelle's arm off of her. Michelle pushed back.

"What's that mean?" Uncle Jimmy sat back in the seat, his eyes on Pete's hand, which was flipping through the deck while he was shuffling. "Don't be funny with that shuffle, bro, I see you."

Pete smiled.

"Monique," Uncle Jimmy's eyes returned to her, the smile in his voice gone. "What does that mean?"

"It means I belong to you. You belong to me. Family." Her voice was flat, her eyes wondering around the room, searching for an escape. She was tired of saying this back and forth to Uncle Jimmy every time she saw him.

"We are one." Uncle Jimmy picked up the knife he was using to cut cheese, a slice still on its end. He pointed the tip at her before eating the cheese from the blade. "Me and you. Mikki and you. Me and Pete. You understand that?"

Monique didn't know what he was talking about, but he said it whenever she was over here, and she knew the answers, whether they made sense or not.

"It means that Michelle belongs to you and you belong to her. Someone do something to her, they just did something to you. Right or wrong. Don't matter. Family is always right, even when they're wrong."

Monique shrugged. "I don't know what—"

"Family always comes first." Uncle Jimmy coughed, choking on the cheese wedge.

"Even when they are dead ass wrong," Pete chimed in, a smirk on his face.

Uncle Jimmy took in a deep breath and stared at Pete through watery eyes. "Yeah, how many men have I took down for you, knowing you was dead ass wrong?" Uncle Jimmy took a swig of beer. "Whatchu trying to say?"

Pete started laughing. "I ain't saying nothing, damn Jimmy, just deal 'em." Pete sat the cards in front of his eldest brother. Monty shook his head.

"Michelle, who you?" Uncle Jimmy asked, never taking his eyes from the cards.

"I'm Waters," Michelle piped in, loud and happy, like she had been waiting for her chance to shine.

Monique wanted to pinch her for being a showoff.

"That's right, baby girl." Uncle Jimmy laughed. "That's what I'm talking about. That girl there, she got it. She is us. "

"Yeah," Pete shook his head, admiring his eldest daughter. "It come natural to her."

"Listen Monique," Uncle Jimmy looked fully at her, his entire tone shifting. Obviously he didn't think Monique had "*it*." She didn't think so either, since she never knew what he was talking about. "You are the second generation of the Waters, we are the first. You are descendent from the Freedmans, from the Portsmouth area. The plantation was the Cromwells. The land is still there. Our people are still there. But we," he pointed at Pete…"are all that's left of the Waters. My daddy's folks. Until now. You, Michelle, my seed—"

"Yeah, ain't no telling how many kids you got out there," Monty sputtered.

"Shut the fuck up!" Uncle Jimmy stood up, reached across the table and grabbed Monty by the throat, lifting him out the seat. "Don't nobody talk when I'm teaching mine about our future! You hear me? You ain't blood, boy! You ain't Waters!"

Monty pushed the thick hand, clutching at Uncle Jimmy's arm. But he didn't seem mad at all. Michelle yawned as Monique looked toward the kitchen, plotting an escape. Pete chewed on his cigar and then laughed. "Put him down, Jimmy, you need to roll a spliff and calm down." Pete laughed.

Uncle Jimmy looked at his brother and the fire immediately left his eyes. He dropped Monty back in his seat.

Monty shook his head and drank some beer. He and Pete exchanged glances. Pete nodded and Monty shrugged it off.

"Mo Mo!" Now her wild uncle was shouting and stomping his feet. "Who are you?"

It was time to stop messing around. "I'm Waters, Uncle Jimmy."

"What's that mean?"

"It means I belong to you, you belong to me."

"Family."

"Forever," Monique said, the mantra branded in her subconscious. "Waters, forever."

He stared at her for what seemed like forever. "I love you baby girl, do you know that?"

"I love you too, Uncle Jimmy," Monique said.

Uncle Jimmy took another drink of beer. "Forever…Waters."

CHAPTER TWO

The Cookout

Monique, age 6
Michelle, age 8

"Ants don't have teeth."

Monique stood next to the group of kids, all of them watching the thin line of ants marching neatly toward the anthill. She looked up and stuck her tongue out at the tallest child.

"Chew, shut up, I know that."

"You said they was going to chew up that piece of Now and Later—"

Monique stomped her white sneaker with red roses trimmed along the side of it in the dust. "No, I didn't. I didn't say they had teeth. I said they was going to eat it. You make me sick."

"Yeah, you did, Mo." Michelle laughed and pulled her little sister's braid. "That's why I broke up that piece of candy like that. You said they was going to chew it."

"No, I didn't. I hate both of ya'll." Monique stepped on the lead group of ants who were carting the Now and Laters crumb back to the hill. The group of children protested with shouts and moans. Monique smiled proudly. "Now what?"

Both Chew and Michelle stared at her, shock sprayed over their faces like a bad paint job. "What would you do that for, Mo—?" Chew started.

"You are such a spoiled brat, Mo. Always ruining something." Michelle pushed Monique. "We sat here all this time getting them ants to come this way and then you going to stomp them out?"

"I don't care. That's what you get. And you better not push me again." Monique pushed back.

"Or what?" Michelle was older than Monique but shorter than her and much smaller. "Why did you have to step on the ants just because—?"

Monique pushed past her sister to the remaining line of marching ants, who were rapidly scattering, and started jumping on them all. "There," she shouted, as she hopped over to the anthill and stomped on it, demolishing the opening. "You want a brat, now I'm a brat."

"Mo?" Chew pointed down at the ruins. "What's wrong with you?"

Monique ignored him and stared at her sister, a sinister smile on her face.

"Sometimes I can't stand you." Michelle narrowed her wide eyes. "Always ruining everything when you don't get your way."

"Next time mind your own business." Monique could smell the barbeque from the grill behind her. Her stomach growled. It seemed like they had been at the cookout all day while the grownups set up and got the grill going. She was ready to eat. Her anger at Chew and Michelle evaporated just like that, her focus changing. She wanted some food and could see her father, Pete, standing near his best friends Monty and Marshall and her Uncle Jimmy at the grill, talking and drinking beer while they flipped the food. "I'm hungry."

Groups of other men hung around, listening to music and playing cards. Most of them worked for her dad. Their girlfriends and wives were scattered at the picnic tables, all of their kids were several yards away playing football, jumping double dutch or standing there staring at Monique, pissed off at her, as usual.

Michelle pushed her from behind. Monique pushed back and stuck out her tongue. She tried to walk away; Michelle twisted her arm.

"Owww." The next thing she knew Michelle had her in a head-lock. Monique tried to elbow away from her.

"That's what you get." Chew laughed as Monique tried to push away, bent over at an awkward angle.

"Get off of me, Mikki!" The girls struggled, Monique punched Michelle in the side. "Chew, get her off me!"

"Catfight!" Chew laughed and clapped.

Monique knocked into Michelle and they both fell over. Michelle reached for Monique's skirt, she twisted out of her grasp and ran. Michelle ran after her; Chew laughing, followed behind them. His baby brother, Rodney, was far behind, running on short pudgy legs, trying desperately to keep up. "Wait Bubba," Rodney called out to Chew. Chew never looked back.

"Stop playing, Mikki!" Monique screamed, desperation dotting her face. "Get away from me." Her sister was stronger than anyone she knew; Monique pretended she didn't care but the truth was she didn't want to fight Michelle. In the middle of rumbling, Michelle could flip from playing to deadly serious; Michelle's eyes would go blank and then Monique would be fighting for her life. It had happened before. Monique wasn't fooling with her crazy older sister—she was going straight to her Daddy for help.

Michelle didn't say a word, her thin lips pressed together, chasing Monique with a sheer look of determination.

"Daddy!" Monique screamed, ducking through people and running as fast as she could to the three men that held up her entire world.

Pete looked over his brother's shoulder, making eye contact with Monique. He squinted, a small smile creeping at the ends of his lips.

Michelle was close on her heels.

Monique pushed with all her might to go faster, to get to Pete before Michelle got to her.

"Here they come," Uncle Jimmy held up his beer. "That little one of yours is hell on wheels, Petey...gotdamn!" He looked at Michelle and laughed. Even though Monique's mother, Miriam, had done Michelle's hair and squeezed her into a girly one piece yellow and white jumper with matching sneakers with daisies on them, and her face was stunningly perfect—like a brown china dolls—Michelle still managed to look wild, like a baby tiger in doll clothes.

"Michelle, leave baby girl alone." Pete called out. "And don't play by the grill."

Marshall shook his head. "Better get them from over here before they get burned."

Monique shifted sideways; Michelle grabbed at her and missed. Monique had learned some football moves from her Uncle Jimmy and they came in handy now. She pivoted her hips, slid past Michelle and ran up to Monty, who scooped her up in his arms. Uncle Jimmy reached out and grabbed at Michelle, who swung wildly at Monique. Uncle Jimmy laughed. "I love this one, Pete, she got the Waters' fire in her, for real."

"You gonna get it Mo!" Michelle huffed and puffed, her little chest poked out. "You make me sick!"

Monique arched her eyebrow and stuck her tongue out at Michelle, bold now that she was wrapped in Monty's arms.

Chew stopped a few steps away, watching the girls wrapped in the protective arms of the men who loved them.

Michelle and Monique always begged his grandmother to let him come to their family events; they always looked out for him. Chew forgot all about Rodney, who tripped and stumbled, running up the grassy hill behind him.

Monique scrambled down from Monty's arms, careful to keep her body behind his and away from Michelle. "I'm hungry, Daddy, can I eat now?"

"Naw," Pete wiped his forehead with the white towel on his shoulder. "Not yet. Hamburgers will be done in a few."

Monique stomped her foot, the white sneakers with the red roses on them getting splattered with more dust. "But I'm hungry now—" Monique started to whine, but the look on her father's face changed her tone. Sometimes it worked, sometimes it didn't. Today, it didn't look like Pete was having it. She bit her lip and looked around for another ally, someone else to get her way with. Where was her mother? Miriam would give her something to eat.

"Go on back over there with the kids," Uncle Jimmy said to Michelle. "Someone get that boy before he fall again." He was looking at Rodney, who was struggling to get to them.

"Rodney!" Michelle ran back over to him. "Chew, why did you leave him?" She was always the care taker, playing mommy and making sure that the younger ones were alright. Even taking care of Monique, although she did that out of sisterly love only. She loved Monique, but she still couldn't stand her.

Chew ran behind her. They grabbed Rodney's hand and walked back to the fields where the other kids were throwing a football. Michelle took a long band out of her pocket, looking for someone to play Chinese jump rope with.

"Go on, Mo." Pete shook his head, smiling at his youngest and most spoiled child. He followed her eyes to the table of women next to the pavilion. "You gonna wait for food just like everyone else," Pete said, and took another swig of his beer. "Don't go over there messing with your mother."

Monique ignored him, making her way over to the pavilion. "Mommy," she called.

Pete chuckled, "That one there don't listen worth a damn."

"Beautiful females never do," Monty answered, shaking his head. "That's why they run the world."

"What world?" Uncle Jimmy coughed, stroked his beard while he watched his niece walking away. "Shit, a hard head makes a soft ass, Pete. I done told you, you better get that baby girl in check before it's too late. That shit ain't cute when they grown."

"Yeah yeah yeah." Pete lifted the lid off the grill and started flipping the meat. He didn't have it in him to correct Monique, just like he didn't have it in him to so much as argue with her mother, Miriam. They both had his heart. It was simple.

"Mommy, I'm hungry." Monique bumped into Miriam's hip as she spread out the salads on the picnic table and covered them with individual platter tents.

"We are all hungry, Monique. But you have to wait to eat like the rest of us."

"Mommy!" Monique pulled on Miriam's thin waist. "Please, I didn't even eat nothing this morning!"

"You didn't eat anything this morning, not nothing." Miriam corrected. "And that was your choice!"

"Girl, give that chile some food!" Uncle Jimmy's wife, Lela, grabbed a small bowl and started scooping potato salad in it. "Where I'm from, we don't deprive no child of food." Her southern accent made Monique smile. "You want some salad, lovey?"

"Yes Auntie," Monique gave her brightest smile and scrambled up on the picnic bench.

Miriam sighed, but didn't say anything. Monty's wife Sara chuckled and shook her head before she went to get supplies. The other women nearby rolled their eyes at Monique, but she could care less.

"Here Monique," Miriam lifted her narrow body and sat her at a table near the end of the pavilion, farthest away from the men playing cards and her father at the grill. "I have to go to the car to get the rest of the coolers and ice. I don't want you listening to grown men conversation. You stay right here until I get back, understand?"

Monique nodded, eyeing the bowl of potato salad. Her mother sighed and plopped the food in front of her. "Plus, the other kids don't need to see that you are eating before them. It's not fair. You are going to wind up with no friends at all if you keep this up."

Monique started to shrug. She didn't care about having friends. She didn't need them. Michelle, Miriam, Pete and Chew were just enough. She would always have them so she would always be just fine. But she knew that shrugging might push Miriam over the line, so she just sat there.

Monique took the fork and dug into the bowl in front of her, humming to herself. She watched her mother and Lela walk away and then looked over at Michelle playing Chinese jump rope with her cousin Stacey, with Rodney watching, while Chew played football with some other boys. They seemed far away, she couldn't hear anything they were saying. Michelle was mad at her, but she would get over it. She always did. Monique glanced at the wide oak trees. It was a good day. She smiled to herself.

A shadow fell across her table, blocking the sun for just a second. Monique looked up, squinting to see the face of the man standing in front of her.

"Hola, boricua morena."

Monique looked into pitch black eyes surrounded by almond skin. The man looked pleasant, but something about his body language mad her uncomfortable. It was hot outside and he had on leather gloves. Immediately, everything felt all wrong. "Which one is your daddy, little pretty?"

Monique had been taught better. Anyone who needed to know Pete already knew him; she wasn't pointing him out. Monique shrugged.

He leaned over the picnic table and placed one gloved hand on top of hers, pinning her hand down. "That food looks good."

Fear pushed her back. He grabbed for her as she fell off the bench. Shouts rang out around her. The noise was deafening, there was more than just this one man—people were coming out of the woods. The man flipped the table over as she scrambled and crawled to the table behind her.

"Daddy!" Monique screamed. She looked toward Pete. The chaos all around her seemed to slow down time. Pete was pulling out a shot gun from behind the grill, Monty had a gun in hand shooting in front of him. Uncle Jimmy screamed, the guttural sound like a lion roaring, as he charged another man running toward him.

The family was ambushed.

Monique scrambled to her feet, her hands and knees bloody from the pavilion concrete. The man grabbed at her and his leather hand clamped around her ankle.

She screamed and twisted. He flipped her on her back. Her head hit the pavement and for a second it felt like the lights went out. His grip lessened on her ankle. Monique squirmed out of his grasp. She pushed herself over and ran in the direction of her father, her head spinning, her vision blurred.

"No, Mo, not this way." Monty let off a shot in her direction. "Run away!"

The man chasing her shouted in pain. Monique doubled back. She had no idea where to go. She spotted Miriam running toward her.

"Mommy!" She ran toward Miriam but stopped short when she spotted a man behind Miriam. "Mommy no!" He grabbed Miriam, one of his arms around her waist, the other around her neck.

Miriam screamed, swinging her arms wildly, elbowing him in the face.

Monique turned around and saw Pete cock back the shotgun and unload, the powerful explosion pushing one man off his feet and against a tree. Uncle Jimmy was fighting, in a wide armed stance, a barbershop razor in one hand, a knife in the other. Blood poured from a nasty gash in his chest. Monty was still firing shots.

Monique had no idea where Michelle and the other kids were. It was all happening too fast. The gloved man was limping in her direction. Her mother's car sprang to mind. She ran for the parking lot. Lela ran toward her, a small gun in each hand, running toward Miriam and the men.

"Get down!" Lela screamed and used her forearm to knock Monique down. Monique hit the ground and tumbled forward, her tooth tearing into her lips as tears poured down her face. She rolled into a bush.

"Stay Mo!" Lela screamed over her shoulder, running forward and firing shots in the air. "Stay there!" Lela pressed on.

Monique pressed her face flat into the grass, covered her ears with her hands, trying to drown out the shouts, the bullets, the screams.

She counted, from ninety backwards, like her Uncle Jimmy had taught her, to calm herself down whenever she was angry. She counted slowly, focusing on the numbers and making herself remember what each number looked like, as if watching it flash on a screen.

"Where is she? Little puta!" The gloved man was still looking for her, standing only a few steps away, shouting over all the noise. "He said get the girl! We don't get paid without her! Find her now!"

Monique didn't dare move. She clenched her ears tighter and focused. *Sixty seven…Sixty six…Sixty five.*

More shouts. Uncle Jimmy's screams, "Bring it. I'm Waters, fucking punks!" Monique opened her eyes and watched her favorite uncle through the leaves. Saliva flew from his mouth and the muscles in his arms were bulging, as he shouted, "You can't do nothing to me! Bring it you fucking cowards! I ain't afraid to die!"

She wanted to run to him. Uncle Jimmy could keep her safe. He was huge. He could protect them all. But she knew better. Uncle Jimmy didn't play games with her, he would be mad at her if she disobeyed Lela and he found out. So she lay there, blood and tears running into her mouth, surging down her throat, the taste of salt and iron making her gag. She stifled back the coughs. *Forty Two…Forty One…Forty.*

The gunshots stopped. Screams filled the air. It was Lela screaming. Monique didn't hear Uncle Jimmy anymore. She already knew the worst had happened, without looking up, without stopping her count. She could feel death. Maybe her daddy and Monty were gone too. Maybe Marshall. Maybe her mother. Maybe

Mikki and Chew. What if she were the only one, when she finally got to zero, who was still alive? What would she do then?

Even then, she didn't stop counting because Uncle Jimmy had told her to always finish what she started. *Twenty Four…Twenty Three…Twenty Two.* Someone picked her up by her waist. Monique balled herself up and then jackknifed, her body slamming into their gut as she tried to fight her way out of their grasp, her eyes closed. *Twenty one, Twenty…*

"I got you, baby girl," It was Monty. "We got to go." She wrapped her arms around his neck and held on as he ran to the car.

Pete pulled up along the curb and Monty threw Monique into the car and jumped in.

"That's how they want to do, huh?" Pete's voice was so loud that Monique clasped her hands to her head again and continued counting. "That's how they want to bring it?"

"Mother fuck!" Monty punched the roof of the Cadillac. "I told you! I told you not to do this thing today! I told you it was too tight right now!"

Pete screamed, "I don't want to hear that shit! You think I want to hear that right now?"

Twelve…Eleven…Ten.

"I had that bastard over my house, let him meet my family!" Pete shook his head. "Never before…I never let no one in before…and this is what he does?"

Nine…Eight…Seven.

"They was going to take my baby girl?"

Monty took a swig out of a flask. "That was the play, you saw it!"

Pete punched the steering wheel. "I'm killing them all…the entire crew! His mother, his wife! The family! They're all dead!"

"Stop at a payphone and let the team know what's happening! Get baby girl to the safe house!" Monty was flinging words in the air.

"Joni's. That's the only place they can go. Tell Marshall to take the others over Joni's. Fuck!" Pete glanced at her in the rearview. Monique was sitting in a tight ball, her hand clamped over her ears, her eyes shut. "You okay, MoMo? There's blood on you baby. Are you bleeding?"

She didn't answer. *Six…Five.*

Monty pointed his gun toward the floor, slapping the chamber out and checking the bullets. He ran his hand against the chamber, letting it circle around, listening to the clicks. "They did the big move today, Pete, firing on the annual cookout. Going for your baby girl. This is bigger than us. This had to come from the head ones…them Italians."

"Naw, not like this. It wasn't them, Monty. Those was them Ricans."

Monty tapped the dash with the pistol. "Yeah, only they would go this far man, in broad gotdamn daylight, trying to wipe out the daughter of the game. Making some kind of a statement."

One…Zero.

Monique finally opened her mouth and screamed.

CHAPTER THREE

New Waters

Her dress was beautiful. Monique twirled in a circle, watching the ripples across the smooth material. The lobby of the funeral home was small and cramped. But Monique didn't know what a funeral home was, and she liked the pretty white tile floor that sparkled and matched her white patent leather shoes. She could even make out her reflection in the dark diamonds in the center of the tile.

She was a ballerina. Monique raised her hands over her head, just like the ballerinas in the Nutcracker ballet that Pete took her to see every year at Christmas. She twirled again, bumping into Michelle.

"Stop Mo." Michelle stomped her foot. "You keep bumping me. Stop spinning around."

"I'm not spinning. I'm twirling." She knocked into Michelle again.

"You make me so sick. Stop it!" Michelle forced the words out in a harsh whisper, glancing over at her own mother, Rebe, who was standing next to Miriam. "I hate this dress, these stupid shoes…and my feet hurt."

Monique smiled. Michelle hated frilly stuff. And, as usual, Miriam had bought them matching frilly dresses in different colors.

Michelle sniffed and her eyes watered.

Monique stopped twirling. The only thing in the world that she couldn't tolerate was actually seeing Michelle cry. Michelle was her strength even when they didn't get along, even when she purposely got on Michelle's nerves.

"It's okay, Mikki." Monique patted her arm. "Don't cry."

"I don't want to be here and I told Aunt Miriam I hate this dress."

"I know." Monique stood still, noticing all the people around them for the first time. Chew and Rodney walked in with their mother and grandmother. Chew looked at her and waved, his face solemn. Monique waved back, looking at his mother and grandmother. She watched them disappear through the large doors into the other room. "Mikki, what's going on? Why are all these people here? Is this church?"

"What?" Michelle chewed on her fingernails.

"Why are we here, Mikki? It's not Sunday."

"Mo, Uncle Jimmy, remember? You always forgetting things like they never happened. You're so weird."

Monique thought for a second. She had put Uncle Jimmy's death out of her mind. It hadn't happened. He was going to come back, he was bigger than life or death. She glanced at the door.

"Mo, he's not coming back. Just like Uncle John. They gone forever."

Monique bit her lip. Waters was forever, that's what Uncle Jimmy always said. That he was there for her. That meant he couldn't be gone. Michelle didn't know what she was talking about. He was coming back one day. Uncle Jimmy wouldn't leave her.

Miriam grabbed her hand and Michelle's. "Come on, girls, let's go in."

Rebe had her arms full with Michelle's baby brother. She had been so sick with this last pregnancy and going through so much with the baby's father that Michelle had practically moved in with Miriam and Monique for the summer. "You both look pretty. Did you thank Aunt Miriam for the pretty clothes?"

Michelle sucked her teeth and looked away.

Monique pulled her hand away from her mother. "No, Mommy, I don't want to go in there."

Pete and Monty walked past. Pete whispered something to Miriam, who nodded. Rebe turned her head away, like it hurt to see Pete and Miriam talk to one another.

Miriam returned her attention to Monique. "Don't be scared Monique, we have to go in. The funeral is starting."

Saying "don't be scared" is exactly what had Monique scared. The double doors in front of them opened. Inside the huge room, down the long aisle, was a wooden box. Blood red roses lay on top of the box. The memory of trickling blood from Uncle Jimmy's wound flashed into Monique's mind. She clenched her hands. The front was open and she could see Uncle Jimmy's strong features with his dark brown skin, inside of the box.

She could hear Aunt Lela's deep sobs echoing throughout the room.

"No," Monique began to swing her arms. There was no way she was going in there. "No way, Mommy."

"Monique—"

"No!" Monique screamed, scrambling away from her mother. She bumped into Rebe, who reached for Monique, but she pushed past her.

"Mo Mo, calm down," Rebe adjusted the baby in her arms. "I know you're scared, but you have to calm down."

Tears streamed down Michelle's face. She shook her head and stepped back also. "I ain't going in there."

"Monique." Miriam had on her "*don't you embarrass me*" face. She pointed to the door, toward Uncle Jimmy.

Monique shook her head "*no*" and walked backward. Miriam pulled her forward.

"No! No! No! No!" Monique stumbled backward, Michelle was right next to her.

"Leave my baby girl alone." Pete's voice sounded like thunder. "She doesn't have to go in there. Neither of them do." Pete put his hand on Miriam's back.

"Come here!" Miriam didn't listen.

Monique stomped her foot. "No!"

"Did you hear what I said?" Pete's roar filled the tight space.

Monty fake coughed. Monique glanced up at him.

Miriam turned to face Pete, her face as tight as rubber, her grip on Monique loosening.

Monique took her opportunity to get free and snatched her arm back. She yanked with too much force and tripped over Michelle and lost her balance. She flipped over Michelle and fell backward, pushing Michelle, who tripped also over the threshold and fell. Monique bumped her head against the marble stairs as she fell, while Michelle rolled down a few steps.

***

"Come on, Mo Mo! Tell me you're alright, baby girl! Come back to me!"

Pete's voice scared Monique. She was in trouble for sure. Her head and neck hurt. So did her chest. There was no doubt that she was in trouble. The last thing Monique wanted was for Pete to be mad at her. She kept her eyes shut for a moment, but the pain in her head was too much.

"Come on, Mo—wake up baby."

Monique squinted, the splitting headache made opening her eyes painful. She was in Pete's lap, and he stared down at her with watery eyes. Michelle, of course, was right next to their father. But her dress was torn and her wild hair had escaped the neat ponytail.

"I'm sorry, Daddy."

"No apologies, baby girl." Pete's skin was ashen. "Are you alright?"

"My head hurts."

"They been through enough, Miriam." Pete rubbed his head. "You're right." He lifted Monique and stood up. "Take my girls home. Actually, get Monique to a doctor."

Miriam nodded, pulling Monique close to her. Her grip was tight on Monique's arm.

Pete nodded at Monty. He sighed. "Let's get this funeral over with."

Pete bent over to kiss Michelle on the forehead. That's when they saw the thin white woman standing at the base of the steps, holding the hand of a skinny brown boy with tangled hair pulled into a ponytail.

"Oh my God," Miriam whispered.

Monique felt Miriam's grip tighten. She glanced at her mother, who looked like she was going to be sick.

"What's she doing here?" Rebe said to no one in particular.

"Ricardo!" Michelle ran down the stairs toward the strange little boy with her arms wide open, a huge smile on her face.

Pete covered his hands with his face and exhaled.

The boy's face relaxed just a little as Michelle flung her arms around him. The boy's mother stared at Miriam with a look of fear and envy.

"Who is that?" Monique watched Michelle run away from her, and a twinge of jealousy surged through her body. Michelle shouldn't be that happy to see someone that Monique didn't even know.

Miriam breathed loudly. Contempt was etched into the lines around her eyes. "That's Pete's son," she paused, "your brother."

Miriam shook her head. "Your brother Ricardo and…his junkie mother."

CHAPTER FOUR

Pole Position

Ricardo, age 9

"I ain't stupid. He with his bitch right now. He just think that I don't know." Leslie walked past Ricardo on her way to the kitchen, a cigarette hanging from her thin lips. His young eyes stared at his mother, the closest thing to an angel on earth he had ever seen. He hated when she cursed. It didn't feel natural.

"Girl, Pete don't care if you know." Her best friend, Amy, laughed and shook her head. "Since when did he give a fuck about what you knew and what you didn't?"

Ricardo ate the last of his yogurt, scraping the bottom of the yogurt cup for every drop. This was all he was getting for dinner. It was all Leslie had bought. It was all he had eaten for the past week. A cup of yogurt for dinner. He looked forward to school, just so he could get school breakfast and lunch. But today was Saturday. So it had been toast for breakfast. A mayonnaise sandwich for lunch. And this last cup of yogurt for dinner.

It seemed like Leslie never even bothered to eat. Instead, she was always just sniffing and wiping at her nose. And drinking.

Leslie turned a grey eye toward her friend. "Fuck you."

Amy laughed even harder and shrugged. "If you want to." She snorted and nodded at Ricardo.

Ricardo rolled his eyes and looked away.

"Don't talk like that in front of my son." Leslie glanced at her son. Her face flushed in embarrassment, like it did whenever Pete or Amy were around and talked about unthinkable things in front of Ricardo.

He looked at the floor, averting his eyes to lessen her embarrassment. Her voice returned to softness.

"You finished eating, Cardo?" She put a glass on the counter and sloshed alcohol in it.

Ricardo nodded.

"Go in the back and turn on the television."

Ricardo looked back at the cupboard. He wanted at least one more mayonnaise sandwich. His stomach was turning inside out with hunger.

He heard a long inhale and glanced toward Amy. There was powder on her face. She wiped at her nose, then studied the powder on her hand and rubbed it on her gums.

"Save me some." Leslie said, throwing back the alcohol. The alcohol had released her inhibitions, she no longer cared about playing meek in front of her child. "Cardo, go to your room. Like I said."

Ricardo didn't trust Amy with his mother. Amy was one of Pete's hoes. She stayed with them sometimes, in between working. And when she did, Leslie always got in trouble with Pete. Amy would tell her things that would make Leslie insane with jealousy. Or she would do things that Leslie would join in on. Then Pete would show up and whip Leslie's ass. Ricardo didn't know why Leslie didn't see it, why she didn't stop it. Or why, at least, she didn't stay away from Amy. Ricardo understood one thing: neither he nor Leslie could control who slept at their house or who Pete dropped off there. And if Leslie dared say anything, she could easily be put out, Pete made that clear. The place where they laid their heads wasn't even home, because it could all just disappear by Pete opening his mouth and saying so.

So he and Leslie never really made it home. Just another place to sleep until it disappeared, like everything else in their existence. All dependent on a whim, on what Pete felt at any given moment.

Ricardo wished Leslie were just a little smarter.

"I know this," Leslie pointed a finger in the air, her words slurred. "I'm not just his stupid little bitch. I have his child. A son. That means something."

"Yeah." Amy eyes Ricardo enviously. "You got his son—"

"—I got his son, dammit. No one else can say that. I deserve better. Me and my son deserve better."

"Girl, hit this and relax. Pete ain't going to change. You know that. Plus, Miriam's life isn't perfect. He act like she all that, but she ain't no better than us."

"He goes home to her. She gets whatever the fuck she wants. He not always taking hoes in and out of her house, having this blow all around her precious little baby. Big headed little girl. Fuck her." Leslie threw her glass in the sink and it shattered.

"Shit," Amy jumped at the sound, but then laid back in the chair and rested her head. "You are tripping."

"Cardo, go to your room." Leslie said it with force this time. Not that he was scared in any way. No one paid any attention to Leslie's words—what was she going to do when someone ignored her? Nothing. As usual. But Ricardo finally moved off the stool when he noticed her watery brown eyes.

"But he don't look like his daddy at all." Amy's eyes were still on Ricardo. "Look like a little Puerto Rican boy."

"Why would you say that? You just looking at his color. He looks just like them. The Waters. My boy is a Waters, even if I ain't shit."

"Leslie, cut it out, girl. You are beating yourself up over nothing."

Ricardo walked out of the kitchen and into the narrow hall in front of the bathroom. He eased down to the floor, listening. He wanted to know more. He wanted to know what they were talking about.

"I had his son first, but he married her. He married her." Leslies slurred speech floated in the air.

"I know you ain't think he was going to marry you? You worked the streets for him, Les. His brothers wasn't going for that."

"Why not? He's the one who had me on the street. I did it for him. Plus, I know the real him, the streets and the gutter. She don't know the real him."

Amy shook her head. "You are so backward, I swear. That's what happens when you grow up in the country."

Ricardo heard a pause and another long inhale. Then Amy's voice: "They marry the image, not the ones in the gutter with them, Les. Knowing the real him ain't good; it means what you think of him don't matter. The woman he marries is the one whose opinion matters."

Silence. Ricardo could hear Leslie walking. "I know where they going tonight."

Amy sounded like she was in another world. "What?"

"I said, I know where he is taking her tonight. He was whispering on the phone. I heard him."

"Bitch, please stop trying to boost yourself up. Pete wasn't whispering. He don't care about hiding nothing from you! You are crazy."

"It's her birthday. He's taking her to the Charlamaine Club, over on Main Avenue. I heard them."

"And?"

"I should go over there and confront him."

"Picture that." Amy chuckled. "You confronting Pete. That happens in your dreams, right before you get stomped out."

Ricardo crawled into his room. He pulled on his pajama pants that sat on the mattress on the floor that served as his bed. Rebe, his sister Michelle's mother, had bought him the pajamas—every few months she gave him a new bagful of pajamas, underwear and socks. Sometimes he would go with Pete to visit them and Rebe always had a bag of something for him. The last time it had been these special pajamas and some toy cars. He wondered how she remembered him. Michelle had a crowd of cousins and there was always someone over her house. But, no matter what, Rebe would give him a special gift.

Rebe noticed him. He mattered to her.

Ricardo lay on his belly on the hardwood floor in his room, his pillow propped under his elbow. Toy cars surrounded him. He stared at the newest one, red with black stripes down the middle. His cousin Alonzo had taken it from the corner store, he hid it in his book bag until they walked out. Then he handed it to Ricardo with a big smile on his face.

Ricardo smiled back. Alonzo was the only other person in the world who gave him anything. He had been lucky that week, Leslie had let him stay with Alonzo and his Aunt Nellie for an entire week that time. Ricardo had never wanted it to end.

But, inevitably, Leslie showed up at the door for him. Pete had wanted to know where his son was, why he wasn't at home. So his temporary feeling of a real home had to be destroyed so he could be dragged back to the dank, empty, lonely apartment for when Pete arrived. For a couple of days a week that Pete bothered to come by.

Just as sleep claimed his body and the view in front of him became hazy, Ricardo felt a sharp jolt of pain tear through his elbow and down his side as his body was dragged up from the floor.

"Come on." Leslie's face was covered with tears, her purse was under her arm and keys were in her hand.

"Mommy, what's wrong?"

"Nothing, let's go."

"Leave the boy here, Leslie." Amy's voice was full of excitement, her eyes wide open and wired with excitement. "Why ain't you just let him sleep?"

""Cuz, I don't leave him here alone. Ain't no telling what fiend will show up at my door."

"Still," Amy shook her head, "Are you taking him to the club?"

"No," Leslie pushed forward, still dragging Ricardo, who was trying to pull away from her. Amy followed. "You going to have to come too, to stay in the car with him."

"Like hell I am. Pete ain't whipping my ass tonight."

Leslie finally let go of Ricardo's arm. "He's not going to even know you're there. I'm just going in, saying what I got to say, and leaving."

"You think I'm stupid. You think he's going to let you just walk up in there—" Amy started smiling. "I don't know why I am listening to your high ass. You ain't going to do nothing. Okay, I'll ride. 'Cuz you're going to chicken out before we get anywhere near there. "

"She need to know. Miriam needs to know that she is not the only one. And she ain't nothing special."

"What have you been drinking?" Amy chuckled as Ricardo scrambled into the back seat of the car. "You are high out of your mind."

"Mommy, I don't want to see Daddy." Ricardo wrapped his arms around the seat in front of him. "I don't want to go."

"Shut up, Cardo." Before the doors were all the way closed, Leslie was speeding off into the night.

"Mommy, stop. I don't want to go!" Ricardo screamed.

"Slow down the car, Les!" Amy was clinging to the door with both hands.

"I hate him." Leslie shouted out into the night, not hearing her son or Amy. "I hate him. That should be me. It should be me." She punched the steering wheel."

"Mommy!" Ricardo wailed as they drove through a red light.

"Pull the damn car over!" Amy shouted, "I can't catch no charge fooling with you, you going to get us put in jail."

"Pete fucking Waters. Damn Waters think they are everything. He promised me. Anything he said do, I do. And he marries her."

"CPS gonna take Cardo if they catch us! Les, slow down. They will put his ass in foster care!" Amy screamed.

Those words sunk in, Leslie slowed down from hyper speed to regular speeding. She still blew through the lights.

In minutes they were pulling into the lot.

"This is a bad idea." Amy's eyes were watering as she dug around in her purse. "Let's go to Doug's house. He is having a house party, Cardo can sleep upstairs with his kids. It will be better, Les. Men are there. Take your mind off Pete. Get some paper."

Leslie rolled the car through the parking lot. She honked the horn. A tall dark brown man was leaning against a Cadillac with his hands deep in his packets, two men were standing in front of him. All three looked back at Leslie's tiny car.

She rolled down the window. "Marshall."

Marshall did a double take, as if he were seeing a ghost. He jogged over to the car. "Les, whats up?" His steady glare absorbed all the information he needed to know. Ricardo watched his eyes raked over Leslie and Amy, assessing the situation. "What are you doing out?"

"I know Pete is here." Leslie tried to open the door.

Marshall shut it closed. "What do you think you are doing?"

"Fuck him, Marshall. I want him to see his son. To remember his family."

"What?" At that moment, Marshall's eyes searched the back seat. Ricardo leaned forward and met eyes with the man his father always brought over to the house. "You got Pete's son out here? At 2 in the morning?" Marshall slammed the door again and pushed down the lock. "Go home."

"No!" Leslie pressed on the gas and the car hopped forward.

Marshall jumped back, still shouting into the window. "Don't do this, Leslie. Not tonight. Take your ass home."

"No!" Leslie screamed and laid on her horn.

Marshall shook his head and shrugged. "You're creating a situation I got to handle. Because you got that boy in the car." He walked next to the car as it rolled in the parking lot. "Don't make me do this. Take your ass home now."

"Tell him Cardo is out here. Bet he come out then. Bet he come for his son. Fuck me, huh?"

Marshall looked at one of the men that were near his car. Ricardo saw the guy nod and head for the club. Ricardo's stomach balled into a tighter knot. Ricardo had seen Pete knock Leslie into a wall so hard that her forehead split open and bled. He had seen Pete press the tip of his gun against her cheek, while she cried, telling her to lick the steel. Ricardo had listened to Leslie suck off strange men in their living room while Pete fucked her, because Pete said so.

Ricardo, more than anyone else, knew that once Leslie was no more useful, Pete was cold enough to easily discard her. And then they would both be in trouble.

"Mommy, please....please...I want to go home."

Amy threw herself out of the car as it rolled along.

"What the hell?" Leslie slammed on the brake. "Where did she just go?"

Ricardo peeked out of the rear view. Amy was slowing standing up, wiping bits of gravel from her arms. She began to limp away from the car, glancing back.

"Amy, I see you. Get your ass back in the car." Marshall called out. "Don't leave her in this alone. You was in on it."

Amy shook her head, walking away. There was a crowd now, people hanging around the outside of the building were focused on them, on the scene Leslie was making.

"Leslie," Marshall turned his attention back to Ricardo's mother. "You're high. You're not thinking straight—"

"What the fuck—?" The voice that terrified Ricardo carried over the baseline of the music and Pete was standing in the doorway, his eyes taking in the scene.

"Shit!" Marshall shook his head and turned away. "Pete, she is tripping off something."

"You got my son out here?" Pete's voice seemed to rumble like thunder.

Leslie was suddenly speechless. Of course. Ricardo slid back onto the floor into a tight knot.

"Les, you got my boy out here?" Pete walked over to the car.

"Mommy—" Ricardo pleaded.

Leslie put her foot on the gas pedal too late, Pete had already reached through the window, his huge body leaning into the car, both hands around Leslie's throat. "You stupid bitch. You do this to me? You bring my seed to the club in the middle of the night?"

"No," Leslie gasped for air, "I needed to see you. I just needed to tell you—"

Pete shook Leslie back and forth like a rag doll. Leslie's foot hit the pedal. The car rolled forward, almost hitting Pete. He shouted in agony as the bumper scraped his hip.

In seconds, he had pulled Leslie from the car and was beating her in the parking lot. Marshall leaped into the car and slammed it into park. Pete punched and kicked Leslie. A few people in the crowd protested, but not too many and not too loud. Ricardo ran to his mother, throwing his thin body on top of her.

Pete paused, pushing Ricardo to the side. Marshall's girlfriend Tina grabbed Ricardo into a hug, turning him from the scene in front of him, shielding her body with his. Ricardo struggled but then stopped, tears of rage blinding him.

"Stupid bitch," Pete yelled as he landed one more kick.

"Get out of here." Monty appeared out of thin air, pulling Pete away from Leslie. "They called the po-po. You got to go."

"My son." Pete looked around for Ricardo.

"I got him," Marshall said, pulling Ricardo's thin body from Tina's. "Just go. Ricardo can stay the night with my sister. He will be alright."

Pete nodded.

Ricardo looked around. The crowd was eyeing him with pity, shaking their heads at him. He felt ashamed. Ricardo pushed away from Marshall and ran to his mother who lay unconscious on the ground.

"Mommy—"

"We got to go," Marshall pulled at Ricardo. He was too little, he twisted away from the large man's grasp. He wasn't leaving his mother.

"Come on, baby." One of the women who was standing in the lot grabbed his hand. Ricardo recognized her as another woman who was always visited with Marshall. "Come on and go with us. Your mommy will be okay. The ambulance is coming. Do you hear it?"

Ricardo didn't answer.

"Fuck this." Marshall picked Ricardo up and carried him to another car. He sat him on the lap of one of the three women in the back seat. Ricardo didn't want to cry, he wanted to be a man. But he stared through the window, looking at his mother's thin figure lying on the ground, and silent tears poured down his face.

Tina patted his hand and climbed out of the car. "I will stay with her, okay?"

All Ricardo could do was nod before Marshall sped off into the night.

Twenty minutes later, they were standing at someone's front door. A mocha colored woman opened the door. Marshall talked softly to her, repeating the story, and Ricardo watched as she nodded her head and clicked her tongue. But she didn't look at him with pity. He was embarrassed, although he didn't know why. He felt ashamed and he didn't know why. Somehow, this was all his fault, although he didn't know why. Thinking about his mother all alone on the pavement terrified him.

The woman put her hand up to Marshall to silence him. "Stop, don't tell me anymore." She took Ricardo by the hand and led him into the house. "Don't say nothing else about that woman in front of her son, Marshall. You know better."

"It ain't my fault, why are you mad at me, Theresa?" Marshall asked.

"Because, what does being with the Waters bring you? Nothing but bad karma."

Marshall sat in the living room. "Yea, and money to furnish this house."

She shook her head again.

Marshall looked at Ricardo. "Make yourself comfortable."

Theresa sat Ricardo at the kitchen table instead. "I bet you're hungry."

Ricardo shook his head "*no*."

"Well, I will warm something up, just in case you change your mind." Theresa turned on the radio on low and began taking out food and heating it up. Ricardo's eyes were as big as two saucers staring at the meal she was preparing.

"When the last time he ate?" she called out to her brother.

"Damned if I know." Marshall pointed at him. "They both skinny like that, though."

Theresa patted Ricardo's arm. "Ignore him. You're going to be tall and lanky. You are a handsome young man."

The phone rang. Marshall answered it. "Yeah, he here. I got him, Pete. Naw, I don't know, they probably took her to the hospital…I know, I know."

There was a pause. "Okay, I will bring him now."

The woman stopped moving "Like hell you will." She grabbed the phone from her brother. "Pete, this Theresa. Let this boy stay the night and get some sleep. I don't know what he saw, but he look like he's been in a war. Let him rest."

Ricardo had never heard anyone talk to Pete like that. He stared in wonder as she said, "I really could care less. This boy stays here.

Send them over to get him tomorrow. Better yet, I will call you tomorrow to tell you how he is doing. He can stay the weekend."

She shook her head. "No, I'm not hearing that. You won't let the boy stay? Now you're trying to offend me?" There was a long pause. "He's around the same age as my son, Pete. He will be fine. Let him stay." She nodded, made a "hmph" sound and handed the phone back to her brother, who chuckled into the phone at something Pete said. "Yeah man, she's one of a kind."

Theresa turned around and shot her brother a look. "Don't talk about me with me standing right here."

Marshall laughed. "You know she's still talking." He shook his head. "About that other thing…" he headed into another room.

She noticed Ricardo staring at her and removed the scowl from her face. She smiled at Ricardo and placed the plate of warm food in front of him. Ricardo looked down at the plate of baked chicken and rice with spiced apples. She placed a mug of warm cocoa in front of him and stuffed the top with marshmallows. "You like chocolate?"

Ricardo nodded. He sat very still. He didn't want to do anything wrong. Theresa handed him the fork. "Relax yourself, child. There is always calm after a storm. You're okay here." She observed him. Ricardo noticed that her eyes were kind. He trusted her.

"Ma." A boy about Ricardo's age was standing in the kitchen door, sleepily eyeing Ricardo. "Ma, what you cooking?"

"Armand, it's too late for you to eat anything else tonight." She chuckled. "Anytime you smell chicken, here you come. So greedy." Theresa pointed to Ricardo. "This is Ricardo. He's staying the weekend with us."

Armand rubbed his eye. "Okay." He gave Ricardo a small pound. "Hey."

Ricardo only spared his hand for a second to receive the pound, then he turned back to the food.

Theresa smiled. "Go to bed. Make sure there is a clean pillow case on the bottom bunk, I already changed the sheets. Ricardo is going to sleep in the bottom bunk."

"Okay." Armand started wandering down the large hallway.

"And put out some clean pajamas for him, Army."

"Okay, okay."

Armand disappeared behind one of the large oak doors, while Ricardo ate and stared at Theresa. Marshall reappeared and sat on the couch facing the television.

Ricardo wondered about Leslie, he was actually sick with worry about her. He was sure she was dead, by the way she was laying on the pavement. And no one spoke of her, making him wonder if he would ever even know whether or not she had died. But some part of him wondered, if she was really dead, or when Pete finally killed her, whether he would be able to come back here, to live in the cozy house with the first real normal family he had ever seen.

CHAPTER FIVE

Real Family

Ricardo, age 9
Armand, age 8

Ricardo stared at the bathroom, during the couple of minutes that Theresa left him alone to get towels. The tub was its own playground. There was a net against the back wall, filled with boy toys, cars, sponges and tub paints. And just above it was another net, filled with dolls, ponies with pink hair and sea shells. The bathroom was covered with colors, pink and blues, reds and greens. Different types of soaps and scrunches lined the shelf above the tub.

Theresa returned, turned off the water and laid out fresh towels on the sink. "Alright son, get a warm bath while I check to make sure your bed is okay. Army went right back to sleep and I know that boy didn't do a thing I told him."

Ricardo just stood there.

Theresa looked over at him. "Are you okay?"

He nodded, his eyes full of tears.

"Of course you aren't okay. Not yet. But you will be. I promise." Theresa wrapped him in a warm hug before she stepped out of the bathroom. "Get in the tub," she said through the door. "It's late, so you won't be in there too long. I will be right back."

Ricardo could hear her house slippers on the wooden floor as she walked away. He stripped off his dirty pajamas and climbed into the tub. The sudsy water smelled good. When he leaned back he noticed the stars on the ceiling, glowing down on him.

He felt another type of pain. Longing. Why did everyone else have so much more than him? Why didn't his mother buy him anything for the tub, or make their bathroom special. The answer was right there in the front of his mind: because her every waking thought was about how to hang on to Pete. Ricardo and everything else in Leslie's life was secondary to pleasing Pete. That's why he was in a stranger's home right now, while she lay beat up in a parking lot somewhere, because of her pursuit of Pete. And while he lay in this tub, wondering about his fate, Ricardo knew, without doubt, that if Leslie was alive, he probably hadn't even crossed her mind. Instead, she was somewhere begging Pete's forgiveness, trying to get back into his good graces.

Ricardo shook his head. He didn't want to think about his mother like that. It wasn't right. It wasn't her fault that Pete treated her like he did. It wasn't her fault that Pete had her strung out.

Ricardo was all Leslie had. He would show her a better life. He would fix things one day. He faded to sleep in the tub, thinking about making life better for Leslie.

Theresa pushed open the door. "Child, don't fall asleep in that tub. The last thing I need is for you to mess around and drown up in here." She pulled him from the tub and wrapped a towel around him. She dried him off and helped him into fresh pajamas. They took a few steps down the hall into Armand's bedroom. The room was big, with a bunk bed against the far wall, next to the desk and dresser. Ricardo tumbled into the bottom bunk. Theresa left the door cracked open as she walked away. Ricardo watched her shadow fade away and then sleep overtook him.

***

More people lived here than Theresa and Armand. Ricardo heard voices fade in and out all around him. Armand's voice, then Theresa's. Then a young girl's voice cracked his dreams. He tried to open his eyes, but his body felt like he had been beaten with a bag of nickels. So he turned over and covered his head with the blanket. That led to the older woman's voice, fussing, clearing out all the noise. Then quiet.

When Ricardo finally woke up, the sun was going down. He felt disappointed when he came to, disappointed that he was returning to life. Sleep was where he could hide from the truth.

"Damn, boy, you finally waking up?" Armand was sitting on a bean bag in the middle of the room, facing the television against the wall with a game controller in his hand.

Ricardo just looked at him.

"You slept all day. Me and my uncle went fishing and everything." Armand shook his head. "We was going to take you, but my mom said to let you sleep."

Ricardo didn't know what to say to that. He yawned. He really wanted to go back to sleep. "You went fishing?"

"Yep." Armand leaned back in the bean bag. "How you know my uncle?"

There was something in the way he said it. Something territorial. Ricardo didn't understand it. "I don't." Ricardo didn't answer questions about who he did and didn't know. Pete didn't allow that.

Armand looked away from the television. He fixed his gaze on Ricardo. "What you mean?"

Ricardo shook his head. "Your uncle knows my dad." That was all he was going to say.

"Oh." There was a few minutes of silence as they both watched the screen. "Are you okay?" Armand pointed at Ricardo's skinny arm. There were black and blue marks up and down it.

Ricardo rubbed it. "Yeah."

"Are you hungry?" Armand put down the controller. "My grandma said to make sure you eat."

Ricardo was starving. He jumped out of the bed. "Yeah, but I got to go to the bathroom."

Armand nodded. "Come on."

They headed down the hall together, Ricardo a step or two behind Armand. He went into the bathroom as Armand ran his hand along the wall on his way to the kitchen. Armand was nodding his head, his fingers tapping out a beat on the wall.

When Ricardo entered the kitchen a few minutes later, a light brown, slightly older, female version of Armand was standing at the table with an apron on, stirring a wooden spoon around in a big bowl. An older woman sat at the table, her head buried in a huge cookbook, and spices and ingredients were all over the table.

"Who are you?" The girl's high voice forced Ricardo to look directly into her large light brown eyes. She turned to the woman. "So Army can have company over but I can't? That's not fair. He is the one on punishment—"

"Hush up, Camilla." The older woman smiled at him. "You must be Ricardo. Are you hungry, baby?"

Ricardo nodded.

"Of course you are, you been sleep half the day. You missed them going fishing."

A door slammed and a second later, Armand's head appeared in the kitchen from the back porch. "You want to see what I caught?"

"Boy, don't no one want to see them dirty fish. Nothing but sun fish. I done told Marshall to throw them back—"

"No Grandma, they aren't all sun fish. Please, you gotta clean them for us. We gonna fry them tomorrow."

"I'm having fish tomorrow," their grandmother snorted. "But it ain't going to be no radioactive fish from out of a pond around here."

Camilla snorted. "I am not cleaning fish."

"Yes, you are, too." Armand let the screen door close, but his voice was still clear. "Uncle Marshall said you have to."

Camille went back to stirring the bowl, her lips set in a defiant frown.

Grandma started making a plate of food for Ricardo, who just stood in the middle of the room, lost in all the conversations happening around him.

Armand reappeared. "Come on." Armand nodded at him. Ricardo stepped onto the back porch and looked down into a bucket, filled with live fish furiously swimming in a circle.

Ricardo jumped back.

Armand laughed. "You ain't seen fish before?"

"Yeah, I have." Ricardo smiled a little, peeking back into the bucket. The smile felt foreign on his face. "I just didn't know you actually had them here like that. When did you go?"

"This morning. Real early. Left right when the sun came up." Armand moved over to the corner. "Look at this. It's the bait." In another small bucket there were worms. Ricardo moved back. Armand laughed. Then he held up a can and moved the lid back, holding it low so Ricardo could see the crickets jumping around.

Ricardo was impressed.

"Army, you better not let none of them crickets loose. Bring that boy back in here to eat. Lay newspapers out on the floor."

Ricardo went back in the kitchen, leaving Armand to prepare for cleanng the fish.

He sat down to eat. He watched Camilla adding ingredients as her grandmother measured them and listened to the back and forth of their easy conversation. Ricardo was enjoying himself. When he was done eating, he sat on the back porch with Armand and Camilla, catching the fish out of the bucket and watching them flop around on the newspaper until the fight finally left them. Then the three of them scaled the fish, scales flying through the air and landing all over the place. Ricardo was impressed that they didn't cut themselves. When they had cleaned the scales off, they put them in another bucket for their grandmother to filet them.

She sent them to the bathroom one by one. Another long hot bath for Ricardo. More food. Armand disappeared in his room to play video games, while Ricardo, Camilla and Grandma watched television and snacked on popcorn. Ricardo felt so warm and comfortable that he fell asleep on the couch, his body leaning into Grandmas. He didn't even wake when Marshall entered the house later on to find them all asleep and put him back in the bottom bunk bed in Armand's room.

It was still dark outside when Ricardo was awakened. He heard a soft angel calling his voice and shaking his shoulder. Ricardo missed her. Leslie. His mother. She was alive. He sat straight up when his brain realized that it was her voice he heard.

"Cardo," she sat on the bed next to him. "Hey baby."

A deep relief swept across his body like a tidal wave threatening to drown him out. All the terror he had felt over the last two days that had been bottled deep inside of him released itself.

"It's okay," she whispered into his curly hair as she hugged him. "Don't cry, Cardo. I'm sorry. I'm so sorry."

After a few minutes, she gathered him out of the room. He glanced up at Armand, who was sound asleep. Theresa was standing at the bedroom door. The three of them made their way to the front door.

Ricardo noticed that Leslie's light skin was marked black and blue and she had huge bruises around her mouth. He watched Theresa talk to her in hushed tones, watched his mother nod, keeping her eyes lowered, like she was embarrassed.

It made Ricardo angry, that his mother was less than Theresa, that she couldn't even meet her eyes.

Theresa kissed him on the forehead and told him that he was always welcome. She hugged Leslie and told her to remember what they had discussed, to know that she had help if she ever wanted it. Ricardo knew, deep in his gut, that he would never see her again. Or Armand, with the carefree life, and bunk beds, and video games in his room and an uncle who took him fishing on the weekend. He would never again see the pretty brown eyed girl who smiled and giggled at him, pretended to pout to get her way, cooked cakes with her grandmother, mixed peanuts in her popcorn and fell asleep at the beginning of movies. He knew, by the way Leslie moved, that she didn't feel worthy of the company of this woman and would avoid them and, because of that, he would never see them again. Some part of him felt a little sad. Ricardo thought of his sister, Chanel, who he never saw anymore. She lived with her godmother. Chanel wasn't Pete's child, so Leslie left her. She told Ricardo his baby sister was with a family that could take care of her, but Ricardo knew that it was because she wasn't Pete's child. As Ricardo looked out of the window, he realized that he had been hoping that she would leave him too, like she had done Chanel, with a better family. But he belonged with Leslie, in their dingy apartment with their empty refrigerator. He didn't belong in a big house with back porches and buckets of fish, large yards and driveways and uncles and parents and grandparents.

Theresa stood by the door and watched them walk to their car. Ricardo climbed in the back seat. He looked at Theresa as Leslie started the car. She waved goodbye. He waved goodbye back. He was glad to have his mother, but something deep in him ached. Ricardo sat back in his seat and looked straight ahead. While they rode home in silence, he forced himself to forget everything that had happened over the last couple of days, including everyone in Marshall's family.

CHAPTER SIX

Children First

Monique, age 7
Michelle, age 9

Monique hadn't seen her father in two days. She sat on the edge of the bed, bored with the inside of the hotel room.

"There is nothing to do, Mommy. We been here too long, I want to go home."

"Go to sleep, Monique." Miriam's voice was muffled by all the pillows around her head. Michelle was in the other bed, her wild hair having escaped the barrettes, pouring over the sheets like an untamed thicket.

"I can't." Monique watched the movie channel, but she couldn't focus. Something was wrong. She kept having dreams, bad dreams, about the man who had grabbed her hand. About Pete. About Uncle Jimmy. Especially about Uncle Jimmy. How he had roared, looking like the lion that she always thought he was.

"Where is Uncle Jimmy?"

Miriam sighed and sat up. "Monique, baby girl, come on and get in the bed. Go to sleep."

"When is Uncle Jimmy coming to get me?"

Miriam pulled Monique under the sheets. "Uncle Jimmy is gone, Monique. He isn't coming back. He is in heaven."

Monique hated when Miriam said that. And she didn't understand what that meant. No way was her wild Uncle Jimmy getting into the fluffy white clouds of heaven with white baby angels all over the place, like the paintings Monique had seen. The statement made no sense.

"Where is Daddy?"

"I don't know, Monique. He is keeping us safe, okay?"

"But why? Why does he have to keep us safe? What did we do?"

"We ain't do nothing, Mo Mo," Michelle's tiny voice floated through the air. "They want to hurt Daddy by hurting us. So we got to stay here, so no one will hurt us."

Miriam shook her head, her eyes full of tears. "You are both too young for this." She drew in a deep breath. "This is too much."

Monique had heard her mother say that before, anytime she was about to put Pete out. That was the last thing she wanted to hear. Her mother wasn't nice, she wasn't sweet and kind to anybody when Pete left them. Everything felt empty when Pete wasn't there. Monique decided to shut up, to pretend that everything was okay, so Miriam wouldn't start a fight with Pete.

"I'm okay Mommy," Monique rolled out of the bed and climbed into the bed with Michelle, who refused to move. "Move over Mikki, gosh!"

They lay in the small room, the sounds from the movie filling the room. Before long, Monique could hear Michelle's heavy breathing. A few minutes later, Miriam's light snore filled the air. Monique was left alone in the dark.

She hummed along with the movie theme song, when it finally ended. Then she sipped on her mother's soda, which she was never allowed to drink. It didn't take long before her bladder was full. Monique slid out of the bed and padded her way down the narrow hall to the bathroom opposite the closet. Her father always made them stay in this same room, in this same hotel. Anyone who broke through the door would have to come down the hallway, giving Miriam time to protect them.

Monique tiptoed into the bathroom, the cold tile stinging her toes. She sat on the toilet and tinkled, then cleaned herself up, careful to wash her hands. Monique tiptoed back down the long hallway. The door behind her flew open, hitting the wall.

Monique stumbled backward, "Mommy!"

Pete stumbled into the room, his huge body leaning into Monty's, while Marshall held his arms up. Monique's eyes trailed down from Pete's arm to the blood trickling from his side.

"Miriam, where you at?" His raspy voice caught as he stumbled into the wall. Monty grabbed him.

Monique stepped back. Her eyes followed the trickle of blood from his side to his hands to the wall.

Miriam flipped out of the bed and was in front of her instantly. "Oh my God, Pete, what happened?"

"Nothing." His speech was slurred and slowed.

"You're drunk."

"Nope. Stop asking stupid questions…and help me…damnit." Pete pushed Monty away and stomped toward the couch. "It hurts. I'm a man, though. Imma be alright." Pete collapsed on the couch.

Michelle sat up, wide eyed in the bed, her hair flying in every direction. "Daddy?"

"Shhh…" Pete lifted a bloody hand to his lips. "Quiet, baby girl."

"Daddy, you're bleeding!" Michelle lunged out of the bed to her father. Miriam met her halfway, stopping her and diverting her to the hallway.

Michelle pushed past her.

"Stay." Miriam's firm tone made Michelle stay put, her arms crossed and lips poked out.

"Why did you bring him here?" Miriam gathered towels from the bathroom and wet them, her shaky voice close to screeching. She looked at Marshall and Monty as she moved past them. "Why?"

Marshall shook his head. "What kind of question is that?"

"You don't want me here, I'll leave." Pete tried to stand up. "Don't need to be where I'm not wanted. I can go."

"Pete, sit down, baby." Miriam pressed a towel against his side.

Pete shouted in agony.

"Why the hell wouldn't you take him to the hospital?" Miriam glared at Monty as she wiped Pete's blood away. "Why here, when you know I have these babies in here?"

"Them my baby girls." Pete pointed a finger at Miriam. "Damn women always acting like my kids belong to them. They mine!"

"This where he said take him," Monty shrugged.

"And you actually did what he said?" Miriam shook her head and planted both hands on her hips. "Do I look like a doctor to you, Monty? What do you think I'm supposed to do? And I have these girls here. Do you think they should see their daddy like this?"

"You can't help me, always complaining. It's okay, if you can't help me, Miriam, one of my other women will." Pete shook his head with those last words, like he was making a profound point.

"What?" Miriam's eyes turned to stone.

"Pete, shut up man," Marshall glanced at his pager. "Look, we can't take him to the hospital right now. He's got a…situation."

"Oh my God," Miriam's hands were shaking. "What do you expect me to do?"

"I'll get someone to come, Miriam," Monty spoke slowly. "The doctor can stitch him up."

Michelle started crying. Monique didn't move a muscle.

"With these girls in here? Hell no." Miriam started moving around the room, gathering clothes and shoes and tossing them toward the girls. "Put your clothes on. We are leaving."

"You leaving me, Miriam? Again? That's what wrong with you—always thinking you going somewhere. Go on and leave then, since that's what you do." He leaned his head onto the armrest of the couch, drool escaping his mouth. "That's what you do. A damn leaver. My other women don't leave. They are happy to have me, damnit. But you gonna see though."

Miriam never looked at Pete. "Girls, let's go."

Monique stepped into her shoes and pulled on her robe. She didn't want to leave her father, but she wasn't going to disobey Miriam. Michelle shook her head "no."

"Move it." Miriam headed for the door, daring either of the girls to show more resistance. Both girls followed her.

"You gonna just leave him like this? What's wrong with you?" Marshall jumped in front of the door and grabbed Miriam by the arm. "You not going nowhere. We got to figure out—"

"Get off me!" Miriam yanked her arm away, stumbling backward into the door. "Don't you ever touch me!"

"What the hell is going on?" Monty ran into the hallway.

Marshall snatched his hand back.

Miriam stood back, her eyes wild, her body shielding the girls as she rubbed her arm. "Don't you ever man handle me!"

"Did you just touch her?" Monty looked back and forth between Marshall and Miriam. "Did he touch you?"

"He bruised my damn arm!" Miriam snatched both the girls and pushed them out into the hotel hallway, down the stairs, and out the door where her car sat directly in front of the exit. Like always. Backed into the spot, ready to peel directly out of the lot.

"I don't want to leave my Daddy." Michelle's little body shook with hiccups in between tears.

"He will be alright, baby, trust me. He was drunk. He wouldn't want you to see that."

"Still," Michelle gripped her blanket. "He's alone."

"No he's not. Monty will take care of him."

Miriam strapped both the girl's seatbelts and then jumped into the car and pulled out of the parking.

"You are going to be a woman one day, Michelle. You have to be able to protect yourself and your kids from the person you love. No matter what."

"Daddy won't hurt us."

Miriam sighed, "That's not what I mean."

"I want to go back." Michelle kicked the back of the passenger seat.

"I am **not** going back." Miriam's voice removed all doubt.

They rode in silence. Monique glanced back and forth between her mother and her sister. Both of them were strong willed and neither would back down. Fear pressed against her stomach…the same fear she had felt when that man touched her at the picnic. Again, she wanted to escape. But there was nowhere to go

When she glanced up, she caught Miriam's eyes in the rearview mirror. Monique wanted to look away, but couldn't.

"I know you don't understand this now, girls, but never let a man nor his bullshit bring harm to you or your children. Never. I should know better…but…" Miriam shook her head. "Always put yourself first. No matter how much they claim they love you, you have to be the one who loves you most. Do you both hear me?"

Silence.

"Men love women who love themselves. Who have standards and beliefs, even when that man doesn't have any his damn self.

You better know that before you think you know anything else. Always stand for what you believe."

Silence.

"Michelle Naomi Waters. Monique Simone Waters. Do you hear me?"

They glanced at each other. "Yes," the Waters girls chimed in unison. Monique grabbed Michelle's hand and closed her eyes, trying to forget the sight of her father's trickling blood.

CHAPTER SEVEN

Annihilation

"We can't do this." Monty's foot slapped against the brake pedal.

"Why the hell not?" Pete rubbed his hand across his forehead and leaned forward. "Me and El don't worship the same God. I handle mine like a man, he comes after my women, my children." Pete pulled leather gloves onto his hands. "Fuck his Sunday."

"It's not just him, Pete. Something like this, done on the Sabbath, it crosses the line."

"Whose line?" Pete opened the door to the car, but didn't climb out. "No one gave a fuck when they killed Jimmy. My brother and I worked hard for this territory, and El just ran over my family." Pete shook his head. "Let the chips fall where they fall."

Marshall piped in from the back seat. "It's the first chance we've had to touch him since the cookout."

Monty coughed. "Been a lot of blood spilt already though."

"What?" Pete looked at Monty like he was hearing things. "Blood spilt? Nothing but street hustlers. Pawns in this game. They are expendable – nothing but a message that we are coming. This," Pete pointed to his rifle, "this is our answer."

Monty glanced out of the window. "What are we doing? Waiting until they come out of the church or spray up the cars?"

Pete shook his head "*no*." "Did they wait until after the cookout to get us? You remember my baby girl screaming?" Pete bit his lip and paused. He opened the door and spit on the sidewalk. "Did you hear Monique scream?" Pete pushed out of the car. "I'm done talking."

The small Catholic church sat back from the street, with a plush green lawn in front of it. On the side of the stone building, near the street, was a neat cemetery. Thin crucifixes marked the modest burial grounds. Pete stomped across it, his feet knocking over the placards and destroying the thin markers.

He was instantly joined by two of his gunners who had been waiting in the park on the other side of the street. The neighborhood was serene, an old city community, self-contained and hidden from the larger population. Pete knew the area well. He had done business here for years.

His men fell into step behind him, flanking in from both directions. Pete turned his head up toward the sun and let the warmth cover his face. He said a quick prayer, like he always did just before he stepped into a war zone, like he had during each tour of duty in Vietnam. Dying was an acceptable option. If he died then he would be united with his brothers again, back in the comfort of his family—whether in heaven or hell. Being left on this earth without them was worse punishment than any enemy should be able to exact upon him.

If God had any sympathy for him, he would die today.

The thought made Pete happy. He turned his face away from the sun and stepped out of the simple graveyard onto the rolling lawn that ended at the chapel steps. He yanked the ski mask over his face.

Two of Perez's men lounged on the top of the stairs, one smoking a cigarette discreetly, the other beckoning him to put the cigarette out and enter the building. Pete was at the base of the steps when they noticed him. As they reached for their guns he bounded up the steps, knocking one in the forehead with the butt of the sawed off gun. He head butted the other one, pushing him back into the double doors. Pete snatched his knife out of the thigh sheath and stabbed him with it. Pete snatched the gun out of the man's hand as he pushed him aside.

"Damnit," Monty muttered as he and Marshall ran to catch up. "He is going to get himself killed."

The other two men who had flanked Pete were just getting up the stairs when Pete entered the church. He took one full second to take in the room, his eyes roaming over the pews, locating his prey. Pete fired the other man's gun with his left hand, aiming directly at El and his family. Screams rang out. Other men around El stood up, Pete shot two of them before a third opened fire. El buckled over as two of Pete's men entered the church, firing into the crowd. People threw themselves under the pews.

Pete threw the handgun down and he walked forward as El and his men scrambled to the door. Pete fired his shot gun. Groans and shouts of pain rang out. Monty passed a group of women, crouched down and shouting. He looked over at Marshall.

Marshall pointed a gun at the priest and the altar boy.

No one else was on the podium. Monty blinked. "What the hell are you doing?"

Marshall pulled the trigger.

The priest fell backward.

"No!" Monty turned to push Marshall away. An older Latina woman with blazing dark eyes and hair covered by a cloth, opened fire with a nine millimeter.

Monty felt a bullet tearing through his thigh. He stumbled backward. Marshall knocked the old woman down. Her gun slid to the floor.

Marshall pointed his gun at the older woman.

"No!" Monty shouted.

Marshall pulled the trigger again. The old woman's body crumbled over.

Pete fired another shot. El and another man fell back over the pew and the bench flipped over.

"Get out! Get out!" yelled one of Pete's men. Pete walked over to the pew, determined to see proof of death.

One of the men tugged at Pete's arm, pulling him away from the pew hiding El. "You're hit, man. Move out. You're bleeding, get out of here. You are leaving evidence. Think, asshole! Move out!"

Marshall scrambled out of the side exit, leaving Monty to limp out on his own. Monty joined Pete. "Let's go."

Something about Monty's voice brought Pete back from whatever haze he was in. He stumbled forward, his shotgun hanging limply in his hand, and pushed out of the side door with the other men behind him.

They slowly ran back over the lawn, and through the graveyard. No one spoke. They could hear the sirens coming. They were out of time. Marshall pulled the car up to the curb, Monty pushed Pete inside. "Go go go!"

Monty and the other two men ran into the park, where their run slowed to a walk as they stripped off the ski masks and handkerchiefs. Monty tied his t-shirt around his leg once they were in the second getaway car.

They drove to Hamlin beach and pulled into the parking lot. All of their clothes and tools went into a plastic bag with weights that they dumped into the water.

"What was that?" The driver, Anthony, finally broke the silence. "You said meet at a graveyard, not shoot up a church!"

"Shit," the other man breathed.

Monty didn't answer. He just sat straight, his mind trying to grasp what had just happened. A priest had been shot. Marshall had walked directly to the podium, for no reason at all, and pulled the trigger on a priest.

They were in trouble. A Catholic church in a White neighborhood being terrorized was going to have repercussions. The Black men having the nerve to do so and shoot a priest for no reason were going to fry. This was still America.

"Drop me at the trap and keep driving. Leave the state. Don't tell no one where you are, not your baby mama, nobody. Call me on this number in two days at 7pm." Monty pulled a wad of money out of the glove compartment. He wrote a number on the back of the registration in light pencil. "Do you understand me?"

They both nodded.

Monty knew the price to get out of this was going to be high and it was going to cost more than money.

CHAPTER EIGHT

The Life

Armand, age 10

"We need a touchdown." Armand wiped the sweat from his forehead. The sun was pounding on his head, making his head ache.

"Shut up," Keith, the quarterback, muttered as he wiped his sweaty palms on his thigh pads.

"No more interceptions, boy!" Armand picked up his water bottle. "And how come you and Jay can't get the snap right?"

Keith shook his head, fumbling with his armband.

Armand adjusted his shoulder pads, which were a little too big. None of their little league equipment fit perfect, but that didn't matter. Armand felt like a warrior as soon as he pulled the jersey over the dingy white pads.

He was born for this.

"Come on, Army. Run it in, boy!"

Armand glanced over at the sidelines. His Uncle Marshall stood there shouting, his hands cupped over his mouth.

"You know what it is, son! Get ya'll heads in the game, boy!"

Armand took a swig from the water bottle. Sweat dripped in his eyes. "I wish he would shut up."

"Man, whatever." Keith wiped his hands again. "My hands are too wet."

Armand handed Keith the ice cold water bottle. "Keep your lips offa it, my grandma made that up just for me."

Keith nodded, pouring the cold water on his face.

"And wipe your hands on the grass or somethin'. You need to get me that ball."

The referee blew the whistle.

Raymond tossed his water bottle at the water boy and pushed Armand in the back of the helmet. "Come on ya'll, we can win this. I get so sick of North Street beating us, man. Ya'll gotta get in on it!"

"Get me the ball, Keith."

"I hear you Army! Leave me alone, dang, I can't get a good grip."

Armand's mind ran through the different plays and routes. He, Keith and Raymond stood in a small circle. "They running cover two defense. I'm open all day." Armand shook his head. "You only throwing to one side of the field. If that's what you call throwing."

"The ball keep slipping, man." Keith looked like he was about to cry.

"Keith, you got this." Raymond's normal goofy smile was gone. He stuck his chin up. "You know we can do this. Either hit Army with it or I will run it. Just put the ball in our hands man. I know you can do that—you got this!"

Keith nodded.

Raymond was always positive. Armand noticed that Keith looked less sick while Raymond talked to him. "We do this all summer long, boy, just imagine when we are in the street. Just like that!"

Two coaches grabbed them and started talking. Armand didn't hear a word they said. His eyes were focused on the sideline and the lines of people staring at them.

The crowd was chanting, shouting at each other. At least 100 people lined the YWCA field on Arnett Blvd, screaming for their kids.

"Army, you better get that ball!" The high voice found Army's ears as his eyes scraped over the dust onto the grassy field. "Go Southwest! Ya'll got this!" Camilla was jumping around with her pom-poms, her back turned from the cheer leading squad, screaming directly at him at the top of her lungs.

Armand smiled. Camilla always had his back. She had abandoned her crew of cheerleaders just to scream at him. She was crazy. He shook his head and smiled.

"Come on, Southwest!"

Armand glanced back over at his Uncle Marshall. Some other players had their fathers there. Most had nobody. He had hoped his father might make an appearance. In school, Armand had told his half-sister Lisa that he had a game, hoping she would pass it on. But, as usual, his father was nowhere to be seen. Pretending he didn't have a child that wasn't from Lisa's mother, Armand figured. As much as Uncle Marshall got on his nerves, he was there. He figured an uncle was better than nobody. That's what his father was to him anyway—nobody. Armand gave Uncle Marshall the thumbs up sign.

He looked around the field. The other team was taking their slow time returning from time out. He hated their colors, hated their swag, hated that they ran over Southwest every single year.

"Army," He glanced over at his uncle again. "Catch and tuck," Uncle Marshall demonstrated, looking like the Heisman trophy.

Armand nodded.

The other team lined up directly opposite them. Armand backed up and moved all the way to the right. He was going long. It didn't matter what the coach had said. This was the route he saw in his head. And his instincts were never wrong. Armand glanced over at Keith. Keith was still struggling, still wiping sweaty palms on those dirty kneepads.

Armand ran over to Keith and patted his helmet. "Nothing to worry about, Keith. Playing Portland Ave. was way harder and it was raining. Remember that?"

"Yep," Keith nodded. "That was way worse."

"You good?"

"I'm straight," Keith shrugged Armand off, sounding irritated, his ego finally replacing worry.

"There we go," Raymond shouted from behind them. "Keith's back, he got this."

"Stop sweating me ya'll!" Keith yanked away from Armand and replaced his mouthpiece.

Armand smiled and trotted to the side of the field. He faced his opponent, Lavar, and smiled.

Lavar gave him the middle finger.

Keith nodded, took a deep breath. Exhaled.

Armand heard the count. It was his play.

Armand ran long, his arms outstretched. It was hot outside…super-hot; just like he liked it. Football was his game. He was going to be a superstar. Ball in his arm, weaving and dodging around the big idiots on the field like they were cast iron statues.

They couldn't catch him. No one could. No one could even come close.

The pass was perfect, the spin on it like a perfect propeller, ripping through the air. He never took his eyes off of it. That's what a true warrior did. He put his eye on the ball and kept it there. Nothing was going to break his concentration; nothing was going to make him look away.

Out the corner of his eye, he spotted Lavar running toward him. Taking a hit from Lavar was like running directly into a brick wall. Armand felt his stomach grip. He couldn't let it shake him—the knowledge that he was going to get pummeled the minute he touched the ball. It was something he couldn't think about.

Catch the ball. That's all that mattered.

The leather ball slid into his hands like a smooth glove. Seamless. He tucked it under his left arm as he headed for the goal line. Lavar was on him in seconds. But Lavar committed too early, lunging at him instead of tackling him. Armand extended his stiff arm, his hand pushing Lavar's helmet as Armand leaped over his outstretched arms.

Northeast crowd groaned, Southwest crowd screamed.

Armand kept running, stutter stepping past one more tackler, cutting inside as that player tripped up and fell.

It was all open field.

"Go Army, go!" Army caught a glimpse of Uncle Marshall, who was running down the sideline next to him. Camilla was running too.

It was too easy. Army looked around, sure a Northside player was about to punish him from some blind spot. All around him were Southwest players, they had been blocking and protecting him, clearing his way to the end zone. That's what a good team did; watched his back and protected him from attacks he couldn't even see. The feeling of protection surged through him, empowered him. Despite his burning legs, he pushed himself forward.

"Go boy! Yeah son!" Raymond was running just behind him now, as his gas was giving out. The goal line just a few steps away. "We did it!" Raymond screamed.

Armand stumbled over the goal line like a track runner stretching out his chest at the finish line. He fell forward, exhausted from the 50 yard top speed run, as he spiked the ball. His teammates all ran around him. Armand jumped up, and they formed a circle around him chanting. "Wildcats!"

Game over.

Armand had never tasted anything so sweet as that victory. It lingered on his mental tongue like the first addictive taste of sugar. The celebration was euphoric. It came at him in images. The team was in a circle, chanting victory and Uncle Marshall was smiling.

Camilla was screaming and jumping up and down. The cheerleaders were running up to him, grinning and flirting. Raymond was by his side, as always. Raymond, who called it success when there wasn't a chance and pumped up Keith when he was weak. The coaches were patting him up. At the after meeting, both teams sat and watched the awards and he received Offensive MVP. The statue was as long as his arm. Camilla ran home ahead of him and told his grandmother. The smell of fried chicken and macaroni cheese greeted him when he finally got home an hour later. He celebrated with Grandma, Camilla and Uncle Marshall. His mother called from work to tell him she was proud of him. Uncle Marshall sat on the porch and retold the touchdown run over and over again to everyone who walked past.

Chandra, the head cheerleader, gave him her phone number.

The hot bath his grandmother made him take with Epsom salt dissolved in the water.

Passing out on the couch, holding his football in his hand, belly full, his family proud of him and the prospect of a new girlfriend to explore.

For Armand, life had never been more perfect than this day. One day, when he became a doctor or lawyer, or, more likely, a professional football player, then every day would feel like today. Every day he would be a winner, with fine girls like Chandra pressing up on him, his family proud and cheering for him, his grandmother at home in their mansion, filling the house with smells of homemade sweet potato cake and pies. When he was grown and a success, every day would be like today. And his mother wouldn't have to work three jobs and miss everything. She could finally be at his games.

Life would be perfect—he could already taste it.

CHAPTER NINE

Throne Envy

Miriam grabbed Monique by the hand as they entered the rear doors to the church. They were running late for Miriam's meeting with the pastor. Monique kept stopping and touching her knee.

"My knee hurts, Mommy."

"Monique," Miriam tugged at her arm. "Your knee didn't start hurting until we pulled into the church parking lot."

Monique wriggled her nose, ignoring her mother's statement. She stood behind her mother, waiting for her to unlock the door with her key. "Mommy, why do you have a key to the church?"

Miriam glanced down at her daughter. "You are so inquisitive." She smiled. "Because the pastor trusts me."

"Oh." Monique rubbed her knee again. It really did hurt. Before her mother had picked her up from Aunt Bee's house, Monique had been playing hopscotch outside with Leann, and had fallen on the pavement. Her knee stung, but she didn't tell Aunt Bee because then she would have had to sit down and miss out on the fun.

But there was nothing fun about going into the church, especially since her crew of friends wasn't there. Now it seemed that her knee hurt even worse.

She and her mother started up the rear staircase toward the office. Monique's eyes began to water. "Mommy, it really hurts."

"Monique," Miriam took a deep breath, "you are working my nerves. When I go in the office you can go to the bathroom, wet a paper towel and put it on your knee. Understand?"

Monique nodded. She had freedom to leave the church office. That was good enough. She kept quiet while Miriam unlocked the church office and sat down her bags. Monique waited patiently while her mother turned on the lights to the office, the overflow room and the hallway leading to the upstairs bathrooms.

Then she looked at Monique and nodded. Monique wondered out of the office, her arms straight out, her fingers running along the wall. She did as she was told, in case her mother checked on her. Monique went straight to the large bathrooms behind the pulpit, situated under the choir stand, and flicked on the light. It smelled like new paint. She touched the wall to check, but her fingers did not get stained by the shiny white gloss on the wall.

Monique stared at herself in the wall mirror. This was the bathroom that the pastor's wife and her armor bearers used on Sunday mornings, it was nicer than all the others. It contained a plush lounge chair and sofa, dressing room quality lighting and mirrors. Monique looked at her reflection. She didn't look like anybody in her family. She wondered where her hair had come from, and her nose. No one in her family had her nose.

Monique finished splashing around in the water, flushed the toilet for no real reason other than habit, and headed back out into the hallway. She felt special, like she was a private detective in a huge museum searching for clues. She walked quietly, rounding the corner behind the choir stand and walking up to the pulpit.

Girls weren't allowed in the pulpit. Her pastor made that clear. He made exceptions on Women's Day, or when there was a special speaker, other than that, only men sat on the throne. Monique thought about that a lot, how only men were allowed to be on the throne and be the head of everything. Like Uncle Jimmy was the head of the Waters, and Pete was the head of her family. There was nothing Miriam or Rebe or Aunt Lela could say or do that didn't require their approval, either spoken or unspoken. They were always tip toeing around the rules set by the male Waters. And then at church, the pastor and the deacons ran things. The deaconesses, the female deacons, were only entitled by way of marriage, not because they themselves had been called by God to that position. And the minister's wives sat on the front two pews to the right of the altar, staring admiringly at their husbands.

Monique guessed that's what she was supposed to do. Find an all-powerful man, put him in his throne and then admire him.

But she didn't really like the thought of that. What did Pete do to deserve all the special treatment? Her Uncle Jimmy deserved it, though, because he would do anything for her and the family. Monique believed that to her core. But Pete…Monique felt sure he could take her or leave her.

Monique wondered what it felt like to be on the throne. For once, to just sit there and be the head and let everyone else be at her feet.

She stepped up the carpeted steps, very slowly, glancing over her shoulder to make sure no one was in the cathedral sanctuary to see her blasphemy. Monique tiptoed, her fingers running softly across the iron rail. There were five steps, she climbed them like a baby, placing both feet on each before moving up.

Monique's heart stopped. She made it to the pulpit. Monique stared at the large high back chair covered in sacred cloth. She reached out her fingers and let the plush fabric run under her nails. It was far nicer up here than she had ever imagined. She glanced over her shoulder, in the direction of the church office, but she didn't hear a sound. Miriam's footsteps on the wood would give Monique a fair warning. Monique lifted on her toes and pushed herself into the large steel chair. It was soft, the padding was comfortable under the deep plush fabric. Monique imagined that she had a crown on her head and a staff in her hand. She glanced down at the throngs of imaginary admirers, staring up at her. She was Queen Monique. Her servants would have to kiss her ring.

Monique giggled and scrambled down out of the seat. She turned to face the sanctuary, placing her hands on the glass podium. Her eyes looked out at the hundreds of empty pews in front of her, up to the balcony overlooking the sanctuary and the second balcony tucked behind it.

Why couldn't she stand here one day and be the head of this place and let the masses sit at her feet? Why did it have to be a man?

Monique smiled.

The next instant, she frowned. She was wicked. That's what her grandmother would call her…wicked and evil for playing on the good Lord's property. She thought of her grandmother, down south in their small church. She imagined the look that would cross Grandma's face if she caught sight of Monique in the pulpit. Her grandmother would spank her with a stick, skinned free of leaves from the huge bush near the door. Then Miriam would give her a second spanking for disrespecting her grandmother by making her have to spank her. Monique was convinced that both women just liked to spank her. Miriam only hit her when her father wasn't around. Monique knew better than to tell. Even if Pete did something, he would eventually leave her all alone with Miriam again, like he always did. And then what? Monique knew better than to think Pete could save her. Monique quickly moved away from the podium, down the stairs, and up the long aisle, making her way back to the office.

"Monique!" Miriam's voice cracked as it echoed off the cathedral ceilings.

Monique's stomach dropped. She was surely going to get a beating. She moved a little faster.

"Monique, where are you?"

"Right here, Mommy." Monique turned the corner, worry engulfing her.

"We got to go." Miriam had more bags in her hands. "Hurry." Miriam began rushing out of the building with Monique on her heels.

"What's wrong?" Monique felt panicked. Had her touching the pulpit been so bad that they had to run? Why wasn't Miriam disciplining her?

"Your dad," Miriam shook her head. "We got to go."

Monique went from running to slow walking. She was tired of always rushing for Pete's emergencies. Pete wasn't normal and there was never a normal day when he was involved. Every day was an emergency, every second was the moment before the floor dropped from underneath them. Monique was tired. She wondered why Miriam wasn't tired yet.

"What happened to Daddy now?" Monique asked, not really caring.

"Get in the car." Miriam held the door open for Monique.

Monique's bottom lip trembled. "What happened? What happened now?"

"Pete got arrested, Monique. I have to find Monty and figure out what to do."

"Where is he?"

"Monique, your father is in jail."

Monique lowered her head. This wasn't the first time. It surely wouldn't be the last. But every time this call came, life for Monique stopped as Miriam worried herself sick trying to arrange and pay the bail and the lawyers through a traceable account. Only to have Pete get out of jail, spend a night home, and be right back in the streets. Monique felt tears stinging her cheeks. She wished she could just disappear. She wanted to remove herself from them both, Miriam and Pete. She wanted a day when fear didn't knot the bottom of her stomach, didn't dance in her gut until the feeling of vomiting became normal. She wished she could magically turn into thin air and float through the window and away from this life.

"Don't worry." Miriam's hands shook as she pushed the car into gear and backed up. She glanced at the tears on Monique's cheeks. "We will figure it out."

Monique wanted to say, "*I'm not worried. I don't care about figuring it out. I just want it to all end.*" But she knew better. Instead, she sighed and watched the city pass by as they sped home.

***

"I know Mom, but this is the way I have to do it." Miriam wrapped the phone cord around her finger as she spoke to her mother on the phone.

Monique sat at the kitchen table, watching her mother's reflection in the mirror. Miriam was so worried. She had been crying. Her eyes were swollen. The bail was high. They had the cash, but no proof of where it had come from. The lawyer said to not show up with cash. Monty thought the case was a trumped up charge, an attempt to stress Pete out. He had said to not do anything for a few days.

Miriam had screamed at him.

So now Miriam scrambled to take a loan as Monique watched her.

"I can pay you the money back, Mom." Miriam glanced at Monique and caught her eye. She looked away. "No, my teacher's salary doesn't cover that, but I have some saved. Yes, Mom, I understand."

This wasn't the first time they had been here. Monique had sat in the car as Miriam gave the bail bondsmen a few thousand last year. And they had waited in the car for hours for Pete to be released. Monique remembered how happy Miriam had been when the bail bondsman had confirmed that he would be released. How quiet Pete had been when he got in the car, kissing Miriam, rubbing her hands, thanking her for her love, telling her how much he appreciated her. Monique remembered feeling warm and loved, watching her parents from the back seat. They had driven home peacefully. Monique had taken a bath and put on her pajamas. Pete had come to her room and kissed her. He had told her he was sorry for making her worry. Then he had left. And Monique had lain in her bed listening to Miriam cry herself to sleep.

Monique knew that words meant nothing more than the air they were breathed on. Pete's words were empty lies. If he were really sorry, he wouldn't keep putting them through this.

Monique put away her notebook and crayons. She might as well take her bath. Pete wasn't coming home tonight, that much was clear. Maybe Miriam would have enough to get Pete out tomorrow.

Monique knew her father was just fine. She had heard him and Uncle Jimmy talking about jail—though neither wanted to be there, they weren't afraid of it. It was just part of life. She wasn't so sure about Miriam. Miriam's skin was sallow and dull, her hair was breaking in the back. Her nails were bitten and cracked. Worrying about Pete was making her look sick.

A small part of Monique disliked the weakness in Miriam. She felt guilty, but the feeling remained.

Monique made herself a promise. She was never going to love a man like her mother loved Pete. If anything, her man would have to love her like that. She wasn't going to be weak making a man strong.

CHAPTER TEN

Price of Loyalty

"Everything has a price, Pete." Monty shook his head as he opened a bottle of cognac.

"Yeah, and I've already paid all of my debts." Pete observed the wad of money on the table in front of him. "They held me over nothing. Suspicion? I just spent a week in jail due to suspicion? That's not even legal."

Monty shook his head. "They are sending a message."

"What message?" Pete stretched his arms. "Perez doesn't have it like that."

Monty snorted. "This isn't Perez." He poured back a shot and let the burn scour his throat.

"Then who?"

"Pete, how much do you think it costs to keep you out of jail on a regular basis? You stomped your bitch out in front of the club. You think I didn't have to pay to keep the police from going too far? You shot up the entire North side of the city, you think there isn't a price for that?"

"You got robbed then, since I still did time."

"A week ain't time," Monty scoffed.

"It's something. It's time I shouldn't have done if you are paying, right?"

Monty shook his head and leaned against the pool table in the office that used to belong to John, the eldest Waters. "You're missing my point. The priest that got shot last year. We haven't paid for that, yet."

Pete looked around the room suspiciously. He stared at Monty as if he were the enemy. Then he walked up to Monty, slapping his broad hand against Monty's chest and patted across his shoulders.

"A wire?" Monty laughed, an incredulous expression covering his worn face. "You think I'm wired?"

Pete didn't answer, his eyes narrowed as he moved back toward the desk and ran his fingertips along the underside of the wood. He moved near the curtain and reached for his shotgun.

"You sonofabitch." Monty poured himself another drink and turned his back to Pete, unconcerned with the gun. "I'm talking about it now because I have no choice. Not because I'm wired."

Pete didn't answer. He held the shotgun in his hand.

"Put that damn shotgun down. They want to meet. You forgot what this is all about, so busy getting revenge. You are back to being a stupid ass foot soldier. We got to get back to business. Death is bad for business, Pete, the working folks fall back. We are losing customers. We got to make this paper, that's what it's all about. And they need promises from you to make it go away."

Pete finally spoke, his words a hushed whisper. He didn't want to deal with the Italians at all. "I don't know them, they aren't my contacts. Those were Jimmy's people."

"No Pete. You are the head man now. You do business with them now."

"What they got to do with this? This is between us and the Perez's."

"Perez tried to wipe us out to get more of this paper. They failed. It's simple. We have responded, drawn clear lines in the sand. But the priest, that was too much. It's the order of things, Pete. I told you, some lines can't be crossed without a price."

Pete swallowed. "When is the meet?"

"One hour."

"What if I say no?"

Monty shrugged. "I don't know. I don't know what they have or what they want from us. I only know that they don't go away."

Pete nodded his head. The emptiness since he lost his brothers was overwhelming him. "It could be a trap."

"It could be." Monty threw back another shot. "Then we're just two more dead Black men. Life goes on."

Pete nodded and grinned for the first time in weeks at the irony of it all. Unfortunately, no matter what he did in preparation of ending it, life kept trudging on.

***

Frank sat at a small booth in the corner of Perkins restaurant in Henrietta, New York, sipping a cup of coffee. He was facing another man, talking in low tones. Monty spotted him first, as Pete stood at the counter looking at the deserts. The waitress seemed too distracted to pay them much attention, both men moved past her and toward the booth. As they approached, the other man stood up and stood behind Frank, clearly his guard.

Monty and Pete stood by the table.

"You made it." Frank looked up, his glance appraised both of the men in front of him.

"Yes." Monty moved to the side and Pete sat down.

"I'm glad." Frank stirred his coffee. "At the outset, I must say I am truly sorry about Jimmy."

Pete met his eyes. "I appreciate that." There was a deep pause. "Really."

“This business, this life,” Frank sighed and raised his hand. “What do we do?”

Pete didn’t answer.

“There comes a time, though, that life moves on for those of us who are left here.” Frank took another sip of his coffee before moving it aside. “A time when you have to decide to move forward.”

“It’s not a choice.”

“Yes, Pete, it is a choice.” Frank shook his head. “We have known each other for a long time. Your brothers and I, we have done business together. Now, it is time for you to decide what it is you are going to do.”

Pete bristled. “My brother’s business is mine. It’s our family. I am taking their place.”

Frank was quiet for a while. “Older brothers, they sometimes let the baby boy stay the baby too long. If they choose. They can let him run the streets and have fun. The person running a business, he can’t do what the baby boys do.”

Pete clenched his hands, feeling an insult buried in those words, but not sure how to react. “What do you mean?”

“I mean lords don’t carry out the work meant for henchman. Everything has a time and a place. If you want to take over the business, then it’s time to be a business man. Let the cleanup crews handle the garbage.”

Pete sat back in his seat.

"I have kids, Pete." Frank coughed, then wiped his mouth with a napkin. "I look at my kids and I decide what future they will have. It's not just about me anymore, about what I feel or what I want." Frank shrugged. "Sure, I take what I want here and there." He laughed a little. "But, for the sake of my kids and my family, I have to put things in their proper place."

Pete listened intently.

"It's time for you to choose. And if you decide on this business, then it's time to order your steps."

Pete rubbed his hands together. He understood what Frank was saying. It was time for him to grow up.

"This thing that happened, it was too much, Pete."

There it was, the pink elephant in the room had finally blown its trunk.

"Killing my brother was too much."

"You exacted revenge. Quite successfully, I might add."

"Not so successfully, or we wouldn't be here."

Frank waved his hand at the air. "Someone has to take the fall over this thing with the priest. We can't have it."

"I didn't do that."

"Pete," Frank gave him a disapproving glance. "You are a veteran. What your men did…you did."

"True." Pete regretted that he had rejected responsibility. It made him feel as though he looked weak and childish. He let the burn of embarrassment pass and pushed forward. "What do you propose we do?" There was a tint of sarcasm in Pete's voice. He didn't feel that he and Frank constituted a "we" in any way.

"Well, you are going to let justice be served on the person who did this."

Pete stared at Frank. That meant giving up someone in his crew and Pete had never done that before. He had no plans on turning into a traitor now.

Frank continued, "And you are going to give the authorities something to hang their hat on. Someone to allow the good people to go to sleep at night knowing justice was served."

Pete definitely wasn't doing that. There was no way he would let the Italians or the Perez's near Marshall. "My people don't get handed over to anyone. I will handle him. And we will arrange for someone to take the charge."

Frank sat quietly for a few minutes, toying with the handle of the coffee cup. He studied Pete then seemed to come to a resolution in his mind. "Okay, Pete. You have five days to handle it."

Pete almost didn't want to ask. "Or?"

"Or, I have no way to continue calming the situation. You know how these things go." Frank signaled to the waitress. "I need a refill."

Sensing he was dismissed, Pete stood up.

"Keep me informed." Frank said between clenched teeth, before turning his attention to the menu and the approaching waitress.

Pete and Monty quietly walked out.

CHAPTER ELEVEN

First Taste

Armand, age 11

Armand tossed the ball in the air and caught it over and over again. He thought about the feel of the leather, the pressure against his hands. He changed how he handled the ball when he tossed it up; how he caught the ball each time it landed into his palms.

He was killing time.

Camilla was in the yard double dutching with Pam and Shanna from down the street. He didn't want to look at Pam. Anytime Camilla wasn't around, Pam was pushing up against him, rubbing her boobs on his arm or trying to hug him. She did too much and he didn't like her at all.

Camilla swung back and forth to the rhythm of the rope before she found her opening. When the closest rope was farthest away, slapping the ground, then she ran in and started jumping.

"Count." Camilla's command was clear. She bent forward, like she was riding a bike and started running in perfect step to the ropes.

Pam twirled like a pro; legs apart and even with her shoulders, chewing gum and popping it in time with the ropes. Shanna counted each time Camilla's left foot touched the ground. "Twenty five, twenty six, twenty seven—"

"Speed!" Camilla's scream cracked the air.

The ropes spun double time with Camilla running in place at top speed practicing her routine. The beat of the ropes sounded uneven.

"You going double handed!" Pam yelled out at Shannon. "Even it up."

"Slow down, slow down!" Camilla was panting.

The ropes went back to regular count. Pam kept talking. "You can't twirl with us in competition, Shanna, I'm just keeping it real. You go double handed every time we do speed."

"That's you, not me. How are you going to blame me?"

"It's you Shanna." Camilla said, her voice low. "I was looking at your hands; your left is off."

Army jumped up, football under his arm and ran through the ropes without getting tangled up.

"Dammit, Army!" Camilla screamed, still jumping. "Stay out of the way! You could have messed me up!"

Armand laughed. "You all serious about jumping rope."

She squinted her eyes at him to show she was serious.

Just to taunt her, Armand jumped into the ropes again. This time, his timing was wrong and the rope wrapped around his ankle as the handle was yanked from Shanna's hands.

"Army, I hate you!" Camilla bent over to catch her breath. "Now I got to start all over!"

He shrugged and went back to tossing his ball.

"Why are you out here, anyway?" Camilla picked up the rope and started untangling it. "I thought you was leaving?"

"Waiting on Uncle Marshall."

"Well leave me alone."

"He don't have to go nowhere." Pam smiled and winked at him.

Camilla went from annoyed big sister to super protective big sister. "Who are you winking at? Girl, don't be looking at my little brother. Friend or not, I will straight up go at you if you go near Army. Uh huh, you are too nasty for my little brother."

Camilla's screechy voice faded as Armand headed to the backyard. He was glad that Camilla had jumped on Pam; she would stay away from him if she knew what was best. Pam wasn't nothing but trouble anyway. He stepped into the garage and turned on the old radio. Uncle Marshall was never this late; especially not on Armand's birthday. His instinct told him something wasn't right, but he dismissed it as worry. More likely, Uncle Marshall had just forgotten and Armand wasn't going to call him…it was what it was.

After another hour of listening to music, Armand decided to grab an orange push-up from the corner store; no reason not to that he could think of.

"Grandma, I'm going to the store," he yelled through the kitchen window.

"Stop yelling into this house." Her calm voice came back at him. "And grab me some pork skins."

"Alright."

"Your uncle come yet?"

"No, he's not here." Armand started walking up the narrow driveway, past his grandmother's rosebushes.

"Humph."

Armand didn't know how to read that. The only response that he ever heard concerning his father was a "humph," so Grandma wasn't thinking too well about Uncle Marshall right now.

He walked past the new group of girls that were now in front of his house. "Where you going?" Camilla said, like she was his mother.

"The store and no, I ain't getting you nothing."

"I ain't want nothing no way," Camilla answered back, rolling her eyes.

Armand noticed that Pam was gone. He knew Camilla well enough to know that Pam wouldn't be back any time soon.

Armand walked along Kenwood Avenue glancing around. Uncle Marshall had taught him to be aware of everyone around him and how many folks were in the cars passing by. He thought about going to get Raymond but decided against it. If he went over there, he would be at Raymond's house all day and would miss Uncle Marshall when he finally came. Armand wasn't about to miss time with his uncle. He could get up with Raymond later.

Armand tossed the ball as he walked up the street. A couple of people called out his name, he just nodded back. He loved his hood; loved the 11th Ward with the huge old houses, the big lawns, the ancient trees and the perfect blue sky. The closer he got to Genesee Street, the louder the hum of the streets; it was the pulse of people walking back and forth on their way to the barber shop or in and out of the store.

"Right here." An older boy had his hands up, calling for Armand to throw him the football.

Army didn't know him. He looked the boy up and down and looked away. He kept stepping, still tossing the ball.

"Young boy, throw the ball."

"I don't know you." Army's throat felt tight. He wanted the teenager to leave him alone.

"Oh, it's like that?"

Armand felt himself getting irritated. He thought about how Uncle Marshall would handle the situation. "Yeah, it's like that."

The three guys standing next to the teenager laughed at him. Armand could tell that the teenager was mad by the way he was glaring.

Armand shrugged and walked into the store. He nodded at the clerk and slid to the side of the store for the cooler. Armand pushed the heavy lid open and looked down in it. "Yo, where y'all pushups at?"

"All out." The clerk stared at the television over his head. "No more."

"Man, what you mean—?"

As Armand turned around, a hand wrapped around the back of his neck and forced his head into the freezer. He could hear laughing around him.

"You gonna clown me, young boy?"

Armand struggled, elbowing the bony body of the teenager, trying to move his face, which was pressed against the glass. He wished Raymond was here. At least Raymond would fight for him.

The boy punched him in the back. "Stay still! I was going to throw the ball back, but now I'm taking it!"

Armand felt a few more blows to his side and pain wrapped around him in spams.

"That's enough, Titan, damn," one of the other guys said. "That's the little wide receiver for Southwest."

The grip around his neck released. Armand pushed himself back and stumbled to the floor trying to catch his breath.

"Stay down," the teenager said, picking up Armand's football.

Armand's chest was rising and falling, but it hurt to breathe and he wasn't getting enough air.

"Breathe." Titan said, tucking the ball under his arm and pressing his palm in the air. "Look, catch your breath young boy! You're hyperventilating! You're not going to get your wind like that!"

The other boys lost interest, floating up and down the aisles. The clerk's eyes were off the television now, watching the boys diligently.

Armand coughed. His eyes faltered. He felt like he was passing out.

"Yo, pay attention!" The teenager shouted at him, pointing the ball at Armand. "Breathe in and out, young boy…slow."

Army finally caught his breath. He stared at the dark teenager holding his ball. Armand tried to remember everything about the boy's face and build, because as sure as he was breathing, Armand was going to get even.

"Lil nigga ain't afraid," the taller boy behind Titan said. "He watching you like he remembering."

"Yeah, this one got a little heart." The thin boy stared at Armand, then back at the football. "Imma keep your ball but you alright young boy."

"You ain't have to whip his ass like that," the taller one chuckled.

"Yeah, I did." He shook his head. "Next time I say throw the ball, young boy, you hit me with it." His voice had a weird tone to it, like it was Armand's fault that he had been beaten.

Armand just stared at him.

"You alright?"

Armand nodded.

"I'm Titan, man." Titan sighed and rubbed his bald head. "My bad, I shouldn't have hit on you like that. My temper is what it is but you gonna be alright. I'll make sure of it."

Titan walked to the front of the store and handed the clerk a few dollar bills. He glanced back at Armand, then told the clerk, "Get him an orange push-up, like he asked for and whatever else he want and re-stock that damn freezer."

Titan disappeared out of the store with Armand's football. His crew walked out behind him.

Armand was as mad as a Dominican being called Haitian. He wanted his football back but there was something else Titan had that Armand wanted—power. Titan moved and the couple of boys with him followed. Titan shouted orders and the clerk who had dismissed Armand earlier was now standing next to him, handing him an orange push-up, letting him grab two bags of pork rinds for Grandma and telling Armand to wait for a complimentary ham and cheese sub to take home. Titan had the power and Armand craved it.

Before figuring out how to get Titan's power, Armand had a much more immediate goal. He was going to get back his football, no matter what it took.

CHAPTER TWELVE

The Hunted

"There he is." Armand tugged on his sweatshirt as he and Raymond walked past the Madison football field.

"Where?" Raymond's head bopped up, surfing the crowd.

"Blend in." Armand wanted to kick him. "Boy, if I wanted him to see us, I would walk right up to him. Put your head down. Stop looking pressed!"

"Man, go on. You are the one pressed all over a stupid football. I told you, my cousin Dut be getting balls from the school all the time. You could get another one that's better than that old one. That one looked like rubber anyway."

"Rubber?" Armand breathed heavy through his nose. "What you saying?"

"I'm saying, we don't need to get shot over no damn football!" Raymond shook his head. "You always making something out of nothing."

"He took my ball. I want it back." Armand wasn't about to explain that the ball was a gift from his father, one of the few gifts he had ever received. He definitely wasn't going into any details with Raymond whose parents were married and had a family that seemed as large as their entire neighborhood. What could Raymond understand about any of it? "You in or out?"

Raymond tossed the candy bar wrapper on the ground. "Word? You in your feelings now?" Raymond shook his head and laughed. "Boy, I got your back. You already know."

"Then let's do this."

"You're crazy." Raymond smiled with anticipation. "Let's do it. Your slow ass better run, because if they catch you he is gonna kill you."

Titan was sitting on the bottom bleacher and two of his friends stood in front of him. A couple of girls stood near them, talking and giggling. Titan was beating on the bleacher with his fists, drumming out a hip hop bass line. There weren't a lot of people on the field, just kids drifting out of the yard onto the street, heading home.

This was the only time Armand had seen Titan with the ball.

This was the only time to snatch his ball.

"What's the plan—?" Raymond's words were lost on the blowing wind.

Armand was already gone, walking along the back of the bleachers, coming up behind the small crowd.

"Shit." Raymond walked in the opposite direction, out in the open, heading past the crowd like he was on his way into the school.

He kept his head down, his hands in his sweatshirt pocket, his eye on Armand as he inched closer to the crowd.

In a few seconds, Armand was right next to them. His hand was on the ball. He took a few steps forward, the ball tucked under his arm. Raymond breathed. No one had noticed Armand.

Then the drumming stopped.

The noisy rattle of the bleachers that had filled the air ended, and in that moment of dead silence, Armand caught his breath. He looked up.

Titan was looking directly at him, a half smile on his lips, an incredulous expression covering his face. "Little nigga, I know you ain't just take my ball."

Armand started running.

Titan jumped off the bleacher and started chasing him.

The small crowd started laughing.

Armand was running full speed. His back remembered the last pummeling he had taken from Titan; he didn't want to get caught but he would fight if he had to.

Titan was gaining on him. Armand was surprised that he was so quick. Armand headed for the gate.

"Gimme back that ball!" Titan shouted.

Raymond came out of nowhere, running at a slant in front of Titan, who stopped for a moment, confusion in his eyes.

Armand tossed Raymond the ball.

"Oh, hell no!" The tall guy from the store, who had laughed at Armand earlier, was sitting on the bleacher. "Y'all are trying to double team my man?" He jumped onto the field, running toward them. Raymond and Armand pushed out of the field and onto Genesee Street, running and dodging through people, with Titan and the other guy right behind them. They crossed the street, dancing between cars, and ran up Frost Avenue.

The sound of the clap made them duck. Someone had fired a gun. Raymond tossed the ball back to Armand. The gun popped again. "Stop running, you little motherfuckers!" Clap! Clap!

Titan and his boy were too close; the gun shots would eventually find a target. They both stopped running.

"Gotdamn!" Titan bent over, his hands on his knees as his chest heaved up and down, breathing hard. His tall friend with the gun tucked it back in his pants.

"You little assholes got me running and shit, I ought to beat your asses!" Titan said in between breathes. He squinted at Armand.

"You're a persistent little asshole. You think I haven't seen you following me around the past couple weeks? I ought to whip your ass again!"

"And you—" he pointed at Raymond. "Boy, I thought for a minute you were going to tackle me. I swear, if you had touched me I would be stomping you out right now!"

The taller one laughed.

After a few more deep breathes, Titan stood straight up and chuckled. He looked into Armand's eyes. "That ball mean all that to you?"

Armand's black eyes didn't falter. "Yeah."

"Why?"

Armand shrugged, feeling a tear in his eye and hoping that it evaporated before he had to actually wipe it away. He wasn't sharing what was on his heart or his mind and if Titan whipped his ass and took the ball back, he would follow him around for another two weeks until he got another opportunity to get it back. He even knew where Titan lived, in case he had to break into the well-manicured house on Post Avenue with the covered porch. He would do it if he had to.

Titan stared back and forth at him and Raymond for a few minutes.

"I told you, little homey got heart." Tall Boy said.

Titan nodded. "What's your name, young boy?"

"Army."

"And you?"

"Ray."

"Ya'll pockets light?"

Raymond's eyes lit up. "Light? Shit, they empty."

"Naw, we good." Armand shook his head. Unlike Raymond, Armand had learned at a young age that everything comes with a price. "We're alright."

"Take your ball, homey. I would hate for you to pull a stunt at the wrong moment and make me have to shoot you. But if you need something, get at me, 'aight?"

Armand nodded. "Aight."

"Say thank you, rude little fuck." Titan and Tall Boy laughed.

"Thanks," Armand muttered. He started to add, "*Fuck you,*" but didn't have the energy to take off running again and he couldn't risk Raymond getting beat up because he didn't control his tongue.

"I'll be seeing you." Titan said, walking away.

Armand and Raymond stood there, watching them walk away.

Raymond punched Armand's arm. "Why did you say we was alright? He was about to give us some money."

Armand shook his head. "No, he wasn't. You don't want nothing from him, trust me."

"Man, Army, you don't know. We could have got something."

"Don't nothing come for free, Ray." Armand waited until Titan crossed Genesee Street before he started walking up Frost Avenue. He hoped he never saw Titan again.

CHAPTER THIRTEEN

Expulsion

Monique, age 9

"I'm not doing that!"

"What! You gonna do what I say, woman!"

Monique squirmed deep down under the covers of her huge white sleigh bed and tucked the blanket around her ears. She imagined that normal families slept at night. But, for some reason, all of her life seemed to happen at night, in the deadest hours of the world, when everyone normal was sleeping. Like she had been before she heard the front door slam and her father's deep voice shake the night air.

"I didn't sign on for this shit, Pete; I swear I didn't. I don't have to deal with this."

Monique reached for the children's Bible her grandfather had given her. He had earmarked a verse for her to read anytime she was scared. The page was already bent and wrinkled, Monique had been petrified more than most kids her age.

Psalm 27 fell open in her lap.

"Woman, who do you think I am? You still don't know what this is, huh?"

Monique traced the bible verse with her finger as she read it slowly and evenly. She didn't count anymore; she had given up Uncle Jimmy's counting technique. At the end of her last count, he had been dead.

Normally, by the time she finished reading verses 1 through 6, her parents would be done fighting and the shouts of anger would turn into groans of passion.

Monique wished that she could crawl inside the bible verse; that she could just find that secret place and hide.

Monique glanced at the picture on the night stand next to her bed. She wished Michelle was in her room sleeping in the trundle bed next to her. Michelle had stopped coming over as often now that her mother had two more kids and needed the help. Plus, Michelle and Miriam were too strong willed to stand each other for too long. Michelle still came over, but only for a couple of days and Pete was always around when Michelle was there.

Ricardo never came over.

Michelle talked about him, though. She told Monique how she and Pete would pick Ricardo up from school and take him to football practice or how they would go to the movies or the amusement park. Pete had even taken them to Niagara Falls. The three of them had a life that didn't include Monique. It wasn't fair. Monique barely saw Pete and now she knew that when he wasn't home, he was having a fun time…without her. That he didn't include her when he spent time with his other children. Obviously, Pete wanted time with the two children he really loved, who really mattered. She thought of Uncle Jimmy. At least he thought that she was a Waters, even if she was different. Pete didn't even try to make her feel included.

Michelle always told Monique that she was lucky, that she lived with their father and had him all the time. Michelle didn't know that the truth was just the opposite and Monique was the jealous one whose father only came home when her sister was visiting.

Miriam's shrieks filled the air. "Take this shit with you and get out. You're leaving? You're leaving me? Then take all your shit with you!"

Without Michelle at home, Pete stayed in the streets leaving Monique to handle Miriam alone.

Monique's solution was to hide out in her large bedroom and read books. She survived by escaping into a world created by words.

Pete sometimes came home at the dead of night.

"Don't push me, Miriam! I'm getting sick of this! You can't keep having one foot out the door and expect me to come home to you!"

"Are you threatening me?"

"I'm telling you, I'm sick of all this noise from you, all this arguing! I don't have to come home to it!"

"No, you don't! Not when you're out sticking your dick in every nasty tramp that looks your way! What, you think I don't know? You think that bitch hasn't called my phone?"

The arguments sounded the same. Monique wondered what the real problem was tonight. She had known it was going to be a bad night when Miriam had started mopping the floors, choking Monique with the smell of raw ammonia and the suffocation of angry energy bouncing off the walls.

"—and let me tell you something else, if you think I am going to take my daughter out of private school while you get money right, you got another think coming! That's the least you are going to do, is make sure her tuition is paid! Your bitch drove past here in her new Mercedes Benz but you're going to come in here talking about my daughter's tuition! My daughter is less important than your flavor of the year?!"

"Don't act like I don't take care about my kids, Miriam and she is OUR daughter, not just yours!"

"Yeah, you take care of them when your favorite is here. You don't so much as look at Monique unless Michelle is around! That's the only damn child you care about; her and your bastard son by that fiend!"

The sound of flesh hitting flesh was so loud that Monique literally felt the house shake.

"Don't you ever call my child a bastard!" Pete was talking through clenched teeth; the words sounded like a forced whisper. The sound of scraping reached Monique and her heart felt like it was going to bust.

Miriam's voice sounded muffled and weak. A sound she had never heard before. She couldn't make out the words. It sounded like Miriam was choking.

Monique jumped out of her bed and ran down the hallway to the staircase. Her parents were at the bottom of the stairs, Pete was holding Miriam by her neck against the wall, and his strong arm looked like it was holding up a rag doll.

Trepidation ripped through Monique like a bullet tearing through skin.

"No!" she screamed, a blood curdling sound, as she ran down the stairs and started pummeling Pete. "Get off my mommy, get off, get off, get off..."

"No," Miriam whispered, trying to shake her head. Pete looked at Monique and his gripped softened but he didn't let go.

"Go upstairs," he said, pointing to her room.

"Get off!" Monique punched his side.

Pete ignored her as if her punches and kicks and screams weren't even happening. He turned his attention back to Miriam. "I keep telling you, begging you…you don't know me; you have no idea what I will do and it's all for my kids. Don't ever threaten taking my daughter from me! Don't ever call my children names!"

His hands were shaking now, and Miriam's body was being shaken with each word. "…but you keep pushing…you keep threatening, keep speaking hate over my son…over my seed! They are Waters! You ain't!"

"Pete, I'm sorry!" Drool ran down Miriam's lips, her eyes were rolling.

"Daddy, let her go…please, God. Please, please stop Daddy. Please let her go!"

"They are Waters! You ain't!" He said it over and over again.

"Monique…go…upstairs!" Miriam barely got the words out. The whites of her eyes were turning red. Monique looked at her father and realized that even though he was standing in the same room with them, his mind wasn't there. He was somewhere else, caught in the family warp, the Waters loyal net woven by his two big brothers, who were now dead.

"I stayed! They said stay with you! They said you were a good woman, the one to stay with! My brothers chose you…but you ain't Waters! That mouth…that fucking mouth of yours! We would be good, we could have it all, a good life, love and all that…but for your gotdamn mouth!"

Monique backed up the stairs, her eyes on Pete. She didn't know him right now. She could tell that he wasn't really seeing Miriam, wasn't really aware that he was strangling the life out of her.

She turned around and ran back up the stairs. She had to get him off of her mother. She thought about calling 911, but that was something that she had been trained never to do. She ran into her mother's bedroom, to the huge oak dresser and pulled out the revolver that Pete kept on the third shelf with his ties.

It was heavy. Cold steel.

Monique ran back down the stairs. Pete was still talking. Miriam's eyes were closed; drool was running down her slack jaw, onto his arm.

"Get off my mommy!"

Pete didn't even look at her. "…and I swallow it…out of love! I let you disrespect my seed…my future! My son can't even come into my home! I let you talk shit about me…about who my peoples is…about my brothers! You got my children separated! I even allow that and you ain't even blood—"

"I hate you!" Monique pulled the trigger. The loud explosion shocked her, knocked her into the wall and she dropped the gun.

Pete snapped out of his haze, letting go of Miriam as his eyes finally saw Monique, saw the gun, saw Miriam dropping to the floor like a sack of potatoes at the base of the stairs.

"Mommy!" Monique pushed past her stunned father, to her mother. Miriam's eyes were closed and she wasn't moving. "No, Mommy, no, don't leave me! I'm so sorry Mommy, please, please don't leave me!"

"No!" Pete stepped back, his face stricken in pain as if he had been shot. "Miriam!"

"Stay away from my Mommy!" Monique screamed at the top of her lungs as she held Miriam's face. "Mommy please, please, don't leave me! Please don't leave me!"

Monique's hysterical sobs overwhelmed her body. She wrapped her arms around her mother, sure she was dead.

"Miriam!" Pete picked up the gun and tucked it into his pants. He ran to the kitchen and returned with a cup of cold water that he splashed on her face. Miriam flinched a little.

"Mommy, please…"

"She is going to be alright, Monique," Pete was on the house phone making a call.

Monique heard his low tone talking into the phone. "I hate you!"

"I promise, baby girl, she will be alright. I will make it alright." He hung up the phone.

"I hate you." Monique wedged her body into a corner, holding her mother tight. "I swear Daddy, I hate you."

Miriam started coughing.

Monique held her tight, still rocking.

"I'm okay, Monique," Miriam whispered. "I just fainted, love. I'm okay. I promise."

"Go." Monique stared at Pete, as if seeing him for the first time. He had almost taken away her entire foundation. Just like that. "Leave."

"Monique, your father—"

"No, she's right." Pete shook his head. "We can't keep doing this Miriam. I can't hurt you like this again."

Miriam pushed herself up. "What are you saying?"

"We can't do this. I can't do this. Not anymore."

Monique couldn't take anymore. She wished she still had the gun, so they would listen. "Go. Get out."

"Monique, stop—"

"My child wants me gone, Miriam. My baby girl doesn't want me around. This is what I am now, a monster to her."

"Get out!" Monique screamed as loud as she could, her hands over her ears, her eyes closed.

Pete held the gun and looked at Monique. He fingered the bullet hole in the wooden banister by his hand.

Monique open her mouth and wailed.

Pete walked out, closing the door ever so gently behind him. Monique barely heard it click.

Miriam wrapped her arms around her daughter and tried to stop the sound of soul destruction that poured from her lungs like molten lava, until Monique choked and gagged, vomit tumbling from her belly all over the steps.

CHAPTER FOURTEEN

The Choice

Michelle, age 11

"I got to make a stop by the laundromat," Pete said. "Then we can go get that other thing before we head to the casino."

"Casino?" Marshall shook his head. "I am not even trying to drive all the way to Niagara Falls. Not tonight, champ." Marshall turned the steering wheel slowly, as if his huge Cadillac were the most delicate machine in the world. "I promised I would take my niece and nephew to Darien Lake tomorrow. No way am I going back and forth on the road like that."

"Stop complaining. I just thought you wanted to hang out. You want to bitch up and babysit, I understand. You do you." Pete laughed.

"Oh, I'm bitching out now, right? Whatever." Marshall coasted down the street. "Just because you can't stand kids…"

"What? I got three kids of my own." Pete went from laughing to be irritated.

"Yeah, and where do you take them?" Marshall turned up the radio. "I ain't never heard you say that you take them on any real trips."

"I gotta explain myself to you?" Pete snuffed out his cigar in the ashtray.

"You are the most sensitive mother fucker! Control yourself. It ain't that serious. You just don't seem to like being around kids."

"That's why they got mothers." Pete rubbed his head. "I stay in my lane. I provide for them. Take them here or there. I get in my time."

"To each his own."

"Yo," Pete shouted. "You ain't even got no kids!"

Marshall laughed. "Yo, calm down." Marshall turned up the music. "You're too damn big to always be acting so damn sensitive."

"What you say to me?" Pete put the cigar down.

"You heard me." Marshall didn't tense up at all.

They rode in silence for a few minutes.

"Which laundry?" Marshall said.

"Over off Atlantic." Pete answered, his irritation subsiding.

He had a deeper issue that he had to handle. He was past the five days that Frank had given him to handle the situation with Marshall. He couldn't do it. He had thought about it over and over again. Pete was loyal, if nothing else. Loyalty was something he was starting to question about Monty, though. Monty wanted it done and had offered to do it himself. The fear of the Italians seemed to send Monty from his normal cool into schoolgirl panic.

Pete didn't like this side of Monty. Monty already had a fall guy setup too, the gunman Anthony. He had convinced Anthony to take the charges in exchange for clearing out his debts and taking care of his family.

Pete glanced at Marshall. It was stupid of him to have shot the priest. It didn't make any sense. But Pete couldn't judge what a man did during an adrenaline rush caused by attacking a church. Maybe Marshall had just lost control. But fighting in the war had also taught Pete that men like Marshall, who did erratic evil acts at crucial times, had to be eliminated. To kill the priest in cold blood was a coward act. It was an evil act. And it made Pete wonder just what Marshall was capable. Why was he the best uncle in the world, but didn't have his own family?

Pete tried to clear his head. He was bouncing back and forth between killing Marshall or facing the Italians. And confronting the Italians was winning, because, at the end of the day, he didn't like the idea of a white man telling him to kill his friend. It went against his nature on general principle alone.

"I forgot," Pete said. "We got to pick up Mikki from school today. Her mother got something to do."

"Cool." Marshall pulled into the parking lot. "Listen, Mikki and Ricardo could come to Darien Lake with us tomorrow. Ricardo and Army seemed to get along."

Pete nodded as he got out of the car. "Maybe." He walked into the laundromat and headed to the back. The manager met him back there and they handled the exchange quickly. As Pete moved back to the car, he watched Marshall sitting in the driver's seat, staring straight ahead. He seemed like a different person, when he was alone and unaware he was being observed. The good guy persona was gone, instead he had a leering look, which reminded Pete of a snake.

It was interesting Pete had never noticed it before. He wondered again whether he was tripping, whether his mind was trying to justify taking the easier route and putting an end to Marshall himself.

Pete shook the thought from his head. He glanced at the clock on the dashboard when he returned to the car. "We're late."

Marshall sat forward, increasing his speed.

"Slow your roll." Pete said. "She will be okay waiting for a little bit. We rolling dirty, don't risk getting pulled over."

Marshall slowed down.

The car slowly pulled up long the front of the middle school. Michelle was sitting on the front steps playing Chain with a smaller girl, teaching her the chant, their hands claps moving in motion to their rhythmic chant. Several children still milled around the front of the school and a group of teachers stood against the front columns, talking amongst themselves.

"Pull up here." Pete motioned to the side, several feet away from the school. He didn't want the teachers to take notice of the car or Marshall. He glanced around at the parents walking to get their children and the other parked cars.

Pete climbed out of the car, brushed off his shirt and tucked in his pants. Teachers could be very judgmental people, Miriam had confirmed that. He didn't want Michelle suffering any disadvantage because a teacher smelled smoke on him or because he looked like he had been in the streets all day. He hated coming to these schools and tried to avoid interacting with teachers, but sometimes it couldn't be avoided.

As Pete moved toward the front of the building, he noticed a black Lincoln Continental parked in front of the school, directly opposite Michelle. The window was rolled down. There was a driver in the front seat. As Pete stepped closer he realized that Frank was sitting in the rear seat, looking out the window at Michelle.

Pete neared the car. Frank made eye contact with him. Frank looked at his watch and raised his eyebrows.

Pete stopped walking. The moment seemed to last a lifetime.

Finally, Frank gave a little shake of his head. He said something to the driver and the car slowly pulled forward.

As Pete watched the car pull off, he realized he had been holding his breath.

Frank was at his daughter's school. Watching. Sending a quiet message. He hadn't made a move for Michelle, but he was letting Pete know that he could touch her, if he had to.

Pete picked Michelle up and wrapped her in his arms, forgetting that she was 11 years old.

"Daddy," she hugged him back in school girl innocence. She tried to let go and scramble down, but Pete held her closely, grasping her bag in the other hand. Michelle was so tiny that he sometimes forgot how old she was.

"Daddy, what's wrong?"

"Nothing." Pete took a couple of steps. "Listen, has anybody ever talked to you while you are out here waiting for Rebe?"

"Talked to me? A stranger?" Michelle shook her head. "No Daddy." Her eyes were shiny with fear. "I don't talk to people I don't know."

Pete finally put her down and let her walk, but he held her hand. If the choice was that simple—Marshall or his own children—then it was not even a choice. Marshall was going to die. Today.

Michelle chatted to Marshall as they drove to her house. Michelle sighed and rolled her eyes. "But Daddy, why can't I go home with you?"

"I got things to do."

"Daddy," Michelle pouted and pushed her feet against the seat. "You always got stuff to do. Come on, please. I don't want to go home and watch Tonio."

Pete bit the inside of his cheek. Who knew Rebe would turn into a baby factory? She was pregnant again, leaving Michelle to babysit her baby brothers and sisters. It bothered him, his baby girl didn't deserve to be Rebe's live-in caregiver.

"I will come back and get you. You can stay with Lela for a little while." Pete paused. If Michelle said another word against him, it would upset him. He had things to do and had to figure out how to do it.

"Okay, Daddy, I understand."

Her faithful compliance changed his mind. Whatever was going down with Marshall had to be planned and it wasn't happening until the late hours of the night anyway.

"You're right." He nodded at Marshall. "Never mind, she can roll with me for a little while. Take me to the trap off Clinton. Nothing happening over there, I got some stuff to get ready anyway."

Marshall shrugged and changed directions. Pete sighed. "Make sure nobody is following us." He couldn't deny Michelle, just like he couldn't say no to Monique. They were the small holes in his armor, the two places an arrow could penetrate.

Seems like everyone already knew that. First El tried to snatch up Monique, now Frank was sitting at Michelle's school.

The path to dethroning him was too wide open and obvious. Pete had to go underground. That much was clear. The war he had raged all over Rochester to avenge Jimmy had increased his exposure. And his circle was too wide, too many people knew that his family cared about itself and its children and nothing more. If there was already a price on his children's heads, if they were already clearly identified, then Pete would have to up the ante. He would mark his kids himself, loudly, so that they were easily identified as Waters. But the mark would also be a death warning. There would be no more threats on his children's life—if he marked them and someone dared harmed them, anguish would pour down ten-fold on that person and their own loved ones. Just like he had done to the Perez's, he would extend it beyond El, to the Italians if he had to. If New York wanted to get involved, they were more than welcome. Pete could fight them, also. He had other ties that were unknown to anyone, even to his brothers, that extended across the south and to the mid-west. Fighting in Vietnam had given him some valuable collections, if nothing else.

The days of threatening his children were over. He would take steps to eliminate that, immediately.

When they got to the house on Clinton, Pete let himself in. Sheila's house was empty, as it had been for months, ever since she had gone down to South Carolina to help her mother. Pete paid the bills and ran things out of her house on the low. It was a mutually beneficial relationship that he had with Sheila for a couple of years. This was where he could often rest his head when the tension everywhere else was too thick.

Michelle slung her bag on the couch and headed for the refrigerator. "Daddy, you want me to make you a sandwich?"

"Yes, baby girl." Pete slumped into the couch. He was tired. He hadn't slept in a couple of days.

Marshall went to the bathroom. A few minutes later, he came out. "I got some runs to make."

Pete nodded. He didn't want to be left in the house without any soldiers, especially with Michelle here. The tension in the streets was too thick right now. "How long you gone for?"

"Not long. I will call Monty to come through."

"No, don't worry about it." Pete felt his teeth grinding against themselves. "I'm good." Pete pulled out a large blunt, snapped open the blade he always carried and split the cigar open.

Marshall motioned to the kitchen. "Baby girl's in there."

Pete felt his earlier irritation rise up. "I know my damn daughter is here, nigga. Who you talking to?"

Marshall shook his head. "She going to get contact high."

"I smoke in front of my kids all the damn time." Pete pulled out a small package and opened it with his finger. "You really getting on my damn nerves with this parenting shit."

Marshall sat down.

"What are you doing? Ain't you leaving?"

Marshall shook his head. "Naw. Imma chill for a second." Marshall picked up the remote and turned the television on.

Michelle walked back into the room with two sandwiches. She sat Pete's food in front of him and looked at the cigar. "Daddy, can I watch TV upstairs?"

Pete nodded. If Michelle weren't here he would have picked up Ramona on the way over here, so he could really relax. The thought of Ramona made him smirk. She had some tricks that could keep him occupied. He could give her a call in the morning, when he finished other business, though.

Michelle sat a beer on the table. "I'll be in Miss Sheila's room, alright?"

Pete knew that his daughter wasn't really asking; she was reminding them, so that neither of them busted in the room with any females, forgetting that she was in the house. It had happened more than once before. He shook his head and nodded at her. "I hear you."

He was going to get rid of some of these women, too. Not Ramona, of course, but some of the others. It probably wasn't good that Michelle could make herself comfortable in anyone's house, could go from house to house without missing a beat. Something about that didn't really sit well with him either, although he couldn't put his finger on it. That was something that would have to change, too.

Pete sealed the blunt as he watched Michelle disappear up the stairs. He took a few deep puffs and sat back with his eyes closed, waiting for the mellow feeling to invade his mind. After a few more minutes, and a few more puffs, he passed it to Marshall. Marshall puffed away, his prior parenting concerns fading in the presence of the scented smoke. They smoked and watched the television, until Pete's vision became blurry and sleep finally invaded him.

***

The volume on the television was blasting, waking Pete up. He sat straight up and reached for the 45 caliber in his holster.

It took Pete a few seconds to get his bearings. He realized that he had been asleep and shook his head. He had too much to do to sleep. The volume of the television seemed like it was at the loudest pitch. He turned to see Marshall's hand laying on the remote.

Pete sighed and pushed Marshall's hand away. He snatched the remote and lowered the volume.

He stood up and stretched his muscles. He hadn't heard from Monty. Pete checked his pager. It looked like he had missed a million calls. The dull high of the blunt had soothed his nerves, but something in the back of his mind was still bothering him. He couldn't figure out what. Pete checked his watch. It was after 10 pm. He went to the liquor rack in the living room and grabbed a bottle of whiskey. Pete poured himself a shot, running through the mental list that he had to complete tonight.

Marshall coughed in his sleep. Pete looked at him. It returned to him. Disposing of Marshall. The thing he didn't want to do, but had no choice. And it was Marshall's fault. Who kills a priest in cold blood?

Pete stared at Marshall, who slept with his mouth open. He could do it now. While Marshall was asleep, without any explanation. Something about that seemed wrong. Pete felt like he owed Marshall an explanation, owed him to wake him up and look him in his eyes before killing him.

Pete drank another shot. He could just slit Marshall's throat. It would take a few minutes for him to die that way, though. And Pete didn't want him to suffer. He owed Marshall at least that. He could snuff out his breath, but then there would be a struggle. That wasn't a good option because then it would seem like he was be attacking Marshall, and this death wasn't personal. It wasn't an attack. It was the price for the priest. Pure and simple. He would shoot Marshall rather than cut him. But still, did he owe Marshall to look him in the eyes as he brought on death, to explain to him what was happening? Jimmy believed it was better for the soul to have an explanation than to leave it tormented with the question of "why" never answered. Jimmy was always right.

Pete went into the kitchen and opened the bottom compartment under the oven. He took out his tool kit and lifted out the gloc and the silencer. As Pete walked back through the house, he made sure all the blinds were lowered and all the curtains drawn.

Pete tapped Marshall hard on the head with the tip of the silencer and took a few steps back. "Wake up."

"Pete, what are you doing?" Marshall pushed his body back into the chair, his eyes wide with terror. "Are you high? What's wrong with you?"

"The priest." Pete shook his head. "I don't want to do this, but there is a price for the priest."

"No, Pete, come on, man." Marshall shook his head. "You're my brother, man. I took an oath for the Waters. I paid the price."

Pete bit his lip. "I love you like a brother. That's the truth. But if you were blood, I couldn't do this. Me and my kids might have to die for you. Blood is thicker. It's either you or me and mine. I can't have that." Pete exhaled. "You caused this, so man up. Take this like a man. I woke you up because I wanted you to know. I love you, as much as I can. But this bullet you got to take."

"No, there is something you can do. You put Perez over me?"

"They are all Catholic, Marshall. It's not just the Perez's anymore. The Italians are Catholic. You shoot a priest, you get them involved."

"I went into that church for you, Pete! That was your call, what you wanted. And now I got to pay the price?" Marshall motioned forward, as if he were going to lunge off the couch.

"Don't do it." Pete lifted up the 45 from its holster and held it in his left hand. "I am giving you the respect you deserve. Man up and take this fucking bullet."

"Man up? What about my nephew, Pete? Army doesn't have anyone but me, Pete. How could you do this?"

"I will make sure he is covered. You know that."

"Is this because of your woman? You're putting a gun to my head over Miriam?"

"What?" Pete's finger fell from the trigger. "What do you have to do with Miriam?"

"Nothing." Marshall began taking deep gulps of air. "Do it."

They stared at each other for a long minute. Pete stood there. "What about my woman?"

"Do it!" Marshall screamed at the top of his lungs. "Aww!" He screamed as if the agony were so deep he couldn't control himself. "Fuck you, just do it!"

Pete hesitated. "Miriam?"

Marshall sprang off the couch.

Pete pulled the trigger of both guns as he backed up.

Marshall staggered in midair and slumped, falling sideways.

Pete fell backward and hit his head on the edge of the coffee table. He felt his neck twist and pain washed down his back like warm liquid. He dropped both guns.

For a second, Pete was out of it. When he came to, Pete could hear Marshall groaning. He had flubbed the job. Disappointment rang through him. The point of waking the man had been to spare him the agony of a slow death and Pete had failed. Pete summoned all the energy he had to push himself up. He had to finish the job. Pete pushed himself up on his knees. The room tilted. Pete lost his breath, the dizziness was so sudden. It didn't matter. He could barely turn his neck, instead he had to turn his entire torso. Marshall was slumped against the couch, a shot to the neck and to the chest. Pete picked up the gloc with the silencer, which was nearest his hand, and pointed it directly between Marshall's eyes.

"My fault, man," Pete said. In the end, Miriam was just another woman. A conduit for his seed. Marshall was his warrior. Pete put nothing past a woman, and he wasn't going to ask about her again. This wasn't about pussy. It was about him and Marshall and the code of the streets. He owed Marshall the dignity of ending it quickly.

Marshall stared in his eyes.

The sound of the explosion was loud. Marshall's eyes closed, his head snapped back, and his entire body relaxed. Pete looked at the gun he was holding, keeping it away from his face, puzzled that the bullet had been so loud, wondering why the silencer was ineffective. Then he heard the sound of metal falling to the floor and looked down to see his other gun, the 45 without the silencer, falling from Marshall's hand. Marshall had pulled the trigger one last time.

Pete felt the searing pain in his chest as the bullet lodged inside of him. Pete laughed, "You son of a bitch." That's why Pete loved Marshall. Pete staggered over to the chair, his hand holding his chest. This was fair enough. Considering all the lives he had taken, all the pain he had caused, he could accept this fate.

Pete could hear his heart pumping loudly. He closed his eyes. Memories flooded through his mind, each one deeply intimate. Pete knew then, as the memories splashed across his mental screen, that he was dying. The pain was so intense that Pete wanted to shout out in agony, but he didn't. He accepted that this is how it was going to end. Finally, death had come to claim him—she had taken her damn time and he didn't expect it to hurt like this, but damn if he was going to complain. The painful jumbled rollercoaster ride of life was finally over, and he would be with his brothers again.

Pete thought he saw a crack of silver in the darkness. Not the white light he had heard of. But then again, heaven probably wasn't in his forecast. Jimmy was standing there, though, his wild afro swaying in the light. Pete started laughing. John was standing next to him, as solemn and stern as ever. He was more a father than a brother. Pete felt such a deep relief that sobs ripped from him. He could finally have some peace.

"Daddy?"

The angelic voice of a little girl seemed so out of place here. Pete looked at Jimmy and John. Neither of them were looking at him, though. And neither of them were smiling, nor did they look happy. Both looked just over his shoulder, concerned expressions covering their faces.

"Daddy, no! Daddy, oh my God. Daddy, what happened?"

Pete looked back. Whose voice was that? He didn't want to go back. He wanted to keep moving forward to the peaceful silver light.

"No, oh no Daddy! Please don't leave me. Noo!" The blood curdling screams of a child stopped him. He turned around, knowing that if he looked back his brothers and the peaceful space would be gone. But he had to know who was calling him.

"Daddy!" Tiny hands were gripping his face and his arm. Only one person had hands that small.

Michelle. Pete had forgotten Michelle was in the house. It was Michelle calling him as if he were God himself, pleading for his life. Pete had forgotten that he had someone to live for. Three someones, to be exact. He couldn't leave Ricardo, Monique and Michelle just yet, no matter what. He couldn't. With the deepest sense of loss pulling on him like a noose, Pete returned to the sound of his daughter losing her mind.

He opened his eyes. "Stop screaming, Mikki. I'm okay."

"Daddy!" Michelle was hysterical, her wild hair flying all over her head, her tiny features swimming in and out of Pete's line of sight. "Tell me what to do, Daddy, who do I call? Are you dying? What happened? Don't leave me, Daddy."

"No, don't call 911. Okay, baby girl?" Pete tried to speak through her screams. "Mikki, stop screaming." Pete tried to push himself up, but couldn't move. "Close your mouth and your eyes and count to ten. Mikki, listen to me, dammit! Like Uncle Jimmy taught you. Deep breaths."

He heard Michelle counting, heard her voice lowering from shrieks to mere panic. "Listen to me. Do not call 911. Do you hear me?"

"Yes, Daddy."

"Call Uncle Monty. Only tell him where you are. Do not mention me or Marshall." Pete groaned. "Don't say any more than that on the phone. Do you understand?"

"Yes, Daddy."

Pete felt consciousness fading. "Do it now. If I fall asleep, you cannot panic. You have to stay calm and let Monty in the house. Do you understand? Don't answer the door for anyone but Monty. Listen for the code when he knocks."

"Yes, Daddy."

"Listen, if I die or he doesn't come in the next half hour, then you leave. Do you understand me?"

"No, Daddy, I'm not—"

"—Mikki, what time is it?"

He heard her moving around. "It's 10:47, Daddy."

"If Monty is not here by 11:15, you leave. No matter what."

Silence.

"Promise me."

"Go where, Daddy?"

"You know how to get home from here, Mikki. I know you do. Do not be here after 11:15, okay? You leave and go home to Rebe. Talk to no one else. She will know what to do."

"Yes, Daddy."

"Go make the call."

Pete listened to Michelle, who followed his strict orders, her voice shaking. He thought about his little daughter sitting there between a dead man and a half dead man. This was something she should never have had to experience. This was his fault. He had forgotten she was even in the house when he made the move on Marshall. Marshall was right, what type of a father was he?

Pete chased away the feeling of helplessness with a determined promise to himself. Life was going to change for the Waters. It was going to become as normal as he could possibly make it, even if that meant that he had to deny himself the wildness of his life. His children were going to have the opportunity to have something he and his brothers never had: a chance at a stability. His legacy, the second generation of Waters were going to be bonded by his determination, protected by his determination and promised a chance at a real life, by his determination.

CHAPTER FIFTEEN

The Choice

Armand, age 12

"We are gonna be alright."

The soft voice entered Armand's ears, but not his mind. His mind was blank, like it had been for days…weeks…months…years; ever since the fire, ever since he had lost everything. People said the stupidest things in the wake of his loss, promising him that things would be better and life would move on; that someday the pain would lessen, or more incredibly, promising him that one day the pain would suddenly disappear.

It didn't. His mother, sister and grandmother were dead and there was nothing that would change that, bring them back or get rid of the heavy weight that sat on his chest day in and out. The pain wasn't going away. He was just learning to cope with it, to carry it with him like a book bag of emotion sutured to his body. It would be with him forever and words of sentiment meant nothing.

"Army, baby, I'll be able to put some money aside to fix the water heater in a couple of weeks, once my checks come in." His Grandma Queen nodded at him. She was his father's mother and the only person from his father's family that came to get him from the foster home. They had all been at the funeral; both sides of Armand's family, Camilla's father and all her family. News crews and pastors and deacons and tears and the never ending stream of words meant to console that only gave more grief.

Only Uncle Marshall hadn't come. Armand knew, without doubt, that he must be dead somewhere. Uncle Marshall would never have missed burying his own mother, twin sister and only niece and he never would have left Armand without a place to go with no home.

It had been months of floating in foster care. The survival instinct Uncle Marshall taught him had come in handy. His first two foster mothers had been alright. Armand kept to himself, went to school and stayed away from the house until he had no choice. Then, he did his chores and stayed in line but the other kids presented the problem; stealing, playing games for favoritism and lying on him. It made Armand have to get savvy, even manipulative, to think two steps ahead of the people around him to stay under the radar and survive.

Then, Grandma Queen arrived at his case worker's office and he had a home again; a huge old house off Park Avenue that she inherited. It was falling apart around her but it was a home. Armand appreciated it. She didn't discuss his father and he didn't ask. All that mattered was that she had come to get him, to rescue him. So this was life now, he and his Grandma Queen, struggling to make ends meet.

Her old house was freezing and Grandma Queen was sitting in front of him, wrapped in blankets.

Armand tried to keep a crazy expression off his face. He wanted to yell "Rochester New York in the winter without heat? No way is everything okay." Instead, he said, "Grandma, I can't let you sit up in here all day without heat."

"No, boy, don't you worry about me. It's Senior Day at the church. They will be here to get me at 11."

Armand breathed heavily and dropped his head. "That's not the point. We need the heat on."

"Once I get my check, we gonna get some of those space heaters—"

"Grandma, it's below freezing outside. Space heaters are not going to heat up the whole house. Plus, we need to use that money to get the furnace fixed."

"I had Ernest come look at it and he said—"

"Ernest don't know nothing about a hot water furnace, Grandma Queen."

She giggled, a light soft laugh that always made Armand smile. He wished he had grown up knowing her, instead of having to lose everyone else first. He never asked her why she hadn't come around before. He didn't really want to know. As kind as she was, there had to be some reason and he couldn't stand to hear a negative word against his grandmother or his mother. Some things were better left unsaid.

"Sho' you right, son. Ernest don't know his head from his ass most the time." She shook her head. "But he fix stuff for free."

"Hmph." Armand wanted to point out that Ernest had to work for free, because nobody was going to pay him to make things worse, but he didn't want to seem disrespectful.

"Army, we will make it…don't worry, son. You got to have faith."

"I know, I hear you."

"My social security check will be here next week. I can give you—"

Armand felt his heart sink. He looked down at his sneakers, they were old. He had been wearing the same kicks for a few weeks. His clothes were faded from being washed and worn over and over again and his whites were too white, because Grandma Queen used some old school lye that turned white into a neon version of normal.

There was a solution. One that Uncle Marshall had prepared him for, one that he had tried to avoid for years. He didn't have gangster dreams, didn't care about flossing or trying to be the big boss in everyone's eyes, but he did have the dream of a good life. Like the people he saw when he went to Eastview Mall with Raymond. When they drove to Victor, New York, they passed big houses with three and four car garages, the Infiniti SUVs filled with soccer moms and privileged kids. He had an idea of a life, where he went to work every day in a boss man suit, propped up in a cozy office. Armand wanted a banging ass wife, who had her own degree, was also a professional, dressed in sexy tight suits with his picture on her office desk. The two of them would have that good life. That suburban, plush, working the system, kind of thing and his family would come with him.

That's all his dreams had ever been about, but life was swinging that path further away from him, pushing him closer and closer to the only solution that would put food on the table now, turn the heat on now and help Grandma Queen get the $800.00 orthotic inserts she needed for her shoes now. It was a chance for him to get some decent clothes so he could at least be comfortable in public, now.

Armand looked at his hands. He couldn't delay any further. Winter was here and he wasn't going to let Grandma Queen freeze. She wasn't going to be this year's elderly person found dead in the house from Rochester's bitter cold. He was going to miss going to school. If he made this choice then the vision that he so desperately wanted—he and his wife and their professional life, was going to be distorted, warped, or completely eliminated.

What choice did he have? A possible unlikely future for an undercover honor student or the certainty of hunger and freezing now? It wasn't really a choice.

Armand stood up and pulled on his book bag. Grandma Queen handed him a piece of toast. "Have a good day in school, Army." She hugged him. A hug she had given him every morning since she brought him home. A hug that he appreciated more than anyone in the world could have known. He never raised his arms back and never hugged her back. He just couldn't, but she hugged him anyway. "You're a smart boy."

He nodded and walked out the door. Frost had covered the cars and the sidewalks, like a dry coating of white, angled and cracked like a complicated spider web. Armand hated the sight of frost. To him it was the sign of death and doom, creeping across the surface of life. It was a silent killer. He walked up the street toward the school bus, certain that Grandma Queen was watching, but when he got to the bus stop he nodded at a few of his people and kept walking.

There was no more school for him.

Armand kept walking, making his way back to the west side of the city. He wanted to walk; he needed to kill time. He stopped at a corner store and grabbed some juice that he drank inside. After sipping on the bottle and taking in the store's heat, he tossed the bottle and kept moving. When he got to the narrow house on Tremayne Street, he paused and stood out front, still hesitant if this was the right move to make.

He thought of the science laboratory at school and the project he had been working on—creating a nylon substance from nothing but chemicals. If he did it right, his mixture should ultimately create a sheet like stockings. Chemistry had him captivated. He enjoyed mixing substances, simply changing the temperature and creating something from it. Maybe he should give up the thought in his head and go to school, catch the bus and make it in time for class, and get back to life as usual.

Then he thought about Grandma Queen, bundled up under three blankets last night, her swollen feet peeking out of the covers. He thought of the empty refrigerator and how she struggled to create whole meals out of nothing, like the leftovers she would bring home from the seniors luncheon that she would doctor up into dinner. He was sick of looking in empty cabinets until her checks arrived.

"Yo, why are you lingering in front of my spot, young boy?"

Armand looked up. Titan was standing at the front door in a wife beater and some basketball shorts, puffing on a cigarillo, as if it wasn't colder than ice outside.

Titan smiled. "I ain't seen you in a minute, youngin'. You got tall."

Armand shrugged, looked up and down the street. He could still walk away.

"Titan, you letting in the cold!" The woman's voice sounded irritated.

"Yo, quiet that," Titan said over his shoulder, his voice smooth and even. The woman didn't say another word.

"I heard you been through some shit, man."

Armand looked directly at him for the first time.

"The streets talk, especially when it goes down bad like that. I'm sorry about your family."

Armand nodded and looked down at his feet. At least Titan hadn't looked at him with the same pity he had to deal with from everybody else.

Titan studied him for a few seconds. "Come in and talk to me, youngin'...what's on your mind?"

Armand took a few steps toward the door. He could smell bacon and pancakes. He involuntarily licked his lips.

"We got grits happening up in here. Eggs, bacon and pancakes." Titan's eyebrows raised as he shrugged. "She even makes mimosas."

Armand looked confused.

"It's just spiked orange juice." Titan smiled, a sympathetic look on his face. "I know you're hungry. I see that."

Armand didn't deny the obvious.

"Cierra, make some more food for my youngin'," Titan called out. "And my bacon better not be pork 'cuz that's what I'm smelling." Armand moved closer and stepped onto the porch. Titan took his hand in a normal street handshake.

"Damn you are cold, son!" He laughed as he snatched his hand back. "How long you been out here?" Titan glanced around the street. "No gloves on?" Titan shook his head. "No hat? You trying to catch pneumonia, huh?" He was quiet for a second as he glanced up and down the quiet street. "Wait, you walked over here? I thought you was over on the East side now?" Titan's expression changed as if really understanding the situation.

Armand didn't answer. He stood just in front of the door, a deep sense of urgency pressing against his gut, telling him to walk away; to go to school, to hold on and have faith.

He shook his head to clear the fear. That was what his grandmother and mother would say, to hold on and have faith. Where were they at now with all their faith? Gone. No, he couldn't have blind hope only to freeze and starve to death. He owed Grandma Queen, he had to make it worth the sacrifice that she made for him. He owed it to her that she didn't have to suffer. He was a man. He had to make things happen for himself and his grandmother and it had to happen now.

Titan clapped a hand on his shoulder. "Come on, Football, get outta the cold, boy." Titan gestured with his head to the narrow house behind him.

Armand clenched his teeth.

Titan looked him in the eye. "You made the right move, Army, by coming over here."

Armand met his eye. Titan had never called him by his name before. For some reason, something in Armand clicked; the fear fell away and hunger for something better took over. Titan could show him the way to make the money he needed, get the power he wanted and change his circumstances.

Armand was ready. He stepped through the door and entered an entirely different world.

CHAPTER SIXTEEN

Away

Monique, age 10

Miriam's hands smoothed the front of the snug fitting dress. She eyed herself in the mirror. She had gained weight. The bags under her eyes had disappeared and her skin was shiny. Her black hair was shiny also, although the few gray streaks that she had noticed in her mane were still there. She sighed. Gray hair was the burden of being with Pete, worrying about his safety and her own safety. Monique's safety. Funny, she hadn't thought about safety or risk until Monique had been born. Before that Pete seemed all powerful. He spoke and the world moved. He issued commands and others complied. Miriam found that power exhilarating. Her bills were always covered, her needs were always met—without having to ask. Prior to Monique being born, their life together was a whirlwind of dates, traveling wherever her imagination landed, and being fully consumed in Pete Waters.

Then she held his child in her arms and it seemed that the "all-powerful one" had a vulnerability. He loved his child. Pete's love for Monique was more than Miriam had ever seen or imagined. At first it was sweet. Then, it stung at her heart a little, how he looked at the baby with all-consuming eyes, without noticing that she, the child's mother, was sitting right there.

Miriam cleared her mind. She wasn't jealous. That wasn't it. It was just that once the child was born, that seemed to be her only purpose to Pete. Taking care of his child. No more exotic trips, no more long days and nights lounging in each other's arms. No more her. Just Pete and Monique. Another Waters.

And the missing link in Pete's coat of armor was not only evident to Miriam, apparently the entire world saw it. So now, when anyone wanted to get at Pete, it was aimed at Monique. At first it had been Rebe, Michelle's mother, swearing she didn't want Michelle around Monique. Pete had squashed that. But Rebe's hard position softened as soon as she landed another man—her first husband. Then Michelle could spend all the time with Pete and Miriam that they wanted, since they were providing Rebe with free babysitting. Then it had been the brothers, Jimmy constantly trying to tell Pete to discipline Monique, to stop pouring favoritism on her. Miriam agreed with the discipline, but it also made her wary because Pete began to put up barriers around his heart. He always listened to his brothers. Miriam didn't realize that, either, until after Monique had been born. She hadn't known his brothers would have reign over her world.

Now Pete's enemies knew to make Monique the target. Pete gloating about her accomplishments and how successful she was going to be in life displayed his wide open heart for Monique. And those intent to carve out Pete's heart headed directly to Monique.

Miriam had enough. After the last shooting, with Pete laying in the basement doctor's office looking like he was dying, Miriam had snatched Monique out of Rochester. They were in Wilson, North Carolina, safely ensconced in her parent's home. And, tonight, Miriam had a date. Miriam wanted to remember what normal felt like. She wanted to be with a man who didn't have a double life, who could go places without worrying about being followed. She wanted to be bored for a change, swallowed up in the regularity of a man going to work and coming home, watching television with her and grilling in the backyard on the weekends. For the first time, Miriam craved what her mother had, what her sister had. And she was going to find it and secure it for herself and her daughter.

The phone rang. Miriam glanced at the clock. It was 5:30 pm. It was Pete. "Monique!" Miriam called out as she clamped her earrings on. "Monique, get the phone."

She heard her daughter from the other side of the house. "Okay, Mommy."

Miriam smiled. Monique had been happy since they arrived in North Carolina.

The phone stopped ringing. Miriam changed her purse, switching her items from her large day bag into a small clutch. She pushed a 9 millimeter in her purse, just in case. No. Miriam shook her head. She wasn't in Rochester anymore. She took the gun and placed it back in the box that she hid under the foot of the bed.

Miriam stared at her new shoes on the bed. A heavy weight sat on her chest, like she was cheating on Pete. She pushed it back. She refused to feel guilty. She and Pete were no longer a couple, there was no reason for her to stay holed up in the house. Plus, one thing she knew with certainty: He wasn't sitting around, lonely, waiting on her. Nature abhors a void, and human beings natural instinct is to fill a hole. Her removal from Pete's life only meant that another woman, or another few women, had been relied upon more heavily to fill the space that she left. It was that simple.

Miriam no longer believed in love, in "specialness." Life as a Water's woman had taught her better. In the end, it all meant nothing. All the Waters cared about were themselves and their seed. She was just a means to an end, someone by which a child could be born. And clearly even that job wasn't a difficult one to achieve,

Ricardo's mother was proof of that. If Pete was willing to have a child by Leslie, then just how special was being a baby's mother to him? Who knew how many other kids were out there that Miriam didn't even want to know about.

No. She wasn't going to get sucked in to emotion. It was time to be logical about the man she was connected to through Monique and what the real ramifications were. The sooner she faced the truth of it, the sooner she could move on.

Miriam moved toward the kitchen.

"Yes, me and Grandmommy are going back outside into the garden now, Daddy."

Miriam glanced over her shoulder at Monique. She stepped into the kitchen and opened the refrigerator.

"Yes, Mommy is here. She is about to go out." Miriam's head snapped around. She gave Monique a fierce expression.

Monique rolled her eyes at Miriam and looked away. "I don't know. She didn't say."

Miriam shook her head.

"I can't just leave, Daddy, what about school?"

Miriam knew where this conversation was going.

"Okay, Daddy, I love you, too." Monique handed Miriam the phone. "He wants to talk to you."

Miriam covered the phone with her hand. "About what?"

Monique shrugged and ran out of the side door.

Miriam cleared her throat. “Hello?”

“I never agreed to this.” Pete’s voice was low, barely a whisper.

Miriam glanced around the space, noting that her father, David, was in the adjoining family room. He was sitting in a lounge chair, his eyes closed and his mouth slightly open, soft snores filling the air. Miriam rolled her eyes. No way was he asleep. He was the nosiest person in the family.

“Yes, you did,” Miriam whispered, standing closer to the air conditioner, hoping the noise would drown out her voice. “I told you that I couldn’t take anymore. You got shot again, Pete, and Mikki was there. I can’t. I can’t do this anymore. I don’t even want Monique to know about it. She’s already worrying herself sick since you left us—”

“I didn’t just leave, Miriam. You know that. I tried to—”

“Pete, I told you we were going to see my parents for a little while—”

“Visit your parents, Miriam, not move to a different state and never return.” Pete’s voice trembled. “I haven’t seen my daughter in almost a year.”

“You talk to her every day, Pete—”

“Talk to her? I talk to her? You kidnapped my child!”

Miriam's heart skipped a beat. She had been juggling the balancing act between visiting her parents and moving away for the last six months. She had no intention of returning to Rochester, New York. It had been easy finding work as a school teacher in her old hometown, even easier watching Monique play with her cousins and relatives up and down the street, surrounded by family and love and completely removed from urban street grime. There was no reason to return. She had just hoped that she could fade away, blend into the scheme of life and by the time Pete realized what was happening, she would have been settled and long gone.

Sadness tugged at her mind. She still loved Pete. She loved him more than she loved herself or anyone else. With the exception of Monique. But Monique was the most important person, the only one whose life counted. And if being with Pete meant hiding in more hotel rooms, watching strangers snatch at her daughter and waking up in the middle of the night, certain that every creak was an enemy trying to break in, then she would have to be without Pete. Safety, no…sanity, required running from Pete, the Waters and everything connected to their life.

"I will get you a place, Miriam. Is that what this is about? You losing the old house? I shouldn't have cut off the money, but I was mad."

"No," Miriam leaned against the refrigerator. "There isn't anything wrong, Pete, I just need a break."

"Is it the tuition? I will put her back in private school. Tell me what I need to do to get my daughter home!" Pete's voice broke. "This isn't right, Miriam. You can't just take her."

"I didn't—"

"Stop bullshitting me!" Miriam could hear Pete's fist slam into the wall. She fell silent. "You put your shit in storage. You knew you weren't coming back. I will come down there and get her, if I have to."

That scared Miriam more than anything else. She believed Pete, deep down in her soul. His word had always been bond, even when she didn't agree with him. And the last thing she wanted was to open her parent's front door and have Pete standing there. There was no telling what hell Pete would rain down on their house to get his precious daughter back.

Miriam glanced out the window at Monique digging in the dirt of her grandmother's garden, with Lensy, her grandmother, standing over her reading the almanac. This was how her childhood had been, it was what Monique deserved. "Please Pete, we will just finish out the school year and then work out something."

"No." Pete's anger was no longer under control, his voice sounded like the roar of ocean slapping against a rock ledge.

Miriam paused, changing the topic. He had given his final answer and she knew there was no way to persuade him differently. "Are you going to call Monique back tonight before she goes to bed?"

Silence. He wasn't taking this much longer. Miriam had pushed too far. She shouldn't have mentioned school. She sat in silence, waiting on his response so she could measure how much time she had left.

"Have her call me before she falls asleep."

"Okay, Pete, I will—" the click of the phone was so loud that Miriam flinched. "Hello? Hello?"

Miriam softly placed the phone in the cradle and leaned against the counter. She wasn't ready to go back. There had to be a way to convince Pete to let them stay. She had nothing to return to. Monique had Pete, but there was nothing in that city attached to Miriam now that she no longer had Pete.

Her father coughed.

Miriam looked up.

David was looking directly at her.

Miriam looked down at the floor. There was so much her parents didn't know. She had never told them what Pete really was, what his family did. She never discussed her life with him or how he supported Monique. It had never occurred to her, until this very moment with David's eyes bearing into her, that they already knew. That her silence and half stories probably told her parents more about her secret life than her words ever could. They weren't stupid. She was the stupid one, thinking she could juggle a school teacher life and be a hustler's wife with no ramifications and no danger. She was the fool sneaking herself out of town, fooling herself into believing that none of her family knew exactly what she had attached herself to and how silly she was for staying.

Miriam dragged her eyes away from her father's. David stood up slowly and stretched, never taking his eyes from her. He walked slowly into the kitchen and took out a carton of milk.

"Baby girl's daddy, huh?" David cracked the carton open and poured milk into his mouth.

"Daddy, don't drink straight out of the container," Miriam mumbled, opening a cabinet for a glass.

"You don't have to go nowhere, you know that, right?" David put the carton directly to his lips a second time and slurped out of it.

"It's not like that, Daddy, he just misses his child."

David stared at her as he sat the milk on the counter. "These northern niggas, they think they know something. They don't know shit. He ain't coming down to my house taking nobody, you understand that?"

"I know, Daddy," Miriam nodded. David had a range of shot guns and hunting rifles. So did her brothers and uncles. "He just misses us, that's all."

"He miss his child. You, he could take or leave. Don't get it confused. But you are *my* baby girl. And he's not going to just walk all over you."

Miriam wanted this conversation to end. "It's not like that, Daddy," she said, turning to the kitchen sink to wash the few dishes to keep moving. She knew her father was right, it was exactly like that.

"Just remember, you got a home. Can't no one push you from it. Now, if you choose to leave and go into the world, then all I can do is support you and pray for you. But you always have a safe place to return to. That's why me and your mom built this home. You got that."

"Yes Daddy," Miriam nodded her head, but her heart sank. Her father didn't understand how deep she was, how she couldn't hide anywhere without Pete's permission. How crazy Pete really was. Miriam didn't know what he would do, but she wasn't going to push to find out.

She sighed and pulled the earrings out of her ears while she kicked off her shoes. She didn't have the energy to go on her date now. She was cancelling the date. Miriam felt trapped again, miles away from the Waters, but still drowning.

CHAPTER SEVENTEEN

Alone

Ricardo, age 13

The house smelled rancid, like a neglected outhouse. Pete stepped into the kitchen and fought back the sick filling that filled is stomach. He had smelled death before, many times. But this was different. It was pathetic. Pete clenched his teeth as he pushed deeper into the apartment. A little girl in a t-shirt and underwear that were smeared and dirty, turned the corner. She stared up at Pete with eyes of recognition. He didn't say anything, uncomfortable being alone with Leslie's other children, and definitely not about to touch someone else's daughter who only wore underwear. Pete groaned and shook his head. He should leave. But rumor had gotten back to him that Ricardo's situation had worsened. That Leslie had worsened. And he had to come check on his son.

He hated when rumors were actually whispered truths that no one had been brave enough to tell him in person. Pete flipped through the rolodex in his mind of the people he had left in charge of checking on Ricardo. Rebe. Miriam. Marshall. Marshall was gone. Miriam was no longer inside his circle. That left Rebe, his young love, turned baby momma, turned very loyal ex. She had even stuck with him after finding that he had a baby with Leslie before her, while Rebe had officially been his girlfriend. Rebe had to know Ricardo's situation was this bad. But, then again, the distance between he and Rebe had spread from a valley to an ocean after the shooting. She couldn't understand how he had forgotten Michelle was in the house. Rebe barely communicated with him directly anymore, sending her messages through Michelle.

Still, he had thought they were all on the same page. That all the women in his life knew that his children came first. That they had an obligation to make sure his kids were okay. It seems that understanding was only in his mind. Miriam had kidnapped Monique, Rebe had gone for self, and Leslie was no doubt turning tricks somewhere for her next hit.

His children were scattered like dust in the wind. And the only person who understood his value system, who could teach them who they really were, was him. A job that belonged to Jimmy and now was vacant. He had been mistaken to trust anyone else. It was all on him.

Pete followed the sound of the television past the little girl. He couldn't save all of Leslie's children. He could only save his own. And that's who he was looking for.

The smell of feces was coming from the bathroom. Pete stepped over the dirty towels on the floor and glanced in the full toilet. He pushed the handle. It didn't flush. Pete removed the lid from the tank. No water. They didn't have running water in the bottom apartment of this house. And from the looks of things, the water hadn't been on for a few days.

"Shit!" For a second, Pete didn't know what to do.

Another little girl turned the corner, a browner version of the first one, but this one was taller. A few years older. She knew him. She never called him by name, so he didn't know if she knew his name. Or, more importantly, Pete wasn't sure if she understood that he wasn't her father. He avoided her eyes, trying not to make any real connection with her. She never smiled. But, then again, none of Leslie's children smiled.

At least she was clothed. He recognized the summer dress, something that used to belong to Michelle. Pete bit his lip. "Where is your mother?"

The girl's gray eyes looked fearful at the mention of her mother. Like she didn't want to tell. "She went to the store."

Pete shook his head. Leslie was an addict. Every time she hit the streets she probably told them she was going to the store. "Where is Ricardo?"

The girl relaxed at that question, turning over the thick book that was in her hands. "Back there." The girl pointed to the back bedroom.

Sweat lined Pete's forehead. "The front door was wide open."

She just looked at him.

Pete spoke again, trying to convey a point. "Anyone could just walk up in here." It was like talking to a blank slate. She made no indication that she registered what he was referring to.

Finally, after a long minute, her eyes looked up at Pete. "It's hot in here." The girl shrank back against the wall.

It was miserable in here, that's what it was. The house was old, there was no central air condition. "Where are the fans?"

She shrugged. "Gone."

Pete stared at the wall, trying not to punch it. Leslie had undoubtedly bartered away the fans.

He took a deep breath. He had to get out of here, before he suffocated by the filth around him and the anger inside of him. Pete made his way down the hallway, calling as he walked. "Cardo!"

He heard scrambling then his son appeared, his spongy hair springing out all over his head. "Hi Dad." Ricardo didn't smile at him.

Pete noticed that he didn't really seem happy to see him. But Pete dismissed it. Who could be happy in this place? "Where is Leslie?"

"The store." Ricardo made a face as he said it. The child knew the routine.

Pete asked a better question. "How long has she been gone?"

Ricardo shrugged. "She left yesterday."

"So who is here with you and them?"

Ricardo puffed out his chest. "I am in charge."

"I been calling, but the phone is out." Pete explained, but then stopped himself. He shouldn't be explaining himself to a child. But, then again, he had to offer Ricardo some explanation for the shitty life he was leading. "It doesn't matter." Pete looked around. He started to tell Ricardo to pack a bag, but he didn't want anything from this filthy apartment coming into one of his houses. Roaches and other filth were undoubtedly thriving in the mess. "Let's go."

Ricardo's face seemed to brighten. He pulled on some shoes. Pete noticed that the toe of the shoes flapped down when Ricardo pushed his feet into them. If Jimmy saw Ricardo, he would beat Pete's ass. Without hesitation. Shame, or something like it, flooded

Pete's mind. The first stop was to the sneaker store. Not that it would rectify the real problem, but at least he could look at his son without feeling like trash.

Ricardo ran into another room and grabbed a bag. "Come on, Chanel," he said to his sister. "Get your sandals on." Ricardo disappeared into another room and came back with a couple of toys that he stuffed into the bag.

Pete turned to look at Ricardo. "What?"

Ricardo stopped moving. He stood there for a second. Anger spread over his young face. "I…I can't just leave my sisters."

Pete glanced at the two girls. Of course they couldn't just leave them here. What was he thinking? "No, you're right. Of course." Shit shit shit. What was he going to do with Leslie's daughters? Why did he have to even be bothered with this?

Pete rubbed his hands on his pants. He didn't want to touch the little girls, didn't want to take them anywhere, didn't want to do anything that would claim responsibility of them. He didn't need to add to the confusion. He didn't want anyone that wasn't his seed thinking of him as their father. Pete didn't play daddy. Being a Water's was a serious creed, only bestowed upon blood.

But he had created this mess when he had violated the family creed, letting his whore have his first child.

Jimmy had warned him that the results would be disastrous. Pete had ignored him, curious to see what his child with a white woman would look like. He imagined a lighter version of his mother, with long ropes of brown hair. He remembered thinking it, the night he had impregnated her, the night he had repeatedly released fully into her with the intent to create a child. That night he was sober, prepared and determine to create a baby.

When he and Jimmy talked about it, after Jimmy saw Leslie's pregnant belly while dropping off some money, Pete saw no reason to hide. It was something he had done for the fun of it, out of curiosity. And why shouldn't he? Why should he deny himself of something, anything, that he wanted, even if it was just to satiate some indescribable urge? He had fought wars, he had wrestled and tamed the streets. The Waters were indestructible. And he had the money and the influence to do and get whatever he wanted. Pete remembered the arrogance in his heart when he calmly told Jimmy that he wanted to do it, just because. And he remembered Jimmy shaking his head, the wild mane of hair shaking too, a look of pity in his eyes.

Jimmy had put down his blunt and stared at his younger brother. "Have you lost your damn mind?" Jimmy had asked.

Pete had shrugged. "Maybe. But so what?"

"Pete, kids don't just go away. Making a baby, that's forever man. This child is a part of this family, someone you have to provide for and raise. Someone who has to have the Water's knowledge. That's why you don't have a baby with just anybody. All of our women, our baby's mothers, are good women. They are all a certain type of woman. Haven't you noticed that?

"Yeah, but—"

"I don't want to hear no 'yeah buts'." Jimmy observed Pete like he was the stupidest person in the world. "That girl ain't got no values. She don't believe in nothing, Pete, she don't even got a God. What she going to put into your child? What's he going to learn?"

Pete had felt the urge to correct him. "I'm having a girl with her, not a son."

"You need to lay off that loud." Jimmy snatched Pete's blunt away from him. "Now you think you can predict what you create, huh. What…you think that you're God now?" Jimmy had sighed deeply. "I'm telling you, end it. Don't let her have your child, Pete. The damage will be far and wide."

Jimmy had leaned back in his seat with his eyes closed, returning to his cigar. "Pride goeth before the fall, Pete. Always remember that."

Pete had nodded compliance, knowing that he had no intent on terminating the pregnancy. He had visions of his first daughter. This was meant to be. His spirit told him it was right. He had seen the child in his dreams.

Then Ricardo was born. A son. The heir to the Water's throne. And Pete looked at Leslie and knew instantly that he had made a mistake. She was so happy at what she had accomplished, so proud that she had birthed his first son. Pete watched Leslie holding the child, wielding him like a key to a better life. And Pete's heart hardened.

That was twelve years ago. There was nothing he could do about it now, but keep moving and salvage what was left of his son.

"Come on," Pete grabbed the bag from Ricardo and sat it down. "They won't need anything. I will buy whatever they need. Tell her to put some clothes on that younger one."

"Okay Dad." Ricardo rushed past him and pulled his little sister by the arm.

"I'm going to be outside." Pete stepped onto the porch and looked across the street at the neighbors lounging on their own front porch. He didn't speak. He rubbed his head across his face.

Pete called Rebe. Michelle answered, of course. "Hi Daddy."

"Hi Mikki. Where is Rebe?"

"Uhm," She paused in that way children do to keep from telling what they have been expressly told not to tell. "She busy."

"Put her on the phone."

"Okay Daddy."

Pete listened to the shuffling, then baby cries and background noises. Finally Rebe came on the line, her voice sounding tired. "Hi Pete."

"Listen, when did Leslie get back on that shit?"

"What?" There was a pause, as if she was shifting the phone. "When did she ever get off of it?"

"I'm over at her spot now, the damn water is off."

"Pete, she's not in her right mind. You know how that goes."

"I'm going to bring her daughters over there with you—"

"No, I'm sorry, Pete. Today is Elise's wedding, remember, I told Mikki to tell you. We are over here getting ready now and Mikki said you agreed to pick her up later, after the reception."

Shit shit shit. "I forgot. Rebe, I came to get Ricardo and these kids are over here…it's bad."

"I'm sure it is. But Mikki still expects to see her father."

"What?" Pete stared at the phone. It was like she wasn't registering what he was dealing with. "Rebe, these kids are in a house with no fans and no water. It's hotter than hell in here and they been like this for days."

"What's that got to do with Mikki?"

Pete's mouth fell open. What happened to Rebe, the woman who used to care about others? "What do you mean?"

"You know what, Pete. Mikki is always losing out because someone else in your life has some emergency. Then you dump her because you are running around putting out their fires. Or you forget that she is there and she winds up with nightmares for months. It's not fair. Leslie and them kids are always like that. Why does that have to ruin Mikki's day today?"

Pete hung up. He didn't have words to respond. It was like he had never known Rebe and Miriam. They had changed into unrecognizable versions of themselves. They were acting selfish, putting themselves first. It reminded him of somebody, but he couldn't quite put his finger on it. He didn't like it. That was the only clear decision he could make. Pete's mind went through the list of side women he could call. They would all do what he said at an instant, so willing to please him that it was sometimes annoying. But he couldn't trust them in a situation like this. They were only pretending to be compliant to gain something in the end…him. They would use this situation to their advantage.

Lela sprang to mind. Jimmy's wife. She was a true Waters, even if by marriage. It took a few tries to remember the number. He hesitated. He hadn't been by to see her recently, or to visit his nephews. Pete didn't like the thought of being a person who only called when he needed something, but he normally only called when he needed something.

There was nothing he could do about relying on her at his convenience. Either she helped or she didn't.

She answered on the first ring. "Hello."

"Lela, its Pete."

"I know. How is everything, Pete?"

"I got a situation with Leslie over here—"

Lela was quiet for several seconds. "What's wrong?"

"The kids were left in the house. I came to check on Ricardo, but there is no water in the house. Leslie's other children are over here with damn near no clothes on. There is no telling when they last ate. It's crazy."

Without missing a beat, she said, "Bring them over here, Pete."

"Thank you." Relief flooded through him. "Alright, I'm on my way."

"Leave Leslie a note, letting her know they are here. She is on that stuff, but she isn't a monster, Pete. She will go crazy if the kids are missing, when she finally does wake up and notice. And tell the neighbors. Just so she knows."

Pete nodded. He hadn't thought about that. The last thing he wanted was the neighbors giving his license plates to the police claiming he abducted the kids. Pete was grateful to have Lela on the other end of the phone, someone who loved him just because she had love in her heart and who advised him on right and wrong without her own twisted motives obstructing her view.

"Thanks, Lela."

"Of course, Pete."

Ricardo stepped out on the porch, holding both sister's hands. They looked excited, like children who don't often get to go anywhere look. Pete tried to lighten the mood, but he didn't know how. They all needed a bath, some new clothes, some time spent on them. Today, he would do it. For the first time ever, he was putting the game on hold for Ricardo. He owed Ricardo at least that.

"First, let's get you to Lela's. Then we will go the park, maybe grab some ice cream."

"Really?" Ricardo shrank back as if it were a setup, his eyes registering mistrust.

The shameful feeling washed over Pete again. It was going to take a hell of a lot more than ice cream and a day at the park to right this wrong.

Pete thought about what Marshall had said about him neglecting his kids. Marshall had been in Ricardo's life, overseeing Leslie and keeping tabs on them. Marshall had even taken Ricardo in the night Leslie had gone too far and Pete had cut her loose. Pete wondered about Marshall's nephew, Army, and how life was turning out for him. Army's mother, Theresa, was more like Miriam than Leslie. Pete was confident that boy was doing fine. Still, he owed it to Marshall to check on them, too.

Pete glanced down at his son, a million unspoken promises for the future spinning through his mind. He was a man of action, not words. He would show Ricardo rather than tell him.

"Yeah little man," Pete put his hand on Ricardo's shoulder. "Time for you to hang with me."

CHAPTER EIGHTEEN
Alignment

Monique, age 13

"I don't want to go with him." Monique stared out the window.

"I don't have a choice, Monique," Miriam breathed heavily as she packed a night bag. "Your father gets you every other weekend. You know that. Court order." They had returned to Rochester, New York a year ago, after Miriam had been served court papers for alleged abduction.

Pete, of all people, had the nerve to turn to the law to enforce his parental rights. Miriam had been a nervous wreck, trying to scrap together money to hire a lawyer and fight the allegations. She had to move back to New York immediately. Once she did, Pete seemed to lesson his fury, reducing it to extreme anger. Miriam had betrayed him, by snatching Monique and keeping her away for so long. Miriam was wise enough to know that she could never return to Pete now, if he ever got her again her life would be retribution for her betrayal. Instead, she played her role, showing up in court when she had to, waving child support payments and forcing Monique to spend time on these visits.

"If I don't go, what happens?"

Miriam wiped at her eyes. "I don't know, Monique. I am tired of being in and out of court. Your father knows I can't afford it. I had to give in to something." She shrugged. "What do you want me to say?"

Monique wanted to scream. Instead, she swallowed back the fury that lived inside of her now, that seemed to be growing every day. She missed her grandparents. She missed the south. She hated Pete. "I don't want to go with him. He is just going to take me over Aunt Lela's anyway."

"Isn't that better?" Miriam's hands were shaking as she packed clothes. "Isn't that better than wherever he was taking you before."

"Yes, I don't want to go over his girlfriend's houses. Sitting there with kids I don't know while he is in their mother's bedroom making gross noises." Monique said that to hurt Miriam's feelings.

She wanted Miriam to feel as helpless as she felt during these forced visits with Pete, where she spent hours around strangers and their children, while Pete bounced from woman to woman, spending a few hours behind closed doors. When it was time to go the women were always in robes or in different clothes, and Pete always looked relaxed and calm. And Monique wanted to throw up.

Things were better before, when she was safe at home with Miriam, missing her father and wondering where he was with Michelle and Ricardo, unaware of Pete's real life.

The divorce had split open the seams of Monique's life, exposing her to the filthy inner stuffing of Pete's reality. Monique wasn't Michelle, who made friends easily and was welcome in everyone's home and seemed to be friends with all their kids. The strangers would try to talk to Monique, but she would just sit there, staring at the television, wishing that she was somewhere else. Sitting at Pete's girlfriends houses wasn't spending time with Pete. Why didn't the judge realize that when he ordered these visits? Why didn't Pete just leave her alone, rather than drag her around to all of his hoes' houses. He had already ruined her life, what more did he want?

Monique felt like fighting. She promised herself that if he took her over someone's house today, she was going to do something drastic to change things.

Lela came to pick Monique up. Things were so bad between Miriam and Pete that neither wanted to see the other. Lela served as the middle man.

Lela walked in with a bright smile on her face and wrapped Monique into a hug. "How is my pretty baby girl doing?"

Monique smiled, even though she didn't really want to. But she couldn't be mean to Aunt Lela. "Okay, I guess."

"You're growing." Lela met eyes with Miriam. "Have you talked with her about…?"

Miriam shook her head. "No. Damn Pete. He is not going to put my baby on birth control just because her cycle started."

"Birth control?" Monique rolled her eyes. Pete had some nerve. Just because he was screwing more women than she wanted to count, he wanted her on birth control. "Why would I need birth control? I'm not nasty like him."

"He's ridiculous." Miriam exhaled loudly.

Lela shook her head, clearly not wanting to offer comment. "Well, time to start talking to her anyway." She looked at Monique, "It's not about being nasty, baby."

Miriam answered as Monique looked away. "I know, Lela, I know. My child hasn't been able to hang on to any of the innocence of childhood. This damn man and his family have stripped her of that—"

"It's what she was born into," Lela interrupted Miriam, "it's not something any one of us wants."

"But you have boys. And they have had a chance to grow up in the suburbs, without seeing drugs in the house, or having to deal with their father bouncing from woman to woman."

"Yes, and they got to bury their father before either of them became men themselves."

Miriam bit her tongue. "I'm sorry."

"I'm just saying, Miriam, you have to let her know the truth about the life she inherited. For her own protection. You have to start talking to her about her body, boys, sex—"

"Okay, okay…not now, alright?" Miriam wiped at her eyes again. "It's hard enough getting through these weekends when she is with Pete. Only God knows what my child is exposed to, what she sees."

Monique wanted to yell at Miriam if she hadn't pushed Pete away, hadn't forced argument after argument with him causing the divorce, then Monique wouldn't have to go on these torturous visits. It was Miriam's fault for not holding it together, for not keeping Pete at home so she had some control over where her child was.

Instead, Monique stood up and picked up her bag as Lela gave Miriam another hug. Monique walked out without even saying goodbye to Miriam. Somehow, she was once again paying the price for being Pete and Miriam's daughter.

***

Monique smiled at her older cousin Jimmy Jr. He looked just like her Uncle Jimmy, except that his eyes weren't wild and his hair didn't flow like a lions' mane. But J.J. had that uncertainness about him that Monique recognized in her favorite uncle, that spark that made them special.

"Mo Mo, what's up girl?" He walked in the room and grabbed her around her neck. Monique swatted at him, slapping the back of his head.

"Get off me, J.J.!"

"What you doing here?" J.J. said as he stuck his head in the refrigerator.

"Waiting for your uncle." Monique rolled her eyes.

"Oh, visiting day again?" J.J. shook his head. "That ain't going to last. Uncle Petey gonna go home soon. He miss ya'll."

Monique sighed. Of course J.J. misunderstood, and she wasn't going to explain that she didn't "*miss*" Pete. She didn't want to see him. "No, he's not."

Monique didn't want to talk about the fact that there was no more home for Pete to return to. Miriam had made sure of that, selling their house and everything in it that Pete had ever touched. They were in an apartment now, while Miriam saved money. This was the second apartment since she and Miriam had returned from down south. Everything that had anything to do with Miriam, Monique and Pete being a family was gone.

"Where P.J. at?" Monique was referring to J.J.'s younger brother, who had been named Pete Jr., after her father.

"Down in South Carolina with my peoples." J.J. handed her a soda. "He keeps getting in trouble up here."

"That's 'cuz ya'll are wild." Monique laughed. "Just like—"

"Yeah," J.J. cut her off, before she said Uncle Jimmy's name, but he grinned. "Yeah, my little brother can't help himself."

"You look good, baby girl," Pete's deep voice interrupted the easy conversation between Monique and J.J.

Both of them looked up, startled. Monique quickly looked at the floor without answering her father. J.J., on the other hand, seemed to come alive.

"What up Unc," J.J. said. He looked genuinely excited.

Monique stared at him, a sarcastic smirk on her face. He needed to calm down. Pete wasn't a superstar.

"Hey nephew," Pete gave him a pound and a pat on the shoulder. "You holding down the fort?"

"No doubt." J.J. nodded earnestly. "Everything you told me to do, I'm handling it."

Monique never knew J.J. was a kiss-ass. She leaned back against the kitchen counter, admiration for her older cousin oozing out of her like air seeping from a tire. How could Pete be honestly guiding J.J. on how to run a household when he had no control over his own? Pete was a phony.

"Monique." Pete said, noting that she hadn't responded. "How are you?"

She shrugged, looking anywhere in the kitchen but at her father. The hate that she felt for Miriam was nothing compared to the intense resentment that Pete's presence brought in her. She loved her father, but she hated him and feared him at the same time. It was all too confusing. It was easier just to avoid him. Unfortunately, he had dragged Miriam to court enough times so that neither of them could just ignore him.

These forced visits didn't make her feelings toward Pete any better. The only person that Monique wanted to talk to was Michelle, but lately even that had seemed impossible. They didn't see each other as much now that Miriam and Pete were completely apart. Monique felt like an only child most of the time.

Plus, Pete's mouth was like a crap shoot, there was no telling what he would say that would hurt her deeply or terrify her or make her want to disappear. That was how powerful he was, that just a sentence out of his mouth could change the entire direction of her day. She resented his power.

Another reason why it was best to avoid him.

"How is your mother?"

That was always the second question out of his mouth. The first was some comment about how she looked, the second was always about Miriam.

Monique clenched her teeth as she shrugged. "Okay, I guess."

"She is your mother. You are responsible for her. Make sure she is more than okay."

How was that her responsibility? He had some nerve, always telling people what to do. *I hate you.* It wasn't her job to look after Miriam, it was his. He was the one not on his job, running around the city doing anything he wanted when he wanted. Monique bit her lip and looked out into the living room, wondering where Aunt Lela had disappeared to. J.J. took out some leftover fried chicken.

"Do you hear me, Monique?"

She paused, wondering if she had it in her to tell him to leave her alone. Fear bounced around in her chest. No, she wasn't that bold yet. "Yes, Daddy."

"Your breasts are growing."

That's what she was talking about. Why would he say that, especially in front of J.J.? Monique glanced down at what used to be a flat surface and noticed the awful two bumps. She wanted to hide them. She hated him for mentioning it. "I know."

"Have you gone bra shopping with your mother?"

"No, Daddy." *Can you change the topic?* "Not yet."

Pete dug in his pocket and peeled off a few hundreds. “Here. Tell Miriam you need to go underwear shopping. In fact, I will have Lela take you. Miriam doesn’t know about women’s under garments, you are going to need more support than her. The women in our family are heavy up top.”

Monique stared at her hands. She left the money on the table where he put it. She didn’t want anything from him.

Pete stared at her.

She stared at her hands.

“How is school?”

“Fine Daddy.” Maybe he would just go away if she didn’t have anything to say. She remained quiet, her gaze avoiding his.

J.J. glanced back and forth between the two of them. He took his cold chicken and left the kitchen.

“The last time I saw you I told you to look at the family Bible.”

Monique blinked. She didn’t hear him when he told her that. She remembered him talking, but she was lost in her own counter thoughts.

“Have you had a chance to look at it yet?”

Monique considered lying, but then she didn’t want to get caught in a lie if he questioned her. “No. You…you want me to read the Bible?”

"The family lineage is recorded in the front of the Bible. I want you to know it. I expect you to read it when you come over to Lela's."

"Okay."

He sat at the table and stared at her. It took Monique a couple of seconds to realize that he was waiting for her to get the book. She went over to the shelf and pulled down the huge Bible from the second shelf and brought it over to the table. Pete took it from her, his hands holding it gently, as if each page were a leaflet of gold. He started talking as if he were in a trance, about the people listed in the book, where they were from, how they got to Rochester. He named the plantation, the slave families. His great great grandmother and her story. Monique had heard it all before, but she had never seen it written down before. She listened, only because she was afraid to miss it. It seemed Pete was taking over Uncle Jimmy's role of implanting the family history in them. No matter how much she hated him, she knew that the family story was one that she better know, in case he questioned her.

"Who we are is listed right here. All the people who were brought together to form you, they are all here." Pete tapped the large book. "You need to know who you are."

Monique didn't answer, but she did study the pages while Pete went in the other room to make phone calls. And she pocketed the money that he had left on the table. It took her mind off everything around her, the confusion over her parents, the hurt she felt every time she remembered Uncle Jimmy. Instead, she looked at the old portraits of women in 1800's clothing, their long hair formally upswept around their stern faces, each with their children positioned around them. She wondered about their lives when they weren't dressed up, weren't posing for the camera. Monique wondered why their husbands weren't in the portrait, why they seemed well off even though they were black slave descendants. There was so much to learn in these stories.

"Let's go," Pete's voice broke through Monique's studies.

"Huh?"

In front of her was a different person. Gone was the father who was teaching history. Instead, the man in front of her was distracted, patting his pockets for his keys, fumbling through the bill fold to leave money for Lela, and staring around the room with unseeing eyes, his mind running through calculations unknown to Monique.

"Let's go," Pete ordered again. "I got some things to take care of. I am going to drop you off."

"Where?" Monique stayed planted to her seat. She didn't want to meet anymore strange women. She didn't want to sit around strange kids, waiting indefinitely for him to return. She would stay right here at her aunt's house. And, if he tested her and left her with another stranger, Monique might just walk home. She was getting sick of this life with Pete. Sick of being transient, moving from one woman to another, from one household to another. If he didn't have his own place for her to stay, why keep going to the court to demand visitation?

He noticed the quiet dissent. He turned from the door and stared at her, squinting his eyes. "Get your ass up out of the chair. Now." His voice was barely a whisper.

But the fear that Monique felt from those few words made her shake. She bit her tongue, as tears tumbled from her eyes and she moved toward the door. He stepped out into the hall, holding the door for her. Monique walked a step behind him until they reached his truck.

She wanted so desperately to go home. But then the thought of Miriam waiting for her, hitting her with a million questions about what Pete was doing and who he was doing it with, made home a bad option. She just wanted to get away. Away from both of them. College. That was the plan of escape. Monique had figured it out when she was 9 years old and a counselor told her that she could live on campus at a college when she was older. That was her way out, a possible escape from both Miriam and Pete. She stared out the window as Pete drove through the city, her fingertips on the windowsill. It wouldn't bother her if she never saw this place again. Once she was gone, there was no coming back. One day, even if it was a long time away, one day she would escape them and this crazy life. Every day until then was just a countdown.

They rode in silence. Pete stopped at a restaurant and left Monique in the car. Twenty minutes later, they were on the road again. Pete stopped at a laundromat and left Monique in the car. They didn't speak a word in the car together, she locked the doors whenever he left her in the car and diligently watched for any strangers.

Monique's nerves were always shot when she was with her father, the silver streaks of grey hair that coursed through her preteen hair were proof. He stopped at a barbershop and left her in the car for a full hour. Monique knew the neighborhood, she was near Miriam's friend's house. But Monique didn't quite know her way. Still, she unlocked the door. Pulled the handle. Clutched her bag. She could just walk away. She could walk away from both of them. From this life altogether. She wasn't stupid. She could make it.

Monique placed one foot outside of the car. Her sandal touched the pavement. Pete would find her. There was no escaping him. And there would be hell to pay. But so what. Life was hell anyway.

If she did this, if she was willing to walk away, maybe he would stop picking her up just to leave her all over the place, or make her ride around while he made all these stops. Maybe the punishment would be worth the lesson learned.

She swung her other leg out. She was doing it. Just as she moved forward to stand up, the door to the barbershop opened. Pete's huge body was visible behind the glass. Monique threw herself back in the car and slammed the door.

He glared at her through the glass. He had been watching.

Monique bit her lip and looked away.

A few minutes later, he was back in the truck. They continued in silence. After a few minutes, Pete turned into a neighborhood that Monique had never seen before. Her stomach dropped. She pressed her forehead against the window, trying to force back the tears that were about to emerge. Pete drove slowly down a quiet street. The houses were large and neat, each one located on a large yard. At the end of the street, Pete turned down a one way street with only a handful of houses on it. Shaded by huge trees, the blue house with grey awnings sat off the road with a long driveway leading up to it.

Pete pulled into the driveway and turned off the engine. Monique stayed in the car, wishing that she had climbed out earlier, when they were at the barbershop. Now she was stuck. There was no way she could walk back through the maze of streets that they had driven to get out of this neighborhood.

Pete looked at her, a smile on his face. "Come on."

It scared her that he was smiling for no reason. Normally he took a few minutes in the car to adjust himself before entering someone's house, sliding into different personalities like easing into new shoes. Now, watching him jump out of the car looking happy was strange.

Pete never really looked happy before.

Monique picked up her bag and pushed air out of her lungs, forcing the tears back. "Daddy, can I just go home? I don't want to wait over here for you."

Pete was on the porch, approaching the door. "What?"

"I don't want to wait with someone I don't know. Why can't I just stay at Aunt Lela's? Or go back home?"

"What, you want to be with Miriam instead of me?" Pete looked confused.

"Yes. I mean, no, Daddy, it doesn't have anything to do with Mommy—" The door behind him opened.

Michelle stood at the door, a smile as big as the ocean on her petite face.

Monique's heart stopped beating. She hadn't seen her sister in over a year, only talking to her on the phone every now and then. Monique dropped her bag.

"Mikki?" Monique screamed as she ran onto the porch, past her startled father, and wrapped her arms around her little big sister. Emotion released itself and Monique started crying, large sobs of relief that wracked her body.

"It's okay, Mo, dang. Why you crying?" Michelle hugged Monique and shook her head. "Girl, you are so crazy, with your spoiled self."

Monique forgot all about Pete. "I thought I was going to get stuck over one of his women's houses again, Mikki, I swear, I hate it. I just want to go home. And I never see you anymore, and everything is all messed up—" the words were caught between the sobs.

"This is my house, Monique," Pete said in a quiet voice. "I bought this for us. Me and my kids. You, Mikki and Ricardo."

Ricardo stood behind the screen door, his eyes on Monique. She wiped her face. Michelle held onto her, laughing.

Monique hugged Ricardo. "Where have you been?" she asked.

"I'm always around," Ricardo smiled at her.

They had gone to the same elementary school for a year, before she left for the south, when Miriam could no longer afford private school because Pete had cut off the money. Although Ricardo was older and in a different class, Monique had grown to adore him. Monique's relationship with Ricardo was nowhere near what it was with Michelle, but he had been there for her in school, keeping the boys away and having her back when someone wanted to fight her. It was weird, having a brother. Everyone at school connected the two of them. The girls who liked Ricardo would come to Monique, asking about her big brother. And there were boys that Monique liked who never approached her, and she knew that Ricardo was the reason why.

Monique missed having someone around who cared about her, even if he didn't have much to say. Ricardo had been her quiet guardian. Now he was in high school and she was in middle school.

"Aren't you going to Wilson next year, Mo?" Michelle piped in. "That's where Ricardo is at."

Monique looked at him.

"Yep, I transferred," he said.

"Please say you aren't going there. I'm never going to get a boyfriend," Monique groaned.

"That's right." Ricardo nodded. "You don't need a boyfriend, girl."

"I know you aren't talking!" Monique pressed a red spot on his neck. "You got a hickie!"

"No I don't!" Ricardo pulled away.

"Where?" Michelle grasped at his tall frame. "Ugh, you so nasty. What nasty girl was sucking on your neck?"

"Why are you all up in my business?" Ricardo pushed them back.

Monique laughed, as she wrapped her arms back around her sister. She never wanted this moment to end, being tucked between her brother and sister, despite their father and all his women. It didn't matter that they had different mothers, didn't matter that they didn't live together, didn't matter that they only saw each other sparingly. They were from three separate worlds, but they were intractably linked, having survived living in the shadows of the street life, all being tainted by it in different ways.

It didn't matter. As long as they had each other, they had strength. Monique could feel their power, there was no doubting the bond. Tomorrow, when she returned home, it might end. But for right now, she let herself revel in it.

Monique finally pulled herself away from her sister to look around the house. A small piece of envy swept through her as she looked around the large house. She wondered how long Michelle and Ricardo had been here with Pete without her. She was always the odd man out.

As if he read her thoughts, Pete spoke up. "I needed time, Monique, to get myself settled. This house is ours. This is our family. No women. No strangers. This is ours."

Monique looked at the large family room, with individual framed pictures of the three of them placed around the room. "For the longest time I wasn't able to have all my children together at one time. Other people had control over when I saw my kids and how I saw them. I had to change things to make it happen, but that day is finally here.

"This is why I have been fighting for you in court, so that I could give you a home, too. The three of you, you are TW2, the legacy that my brothers and I started. You have to be there for one another. You three have to be what my two brothers and I were. A three cord bind. Unbreakable. All we have is one another, and without each other, we are nothing." Pete moved into the dining room. "Come here."

The table was huge, but only had four chairs, one on each side. "We don't need any extra chairs." Pete explained, as Monique looked around the room for the extra chairs.

"Daddy, this table is too big for there to only be one chair on each side."

Michelle giggled as Ricardo shook his head. "Something only a girl would notice."

Pete kept talking. "This table is for us." In front of each chair was thick padded crimson red table cloth, on top of the cloth was a rectangle jewelry box.

"Mo, yours is over here." She and Michelle changed places. "Before you open them, understand that you are part of a trio that no one can undo, no person can interrupt, no one can break. Waters first and only."

Monique couldn't keep her fingertips from the huge box.

"Open it." Pete said, sitting down.

Michelle shouted. "Daddy, this is so hot!" Michelle held up a sparkling platinum chain, with TW2 encircled in an emblem.

"It's our family crest. Our mark. You wear that everywhere you go, no matter what. If someone touches you, they are tampering with this entire family. And they can't claim not to know."

"Damn." Ricardo opened his but just looked at it.

Monique was already in the mirror behind the table, laying it against her chest and admiring it.

"Put them on," Pete said with a smile, noticing Monique's vanity. "Understand something," Pete met each of their eyes. "If I never said it before, I am saying it now: each of you was wanted, planned for and loved. There are no mistakes standing at this table. You belong to something great, bigger than any one of us. We are the Waters'. You are mine, I am yours and you are each other. Forever."

"Waters, forever," Monique and Michelle said without thinking about it, their old training resurfacing. Monique missed Uncle Jimmy.

"Waters," Ricardo said, his eyes on Monique and Michelle, following their lead. "Forever."

"Forever…Waters." Pete finished it, his hand touching his chest.

Monique glanced around the huge table at each of her siblings and her father. She no longer felt alone and isolated. She was again part of something bigger than herself, she was claimed and loved. Her family had finally returned.

CHAPTER NINETEEN

Pretty Nerd

Monique, age 16
Armand, age 18

"I don't want to be here." Armand looked around at the crowded house party on Congress Ave. It was packed with people, he was bound to have some enemies in there. "You already know I don't do crowds."

"Yo, you owe me," Raymond laughed. "So, you gotta deal with it."

"How I owe you?"

"You can act like you don't remember the bet. It's alright, let me remind you: two stacks and a weekend partying my way, remember?" Raymond adjusted his shirt. "There's a few hotties in here. My cousin is throwing this party and Patrice said she would be here."

"Patrice? Really? Y'all act like an old married couple already. We are going to a party, and your girl is meeting you here? Where is the fun in that?"

Raymond got defensive, his chin sticking out. Armand wanted to laugh. "Ain't nothing wrong with it. I can have my cake and eat it, too. Just because she is here doesn't mean I can't get other numbers."

"Yeah," Armand chuckled. "Okay. Whatever it is you tell yourself…"

"Whatever." Raymond changed the subject as he juggled the chain around his neck. "I'm about to freeze them out. When they spot this chain, it's over."

"I will give you that, the chain is hot. But, I don't think this is the type of place you want to have the chain out at. Too much attention."

"You think?" Raymond looked sincerely concerned.

"Tuck it in." Armand saw a few guys from the Northeast side leaning against a car. "Just in case." His eyes scanned the tree lined street. "We got any more people here?"

"Yeah, Dut is already here with Mike and Chew, somewhere. I can't bring too many people in here, don't want my cousin's mother flipping out. She doesn't really like my side of the family."

"Oh boy," Armand laughed. He had to admit that he was curious. He hadn't been to a party on this end of Genesee Street before. They entered through the driveway and walked around to the back. There was a large paved patio in the back with lawn furniture and burning wick poles. A huge speaker was in the corner of the yard and music filled the air. West side girls were everywhere, clumped in packs like girls like to do.

Raymond openly stared from girl to girl. Armand kept the lid of his hat low, covering his eyes. It was clear they were the "new guys" because they were drawing attention. It made Armand a little uncomfortable to have so many eyes on him, even if they were paired with flirting smiles. Unlike Raymond, Armand kept his attention on the guys chilling on the lawn chairs at the back of the yard, smoking a few puffs under the palm of their hand to keep from getting caught. The few boys near the garage nodded at him in deference and he recognized them from the hood. Raymond slapped a few heads, pointed out some people to him and said their name out loud.

Armand was glad he was with Raymond. Raymond had good energy, people just liked him. It seemed like they could relax, everyone so far was either cool with Raymond or oblivious to them. Armand sighed. He wondered what it was like to be a normal teenager at a normal fall party, without trying to hustle to live. Without having to provide solely for himself.

He shook it off. There was no need in crying over his situation. The past was the past. Now was now.

"What's up Army?" A deep brown girl with a squeaky voice walked right up to him. Most females weren't that bold. She spoke like she knew him and he had no idea who she was.

"What's up?" He glanced at her, watched the way she folded her arms, her neck moving her head side to side as she spoke.

"Oh, so you don't remember me now? We used to kick it back in elementary school." The girl waited for Army to remember her. She widened her eyes to match her crooked smile. "Shawnta, remember."

Armand started to lie and say he remembered. But then he thought about it. There was no reason to lie. He wasn't interested. He didn't like her vibe, or how she had awkwardly walked up to him. She was making him uncomfortable. "Naw, my fault." Army shrugged a little.

The look of expectation on her face fell. "Oh, well, it's been a while."

"Yeah," Armand shrugged again. He wanted her to move, but didn't want to clown her in front of everyone, either. He could feel Raymond listening, waiting to shout out with laughter. "What school you went to?"

"Number 11. We used to walk home together."

He remembered her now. Armand smiled. "My fault, yea, I remember. What's up with you?" He blessed her with a warm smile and lifted his arm a little, allowing her a distant hug. "You had a brother, right? Uhm…Manuel?"

"Yeah," Shawnta smiled. "He gone now, though. He got shot."

"What?" Armand felt loss wash over him. Every death of someone he knew brought back that deep hurting feeling. "I'm sorry to hear that."

"Yeah," Shawnta looked around. Her friends were giggling and watching. "Well, alright then. I just hadn't seen you in a while."

"Yo, hold up." Armand pulled his phone out of the case. "What's your number? I might be around the way."

She smiled, relief on her face. She rattled off the digits. Armand gave her another hug as she walked away. He might actually call her. There was no reason not to. His past life was so painful that sometimes he forgot that he hadn't lived on a shelf in isolation. They had friends, a community, people who cared about them—before the fire destroyed everything. Armand watched Shawnta, the sight of her bringing back thoughts of Camilla.

"Come on, boy," Raymond tapped his arm. "Gotta find my peoples and speak."

Armand followed Raymond through the side door into the crowded garage. The music was softer in here, where there was no speaker. The hum of chatter filled the garage, though. Two girls were standing near the closed garage door, in deep discussion. They caught his eye because neither paid him nor Raymond any attention, and both were beautiful. One was mocha colored with thick black hair pulled back from her face, the other had huge bouncy curls and almond shaped eyes.

Raymond stopped at another group of guys he knew, speaking, slapping hands and making small talk. Armand stood with his back to the girls, but listening intently.

"Listen," the almond eyed girl said. "I told all three of them to meet me here."

"Are you crazy, all three dudes? You want to get busted?"

Almond Eyes laughed. "I don't go with none of them. They don't own me, so there is no way for me to get busted. But I don't know how two of them really look, you know, since we met through other people. It's been a lot of phone time, you know. So, tonight is thumbs up or thumbs down."

The friend laughed. "But you talk to them all the time, Mo. How could you not know which one you like?"

"I like them all," Mo said, her voice sounding so indignant that her friend laughed harder. "Look, none of them is getting any, so it doesn't matter. But, I can never tell if a guy is cute or not. When I think they are cute, you say they are ugly. And when I think they are ugly, they are the cutest one in the room. So, I give up. You choose."

"You are so crazy. You want me to choose who you go with?"

"Yep," Mo said, "Whichever one you say is that one, that's who I am going with."

Mocha sounded doubtful. "Just like that?"

"Yep," Mo laughed. "I know you got my back. Just like that."

Armand shook his head. The things pretty girls did. He chuckled though, he liked her mind set. She wasn't trying to trap a boyfriend, she was playing with guys, like he and his boys played with girls.

"Come on, dude." Raymond pulled him through the garage. He glanced back at the two girls, still plotting on their random game of boyfriend assigning. He wondered who she was.

"I thought you changed your mind." They bumped directly into Dut who was holding a plate of barbecue wings. "Watch the plate, yo."

That caught Armand's attention. The plate was piled high with potato salad, ribs and macaroni and cheese. "Where's the food?"

"In the kitchen," Dut laughed. "I left Chew in there. About to grab a seat outside."

"I'll be there." Armand headed to the kitchen.

"Auntie Lynn," Raymond's voice was drowned out in the music, which was louder now that they approached another speaker. Armand saw Raymond hugging and talking to people. He surveyed the dancers on the makeshift dance floor in the living room and the guys lingering around the food. No threats. Armand grabbed a plate.

He was trying to grab corn on the cob when the bouncy curls appeared next to him. Her head was turned. A boy was standing next to her, awkwardly reaching for a plate. She had two plates in her hand, clearly about to make his plate. Armand watched the two of them as he balanced the corn on his own plate.

Mo put the second plate down. She apparently changed her mind about making his plate.

"Good girl," Armand thought. The boy was obviously a loser. A clear hound. She deserved someone better. More real.

"So, you were waiting for me?" the boy smirked at Mo.

"Hmm," she smiled, almost laughed at him. "I guess. You just got here?"

"Yep." He loaded food on his plate. "Are you going to dance with me?"

Armand dug through the floating ice in the freezer, searching for a soda.

"I don't really dance," Mo said, her face showing that it was an obvious lie. She moved closer to Armand.

Armand saw his opportunity and seized it. "What you want out of here?"

Mo met his eyes. "Ginger ale, please."

The ice was so cold it was burning his hand, but Armand would be damned if he showed it. He handed her his soda. "You can have mine, I will find another one."

She smiled, her eyes lingering on him. "Thanks."

His plate tipped.

"Oh oh, here, let me help." She moved quickly, taking his plate from his free hand and putting it on the table. Her back was to the boy she had been talking to. He stood there for a few awkward moments and then floated back, disappearing from Armand's view.

Armand smiled. He had given up too easily. If he knew what Armand knew, he would have figured out that this girl was worth fighting for.

Armand found another ginger ale and pulled it out. "Got it."

"Look at your hand! It's red."

Armand shook off the water. He was hoping to get circulation back, but wouldn't admit it. "Yeah, it's okay."

She grabbed his hand. "Oh my God, you're freezing." She laughed. He liked her laugh. It was so carefree.

He let her hold his hand while stood there watching her. He liked the way she grasped his hand, as if it were delicate, instead of rough.

She caught him staring at her. "Here," she said, breaking the awkward pause and reaching for a cup.

"I don't need a cup," Armand said. "I'll drink straight from the can."

"Of course," she sat the cup down. "You go to Edison?" She squinted at him and Armand knew she was trying to place him.

"No, I went to East." Armand left it at that. Titan had made him return to school and focus on finishing. Titan had insisted that Armand learn to live a double life to survive in more than one world. Titan was strict about it, stressing to Armand that duplicity was the key to survival. Armand had mastered living two different lives at one time, so that no one from the normal world suspected his street life and vice versa. Armand had graduated from East High a year early, excelling in his classes, but staying very low key. He didn't socialize much, he wasn't there for that.

"Oh," She nodded her head to the music. She let it go.

He was glad. He opened the soda.

Monique lifted his plate and handed it back to him. "You got enough food on here?"

"Ah, you got jokes," he smiled. Most people weren't comfortable enough to tease him. "I have a big appetite."

She stepped back and looked him up and down. "You don't look thick enough to have a big appetite." She was bold with that move, a clear challenge. Her almond shaped eyes sparkled.

"You will be surprised at what clothes hide." He smiled. "I'm thick enough."

She laughed out loud again. "That's what you say." She turned and picked up her plate, then looked back at his. "Well, I hope your food tastes good. You picked the good stuff—we have all the same things."

"Yeah, I always pick the good stuff." He smiled again, before taking another sip of his soda.

This time she didn't laugh, only smiled. "Yeah, I can tell that." She started walking away, which threw him off. Females didn't normally walk away from his flirting.

"What's your name—?"

"Monique, what up!" Chew walked up on Monique, his arms opened wide. He almost knocked the plate out of her hand, he hugged her so fast.

"Chew!" She shouted and hugged him back. Her girlfriend appeared out of nowhere, grabbing the plate from her hand and sitting it on the table. "I haven't seen you in forever." Monique hugged him again, a range of emotions fluttering through her sparkling eyes.

Armand watched closely. Raymond and Dut walked up, standing near but not really listening as they bobbed their heads to the music.

Monique's eyes actually watered. "So you took a break from the thug life to come slum with the regulars?" she teased, wiping away tears.

"Don't do that," Chew shook his head. "You got my number, you could have called."

Armand felt his heart deflate. She was one of Chew's girls.

"I call the house but you are never there. I always talk to Rodney." She hugged him again. "I miss you, man."

Chew was glowing like a prince. Armand wanted to knock him out. "I miss you too, baby girl."

"Who is this?" Monique's friend pressed herself up against them both, obviously breaking up the reunion. Jealousy was sprayed across her face too, her eyes were locked on Chew.

"This is like my brother, Tina." Monique wiped her eyes. "Chew, this is Tina, my best friend."

Chew smiled, clearly interested. "Hi Tina."

Tina smiled, trying to look casual but her body language was way too clear. She was a roller.

Armand coughed as he tried to look nonchalant, swallowing his potato salad.

Chew noticed him. "Hey Army."

Armand nodded. "Whatup." Armand expected for Monique to ask Chew about him. Instead she started talking to Chew about their past life together, reminiscing about people and places Armand didn't know. He tried to pretend like he wasn't listening as he swallowed his food.

After a few minutes, Tina broke up the private conversation. Her flirting paid off when she finally pulled Chew on the living room floor to dance. Monique took a few bites of food and watched Tina and Chew. She stood next to Armand for a long time. When the heavy beat of her favorite song came on, Monique abandoned her plate of food and went out on the dance floor alone, standing in the center of the floor, eyes closed as she enjoyed the music and lost herself in the rhythm.

Armand watched her. She was someone he could get with.

He noticed that other guys watched her, too. The boy she had originally brought to get food was nearby. He moved out on the dance floor and tried to press his body against her. Monique opened her eyes. She smiled politely at him, but she moved away when he tried to touch her. They swayed to the beat a little longer. He grabbed for her again. Armand felt the muscles in his arm flex. He was going to stomp this boy out. Monique moved away again, this time making her way off the dance floor.

Armand finished his plate. She came and stood by him. They watched the people move on the dance floor. Now that she was standing right next to him, Armand had nothing to say. She finally opened her soda and took a sip. Armand almost wanted to ask her to dance, but decided against it.

"You finished eating?" she finally asked him, as she sipped her soda, still swaying to the music.

"I had enough." He tried not to smile, but he liked looking in her eyes.

"Me too," she said.

"You didn't eat."

"I mean, I had enough of the party." She looked around. "I'm about to go."

"Curfew?" He hoped she had a curfew. She looked like she had a parent somewhere who was on her like a hawk. She seemed…protected.

"Not tonight." Monique smiled.

Armand didn't know what that meant.

After a few more minutes, Monique sighed. She glanced at her phone. "Well, it was nice meeting you. Army, right?" She slid away into the crowd, before he could answer.

Armand watched her whisper something in Tina's ear, who was letting Chew rape her on the dance floor.

Tina shook her head "*no*," Monique laughed and kept nodding "*yes*" while pulling at Tina's hand.

Tina untangled herself from Chew's grasp. Monique headed for the garage, with Chew and Tina behind her.

Armand was grateful for Chew, who gave him an excuse to tag along. He followed. When they stepped outside, Monique looked back. Armand could tell she was surprised to see him.

"Can I walk you to your car?" He didn't want her to think he was a stalker.

She smiled. "I didn't drive. She did."

"Why are you leaving the party so early?" Armand pushed a low hanging branch out of the way as they walked.

Monique shrugged. "Just ready to go."

"Yeah." Normally Armand was the one who unexpectedly shut everyone's night down. "I understand."

They walked in silence, with Tina and Chew talking behind them. Armand watched as Monique kept glancing up at the sky. He looked up also. "What are you looking at?"

"The little dipper," she pointed up.

Armand had no idea what she was talking about.

She noticed the confusion on his face. "Look," she pointed to a group of stars. "The constellation of stars, right there. You see, those three make up the handle. Then those four are the cup." She grabbed his hand again, pointing his finger to the stars as she explained each one.

"How do you know that?"

"I love the planetarium." Monique said. "My mom used to take me all the time." She crossed her eyes, "I'm a nerd."

"A pretty nerd."

"Ah, you called me purty!" she said, teasing but also blushing. "Thank you." Her sincerity surprised him. He had expected her to say it the way pretty girls did, as if they already knew it but were saying "*thank you*" to seem polite.

She looked genuinely thankful.

"Well, pretty nerd, maybe you can take me to the planetarium sometime."

"Really?" Her voice was full of doubt.

"Yeah," Armand was genuine. "Really."

"Maybe." Monique said. Armand could tell she wasn't taking him serious. "We'll see."

She climbed in the car with a complaining Tina. Monique and Armand stared at each other as Tina pulled off. Armand felt lucky, it seemed that none of the three boys she was plotting on had won, he had managed to walk her out.

"Shorty is stacked. Did you see that butt?" Chew said.

"Whatever. I'm going to get at Monique, believe that."

Chew laughed, "Boy, whatever. Monique is a good girl, she don't want no thug."

"She want me," Armand answered.

"Oh yeah?" Chew checked his cell phone. "Did you even get those digits?"

Armand stopped walking, surprised that the most vital detail had missed him. He was so used to females pushing up on him that he hadn't even thought about it.

"Yeah," Chew said. "That's what I thought."

"Boy, you giving me her number."

"I don't even have it."

Armand glowered at him.

"Real talk," Chew laughed, backing up with his hands in the air in a sign of surrender. "Serious, Army, I don't have it. She changes her number all the time. You heard her, she called my house and talked to Rodney. I don't know her number. Something with her parents, I think they make her."

"Damn." His instinct told him not to believe Chew, but either way it was his fault for not getting it. Somehow, he had to get in touch with Monique again.

CHAPTER TWENTY

The Streets

"I don't like it." Armand didn't hear his other phone vibrating in the cup holder. He held his personal phone to his ear, hearing the pounding of his heartbeat in the silence between the line. "You there?"

"Yeah." Titan rarely talked on the phone. "Why?"

"Don't know him. He not matching up."

Titan sat in silence. Armand was annoyed that Titan had called him at all, especially just before a meet. Armand had no choice but to answer, Titan was the youngest man running things in the city. And he had made Armand a boss over a crew. But smart phones were the death of anyone living a street life. Everything connected to a simple email address was doom waiting to happen. The damn phones and their location trackers, GPS, navigation--constant beacons putting a person on the map exactly when they needed to be invisible.

Street life without invisibility was like a track star without steroids, bound to be caught.

The first time Armand had inputted his email address and then watched the phone automatically upload all his contacts, emails, pictures and texts messages from his old device, Armand had shut it all down. Now he only used the phone to talk—disconnecting all his social media sites. It wasn't worth the exposure, wasn't worth giving bits of information to those ravenous to piece together his life and secrets. He hated the smart phones. But they still seemed like a irritating necessity, something that he had to have.

Until now.

"Listen young gun," Titan's voice sounded gritty and irritated.

Armand sighed.

"I don't have no choices here. It's necessary. I want this vein."

Armand didn't answer. His silence was as loud as words: He didn't agree. But, who was he to argue with Titan?

"I think this stranger could bring static."

"I hear you," Titan acknowledged Armand. "I'll handle that. I have always got it covered, right?"

Armand didn't answer.

"Call me when it's done."

"Yeah right." Armand shook his head. The battery and Sims card were getting snatched out of this phone, and the phone was getting rolled over by the truck, as soon as this call was over. He would have Regina buy him another phone, or maybe put it in another female's name. A fresh start. Put an old trap phone on this number, for when Titan called it. A nice reliable old flip phone, with no internet.

The other trap phone rang but Armand still didn't notice it. His mind was busy flipping through his thoughts. The connect from New York was a guy named Kane. Armand hadn't been able to connect him to anybody he knew in any way. Kane didn't have ties to any gang, the streets, a borough lord…no one. A bad sign.

Armand busted his phone open and ripped out the battery.

"Where we going?" Dut was Armand's driver. He watched Armand destroy the phone and tuck it under the tires before jumping back in the truck. "Roll over them?"

"Yep. A couple of times. We going to Batavia."

"Cool." Dut shrugged, did as instructed and headed for 390.

"Why Batavia?"

Armand shrugged. He wasn't giving up that much information. Armand knew Batavia like the back of his hand. Titan demanded control of the town from the White boys from Toronto who had taken over. He had a trap there, had a White girl with a small ranch style house where he kicked it. He also had a small crew who helped him run the Toronto crew out. The bloodshed had been minor. The police presence had been manageable. The rewards major. Until the White girl fell in love, then threatened to kill herself when she couldn't have the one thing she wanted. Him.

That's when Armand had faded back rather than hurt her. That's when he set up one of his soldiers, Lonnie, to take over the town, who had his own trap already in the area. That's when he just collected his ends and kept it moving.

It seemed like a lifetime ago, not just a year ago. Every day was like a lifetime, a year felt like a decade. Armand glanced at his reflection in the mirror. His black pupils were emotionless and the dark circles under his eyes surprised him. He looked older than he should.

The vibration finally reached his ears, the rattling sound pulling his eyes away from the dark road for a moment.

"You ain't hear the phone?" Irritation climbed the back of Armand's neck as he missed the call.

Dut shook his head "*no.*"

Armand grabbed the phone. "Yo, put your high beams on." Armand wished he had brought Raymond with him instead. He needed someone who lightened up the mood, not someone always looking for war.

The phone vibrated again. Armand flipped it open. "Whatup?"

Kane's voice sounded far away. "How much longer, son? You should have been here by now."

Armand breathed deeply, the sigh giving him a moment to catch his tongue before he started a war. Malone, the previous contact from New York, had been a stand up kind of guy, someone Armand respected. This new contact felt phony and his tongue was disrespectful.

"We are on our way to you now."

"I don't want to sit out here all night. It's bad enough I had to drive to the country to trade pennies with you hicks—" Armand could hear someone laughing in the background as Kane continued, obviously mouthing off for the benefit of whoever was listening, "—wasting my time with these country ass wanna be gangstas."

Tonight wasn't the night to push Armand. He hadn't slept in two days. "What you say?" Armand clicked the phone to speaker.

"You heard me, boy. I ain't waiting forever, where ya'll at?"

Dut shook his head with his eyes squinted.

According to Armand's calculations, they were only a few minutes away. "I don't know, boy." Armand spat out the word, his sneer evident. "We're lost—could take a while."

Armand met Dut's eyes. Dut wasn't his main man, but he was definitely one of Armand's gunner, and his smoothness with the gat was something that couldn't be denied. With one glance, they were on same the page.

"You better hurry up or you can get what you need from somewhere else."

"Oh yeah?"

"Hell yeah."

Armand chuckled. "You real loose with your tongue, boy, you might want to check that when doing business."

"Whatever, I ain't got all night and this small change ain't worth it. I hate driving upstate any damn way—"

"Yo," Armand interrupted him, "we be there when we get there. One."

Armand slapped the phone closed. "I want to silence this one here."

Dut turned up the volume on the radio. "Permanently?"

Armand followed Dut's movements with his eyes. Fighting paranoia was a daily struggle. No one could be trusted and everyone had their own agenda. Titan had taught him that much. Why the hell was Dut turning up the volume all of a sudden? Armand glanced out the window, his mind running through the unspoken possibilities. Was the truck wired? Was Dut wearing a wire? Armand shook his head—everyone couldn't be against him; he had to trust someone, sometime. No man can operate on the streets alone, that was reality of it and the one flaw that made the game no more than a crap shoot.

"Naw." Armand rolled down the window a little, letting the flapping air drown out his thoughts. "We just gonna teach him a lesson."

"That's cool."

Street lights dotted the road, lending more light to the pitch black night. Stores and plaza's lined the wide street. "Turn into the CVS plaza and park it."

Dut nodded and followed the directions.

"Kill the engine."

Armand pulled both his Beretta's out of the glove department and Dut grabbed a shotgun from under the driver's seat.

"I want them goods," Armand said, his voice quiet. "We can't really touch him, not yet anyway, but we are stripping everything he got."

"No doubt."

"Let's do it."

Armand covered his head with a hoodie and blocked his face with a bandana. Dut did the same. They crossed the plaza on foot, running up behind Kane's Charger, parked in the next parking lot behind a closed Popeyes.

Armand tapped the glass with his gat.

"What the—?"

Dut stood on the passenger side with the shotgun pointed at the passenger.

"Unlock and get out." Armand said, his voice deadpan.

"Yo, calm down—"

"Kane, fuck you, nigga." Armand said. He wanted Kane to know it was him. The hoodie and the scarf was to minimize visibility for any unknown cameras. "You let some wanna be gangstas get the drop on you, son."

"Army, you robbing me?" Kane's eyes were bulging out of his head.

"Nope, I'm showing you how fake gangsters do it. I'm not robbing you, he is." Armand nodded at Dut, whose face was still covered. "This is his practice run."

"Don't do this Army. Not right now. I got other shit to do tonight, don't fuck that up."

"Oh, now you talk with a little bit of respect. I hate folks like you, only decent to people when you need something. You know what Kane, fuck you."

Dut motioned Kane and his partner out the car. Armand stood back in the shadows, covering the entire scene, so no other person could walk up and blind side them. He kept his back flush to the wall while Dut made them lay on their sides and hogtied them both.

Kane's face was wet.

"Boy, I know you are not crying." Armand actually was surprised. "What's up?"

"Don't do this. Damn man, I don't need this tonight."

"Yo, I feel you." Armand nodded his head sympathetically. "I didn't want to do this either. Once it's started, then it's done. Can't be stopped. Wish you hadn't pushed us to this."

Dut emptied out their pockets, throwing the money and pills he found at Armand's feet.

"What's this?" Armand looked through the bag. "This Molly? I don't move this." He shook his head. "I'll keep it, though. I'm sure I can find something to do with it."

Dut took their guns and sat them in the back of his own truck.

"We got anything good?"

"It's okay. Got what we came for." Dut nodded, letting Armand know that he had found the small package of white powder.

"Yea, but now I'm wondering what this man got on him that would have him crying."

"I ain't crying, Army, damn," Kane yelled.

"Pop the trunk." Armand shifted his position to get a better view. "Check under the board, in the spare tire well. No one is dumb enough to hide something there but—"

"Jackpot!" Dut shook his head. "Got a duffle bag in here with it all. Brick, that molly. Pills. Son, it's all here."

"Army, I'll split it with you." Kane's voice was high. "We can go 50-50."

Armand didn't negotiate, there was no need when he was in the power position. "Put it all in the truck. Any steel in there?"

"Nothing major."

"Cool, we'll just take what they got."

Kane spit, it missed the curb and clung to the side of his face. Both Army and Dut grimaced. "Yuck, nigga," Dut said.

"Army, you know they are going to come looking for you to get their stuff," Kane threatened.

"That ain't how it work, boy, and you know it." Armand took out his switchblade and sliced two tires. "But if your people want to get at me on the strength of you, they know where I'm at. Or, they can send someone else to handle business with me from now on and they will get their cut off of this stash. But if I see or hear from you again, it's a wrap."

"So that's how it is?" Kane squirmed on the ground.

Armand shrugged as he jumped in the truck. "Yep, that's how we wanna be gangstas handle it, boy."

Dut peeled off, his laughter carrying out of the open window into the night.

CHAPTER TWENTY ONE

Fate

He had checked for her everywhere. Armand was giving up on ever seeing Monique again. Just the thought of it had him frustrated, he had attended every Wilson football game, gone to parties, hung out with Chew. Armand knew that Monique wasn't a hermit, she obviously could handle herself at a party. He suspected that they were just missing each other and he was probably showing up right when she left or vice versa.

There were plenty of other girls, plenty of other options. But he was curious about her. For some reason, when he closed his eyes, Monique was who he saw. It was a welcome relief, to have her face replace the nightmares of the dead, or the horror in the eyes of his victims. Thinking about her erased the reality of his current life. In every other female that Armand spent time with, he just saw the here and now. In Monique, he saw a future.

Armand wanted a taste of that future.

So, it was shocking when he randomly spotted Monique walking down the street. Armand was rolling past in his Lexus. He almost didn't want her to see this car because he didn't want to explain his life to her. She was clearly innocent, pampered from the street life. He had been driving down Wellington Avenue, looking at his cell phone and thinking about some money he had to pick up. And there she was, walking down the street with a book bag on her back, her hair pulled back into a ponytail and glasses on her face. She really was a nerd.

She was adorable.

He pulled his car over.

She kept walking without even looking at him.

Armand laughed. He rolled down his window as his car slowly rolled next to her. "Hello?"

It took a few seconds. Monique glanced at him, her face devoid of any emotion.

Armand gave a little wave, his expression questioning.

Monique's face relaxed and she pulled her earphones from her ears. "Hey."

That simple word made his heart leap. It was as if they had just left off from a conversation a few moments earlier, not that it had really been a few months.

"Hey." Armand put his car in park. He paused as if searching for her name in his memory. "Monique right?"

She smacked her lips and gave him an "*oh really*" look. "You don't remember my name?"

"I got it right, didn't I?"

She imitated him, putting a finger to her chin and tilting her head in the air. "Uhm…Army, right?" She remained planted in the middle of the sidewalk, not making a move toward his car.

He laughed. She seemed very comfortable in her own skin. Armand waited for her to walk closer to the car. Instead, she stood there, grinning at him. That surprised Armand. There was an awkward pause as he tried to figure out why she wouldn't come closer.

"Where are you headed?" Armand asked, thinking he might offer her a ride.

She shrugged. She didn't trust him, that much was clear. But she smiled at him, a very patient smile, as if she were waiting for him to catch on to something.

They looked at each other.

"So, can you get out your car?" Monique finally said.

"Oh." Armand chuckled. He was so used to girls running up to his car. He guessed she wasn't getting in. He parked the car, turned off his engine and climbed out.

She had on jeans and Uggs with a thick Northface coat. When he stood up, Armand saw her eyes taking in his boots, jeans and coat.

"Why are you looking me up and down?" Armand called her out. "You checking me out?"

Her smile lit up, although she looked a little embarrassed. She recovered quickly. "Just trying to see if you look any thicker than before."

"Well, I got this coat on. You have to see me inside, out of the cold."

"Or I will just take your word for it." Monique adjusted her bag. "I'm walking to the library."

"I could give you a ride."

"Or you could walk with me." Monique shifted the bag again. "It's just right there."

Armand tried to figure out her game. She wanted him to leave his car to walk with her. It was clearly a test. If he refused to walk with her he knew that she would never have another conversation with him again. He didn't mind the test. At least she didn't just run up to strange men in cars. "Okay," he said easily.

She seemed pleased. She stepped forward. "So, how you been?"

"Same ole, same ole." Armand reached for her bag. The smile on her face spread even wider.

His shoulder dropped under the weight of it. "Why is this bag so heavy?"

Monique giggled. "The AP books are huge."

She was in Advanced Placement. She was a winner, which he had suspected. "You're in all AP courses?"

"No." Monique sighed. "Just a couple. I'm hoping to get college credit in History and English."

"That's good." Armand strolled beside her. "The pretty nerd, right?"

"Right."

"So, when do you prove to me that you are so smart? When do I get to go to the planetarium?"

Monique studied his face for a minute. "You remembered?"

"Of course, I want to go." They crossed the street. "How could I forget?"

"Well, you know, you didn't ask for my number or anything. So…"

"That was my fault," Armand followed her through the library.

She sat at a table in the children's section. "Oh," she paused, "I thought you might not be interested…in going."

"I'm interested." He dropped the bag on the table, it landed with a loud thud.

"Shh," Monique said, smiling.

"So, can I have your number?" Armand asked, the words feeling awkward coming out of his mouth.

"Of course." Monique began taking out her books and notebooks and a water bottle. She rattled off the numbers.

He called the number. She checked her phone. "I got it." She said.

His phone vibrated. The money pickup was waiting. He had to go. But he didn't want to leave.

"So, this weekend? We can go on Saturday."

She nodded. "I hear you talking. I want to see if you are going to come through."

"A challenge? I accept that." Armand leaned close to her. "I always keep my word."

She met his eyes, all playfulness gone. For a second it seemed like she was hanging on his words, as if the statement was a weighted promise that her life depended on. "I hope so," she answered.

"You'll see." Armand stood back. "I'm glad I saw you. I have been looking for you."

"You have?" The dimples in her smile drew his attention. He wanted to kiss them.

"Yep. I guess I got lucky today, huh?"

"Maybe I got lucky." Monique set up her tablet. "Thank you for walking me."

"Anytime," Armand said. "Whatever you want." He checked his phone. "I got to go. But, I'll call you tonight."

"Okay."

He looked at all the books spread out in front of her. "What time do you go to bed?"

"I'll be up," Monique said.

"Alright," he smiled, feeling stupid, and made his way out of the library. When he stepped out into the crisp cold air he glanced back through the tinted window to steal one more glance at her. She was watching him.

He was definitely going to call. Armand hoped that she answered.

CHAPTER TWENTY TWO

Expert Strategies

When the phone rang that night, Monique glanced at it. She had wondered whether Armand would really call. Her heart leapt in her chest. Something about him was magnetic. When he was nearby a weird voltage tingled through her body, across her limbs and down her spine. She had saved his number under the name One. Monique coded all the numbers in her phone because she trusted no one.

One. Popped up on the caller Id.

Monique smiled. She pulled her long hair back and folded it into a ponytail. The phone rang a third time. Monique savored it. She closed her eyes and pictured his smile when he watched her talk. She had never seen anyone do that before—actually watch her speak and smile for no reason. The fourth time it rang, she rejected the call.

She was satisfied that he had actually called. She had no intention of answering it.

Monique wondered into the bathroom and spread cleanser on her face. He was something different. She loved that he didn't go to her school. He was cool with Chew, which meant he was in the streets. Monique was alright with that. Her cousins, her brother and even her father were in the street. Plus, it wasn't like she was going to marry him. More than likely, they would never get past a couple of kisses.

No one else had.

Monique had a clear goal: Escape. She had to escape Miriam and the unspoken sadness that clung to Miriam in the quiet moments at home. The harsh eyes and cold words. The uncertainty of a warm mother some days, a distant and detached mother on others. Monique had a solution. As soon as she went to college, she wasn't coming back. She also had to escape Pete. She loved her father, but she was terrified of him. There had been so many things she had seen…things she couldn't erase. She loved being at his house so that she could be with Ricardo and Michelle, the only two people in the world who had any idea what it felt like to be her. But that didn't mean she was comfortable spending time with Pete. In fact, she avoided Pete like the plague. Most of the time spent at his house, Monique managed to avoid him completely. Not that Pete noticed. His eyes were only on Michelle. And Monique was fine with that.

But there were the times when Pete got that distant look in his eyes, with savory smoking pouring from his parted lips as he focused on the high flames in the fire place. And on those evenings, she and Michelle would hear about Pete's childhood being raised by his brothers, or the adjustment he had from fighting a war in the jungle to the tight streets of the inner city. During those few hours, Monique got a glimpse into who her father was and why he was this way. And those lessons taught her who she was.

It wasn't like Uncle Jimmy, with the shouting and the theatrics, throwing phrases at them and forcing them to learn by rote memorization. Instead, it was intimate glimpses into Pete's soul. And in those moments, Monique felt something a little like love for her father.

But she was leaving Rochester. And she wasn't going to slip up and ruin her chances of getting away by getting bogged down with a boyfriend. She didn't want sex because she wasn't risking getting pregnant. She just wanted to have fun and feel the thrill that came when a boy smiled at her with interested eyes and the look of longing. But that was it. She splashed warm water on her face and removed the cleanser.

She would call Armand back tomorrow, maybe after school.

Monique grabbed the nail polish out of the closet hall way and headed back to her room. She sat on the bed and spread a small hand towel out under her toes.

Her phone rang. Monique glanced over at it, wondering whether or not it was Michelle.

One.

That surprised her. She was used to boys playing nonchalant, not calling back too many times because they didn't want to seem pressed. It was cute that Armand had called back. She picked up the phone and silenced the ring. She would definitely call him back tomorrow, maybe during lunch.

Monique turned on some music and plugged her headset in her ears. She painted her toenails thinking about when she first spotted Armand at the party, when he was standing by the table scooping food in his plate. When he looked at her she felt tickles up and down her spine. It was a first. And something in her made her not want to look him in the eyes. She felt like she was telling all her secrets just by gazing at him. It seemed that he could read her. When she imagined touching him, he smiled, as if he knew what she was thinking. And it embarrassed her. So she tried not to look at him.

But she couldn't keep her eyes away. That's why she had left the party early. There was no need staying when he clearly wasn't interested. She had stood by him for several minutes and his eyes had been trained on the dance floor, clearly on some other girl. And no one else at the party even compared to him so there was no reason for Monique to stay.

Monique wondered how it was that she hadn't seen him before, especially if he knew Chew and was from the West side. She paused, thinking about Chew. What had he been up to? He looked different. His lips were dark, his skin was grayish. Monique could bet that he was smoking all the time and not drinking water, not eating healthy. Monique bit her lip. She missed her dear friend. Chew had been by her side as much as Michelle when they were little. It was amazing to imagine that a few years later she would not even know much about him. He hadn't really pursued Tina, so Monique hadn't gleaned any information about him.

Monique picked up the phone to call Tina and ask about Chew.

There were two more missed calls. Monique glanced at the caller Id. *One.*

She dropped the phone. This fool was a stalker. Monique started to call Armand just to ask why he kept calling. She decided against it. Even though she liked him, this was clearly going to be over before it ever started. He wasn't going to force her to answer the phone! Had it occurred to him that she might be busy?

Monique crossed her arms and glared at the phone. She should block him. She picked up the phone, intent on doing just that.

But he was a connection to Chew. She could at least get Chew's number from him, possibly. And, there was something about him…something she just couldn't put her finger on. Monique was curious. And she wanted her curiosity satisfied before she completely cut him off.

Monique picked up the phone and called him back.

"Yo." He answered on the second ring.

"Hello?" Monique said, her voice had an edge to it. Not only was he rude, calling back to back, now he was answering the phone like he was crazy.

"Hey…hello." The voice instantly changed from tight to mellow and relaxed. "I'm sorry, I didn't mean to call you so much." Armand sounded flustered. "I was dialing this number thinking it was someone else—"

Her heart dropped. He wasn't that pressed for her after all. "No problem." She paused for a second. "Uhm, well, I can talk to you later."

"No, no, it's all good." He exhaled. "Are you busy?"

"No, just getting ready for tomorrow." Monique liked the smooth sound of his voice. "What are you doing?"

"Calling it a night." Armand gave a slight laugh. "It's been a long day."

"Yeah." Monique's day actually hadn't been any longer than usual. She just found that she had nothing to say all of a sudden.

"Did you stay at the library for a long time?"

"No," Monique hadn't been able to get much studying done. Her mind had been on him. "I walked home a couple of hours later."

"So, you live near the library?"

He was fishing. She smiled. "Kinda sorta. It's not that far." There was no need in hiding where she lived, all he had to do was ask Chew. But Monique was trained to keep information to herself. If he wanted to find out from her, he was going to have to work a little more. "Where do you live?"

"Downtown," Armand answered without hesitation. "I just got my place. You will have to see it."

"Uhm, maybe."

"No, not like that that," he said, and they both chuckled. The tension on the line finally evaporated. "I just got the place a few months ago. I think you would like it."

"Yeah, maybe." She smiled. "Did you furnish it already?"

"No, it's empty right now. I'm taking my time."

Monique liked that. He wasn't trying hard to impress. "You live alone?"

"Yeah," Armand answered. "I'm kind of a loner."

"Yeah, me too." There was a pause. Monique did not do phone silence at all. She would rather get off. "Well, I won't hold you," she said, "I was just calling you back."

"Okay luv," he said easily.

The word made Monique's heart jump. She tried to think of a response, but he kept talking.

"Are you going to the library tomorrow?"

"Yea, I have mid-terms all week and that's the only place I can really study. If I come home I will fall asleep."

"Okay, I'll meet you tomorrow, same place, same time?"

"Huh?"

"I want to walk you to the library again. Is that okay?"

That threw Monique for a loop. She just sat there.

"Is that okay with you?"

She could hear the smile in his voice. He knew he had impressed her with the offer. "Yes." She answered, blushing. "I would like that."

"Okay, have a good night," he said and the line disconnected.

Monique leaned back into her pillows, confusion dotting her mind. What had just happened? First, she was breathless and her heart was racing. Just from a phone call? Second, he had tricked her into calling him and then downplayed it as if he hadn't meant to blow up her phone. He had broken her game by forcing her to return his call. That was a first. They weren't playing by her rules, he was leading the direction of whatever this was that they were doing.

It occurred to her that this was the difference between a boy and a man. She had finally met a man. Monique smiled as she laid her head against her pillow, images of Armand dancing across her mind.

CHAPTER TWENTY THREE

Reliant

"Ricardo, come on." Monique whined into the phone. "Stop playing and come get me."

"I'm not coming over there, Mo. I already told you, I got plans tonight."

"But I'm not talking about tonight. I just need you to drop me off at the planetarium around two. What's that got to do with your plans for tonight?"

"Because I know you." Ricardo laughed. "I'm going to get stuck waiting for you, or running you somewhere else, or you are going to act like a baby when I drop you off."

"I promise I won't."

"I love you, Mo, so don't take this the wrong way—but your promises don't mean shit."

Monique inhaled quickly. She was completely offended. "That's not true."

"Yes it is, when you want something then everyone else comes second."

Monique sat quietly for a few seconds.

"Come on, don't act like that Mo," Ricardo said, responding to her silence just as she expected him to. "Don't do this today, okay, really."

"Ricardooo," Monique dragged his name out.

"No," he said, sounding more forceful now that her voice was back to normal. "Not today, Mo. I will come get you tomorrow."

"Okay." She relented, shuffling through her mind on what her next move should be.

"I will tell Mikki to come get you."

That was even better. Monique didn't want to ask Michelle because she had just argued with her that morning. "Okay," she said again, keeping her words to a minimum. Now that Ricardo said no, he owed her. She would keep all her interactions short, just as a reminder. Unlike Michelle, Ricardo responded to guilt. He would definitely make this up to her.

"You have money in your pocket?"

His voice was soft and caring. Out of the three of them, Ricardo had the most loving heart, there was no question about that. He didn't show it to the world, but there was nothing that he wouldn't give her and Michelle, he had proven that time and time again.

She had a wad of cash in her stash in her jewelry box because she pinched off a piece of anything that was given to her and put it away, even if it was just a dollar or two. But she would never say no to that question. "Not really." Monique answered.

Ricardo snorted. He knew better. "Okay, I will give Mikki something to give you, okay?"

"Thank you, Ricardo," Monique said his name like a song to make him smile.

"Whatever, shorty," Ricardo answered, but Monique could hear the smile on his face.

"I love you."

"Yeah yeah yeah," Ricardo laughed. "All it takes to get your love is a few bucks?"

"No, of course not. Don't start preaching."

"You don't need nothing from these niggas out here on these streets, Monique. Whatever you need, me or Dad can get you. That's why I keep you with cash, you feel me?"

"I know." Monique wondered why no one thought she might want a relationship for the thrill of having one, like they did. She was just supposed to study and be content with what her brother and father handed her. "Where you at, Daddy's house?"

"Yeah, me and Mikki are both here. I will tell her to get you at two."

"Okay." Monique felt disappointed. She tried to shake it off but she always felt left out when they were there without her, which was most of the time. But both their mothers had other children to chase after, Monique couldn't just leave Miriam for weeks at a time. Even if she wanted to. "Tell her I will be ready."

"Yeah, right."

"I will!" Monique disconnected and started getting dressed for her date.

***

Three hours later, Monique climbed into Michelle's Malibu.

"Why did you honk the horn?" Monique demanded as she slammed the door.

"I wanted you to hurry up. And you get in my car without saying hello? Or how about "thank you" for driving all the way over here to get you?"

"Thank you. But you should have come in. She heard the horn blowing, and now she is wondering why you wouldn't come in." Monique shook her head. *She* referred to Miriam. "It's hard enough to deal with her, now I am going to hear a thousand questions about why you didn't come in and say hi."

Michelle smiled. "Aunt Miriam misses me?"

"No, she just needs something to complain about." Monique pulled down the visor and looked at herself in the mirror. "She almost tried to stop me from leaving."

"Next time, I will come in. I'm rushing. Ricardo said you were going to the planetarium, but I am going out to Webster to meet someone at the movies."

"Who is someone?"

Michelle smiled. "Why you all worried about what I got going on?"

Monique shook her head. "Because, she might be ugly. Or someone I don't like."

"It doesn't have anything to do with you!"

"Whatever." Monique slapped the visor back in place. "Whoever she is, I have to like her."

"This one probably won't get that far." Michelle shrugged. "We'll see." They rode in silence, listening to music. "Why the planetarium on a Saturday?"

"I thought you would never ask." Monique smiled broadly, revealing a mouth full of even pearly whites. "I got a date."

"At the planetarium? What, it's a white boy?"

Monique sighed. "No. He is not a white boy. Although, I am not opposed to diversity."

"So, you must have picked the place." Michelle laughed out loud. "The planetarium? Are you trying to bore him to death?"

Monique stuck her bottom lip out. "I like the planetarium. And, if he is going to be in my world, then he has to deal with what I like."

"Ahh, so you are finally learning a little something, huh?"

"Yep. So, I wanted to ask you if you knew him. He said he went to East. His name is Armand."

"Armand?" Michelle shook her head. "Nope. I don't know him. He might not have been well known."

"I doubt that." Monique looked out the window. Had he lied? If he was a liar, she wasn't dealing with him. "He seems like someone who would have been very well known."

"Wait, there was an Armand, back in the day." Michelle nodded her head. "He was a cutey. Quiet though. Not mean, but not really friendly either."

Monique felt the weight that had landed on her chest lift up. She was relieved. "What happened to him?"

"I don't know. Probably transferred. I can ask around." Michelle gazed at Monique for a second before focusing on the road again. "You seem…pressed. I got to see this one again. I don't really remember."

"No. Absolutely not." Monique did not want Armand to see her being babysat. "You are not going to meet him today."

"Why?"

"Mikki, come on. Just drop me off and leave it alone. Please."

"Mo, I want him to know that you have people in this city. He not just fucking with some silly girl."

"Okay, so if he becomes a keeper, then you can say that. But today is the first date. It might not be anything at all. Please…"

Michelle relented after a few minutes. They rode in silence.

As they pulled into the parking lot next to the planetarium, Michelle said, "I will come get you when it's over. Call me, okay?"

"No," Monique grabbed her purse. "He can give me a ride home."

"Fuck that, Monique." Michelle's voice was as tight as a wire cable. "I don't know this one. I think he fell off the radar after tenth grade and I can't think of anyone who might know him. You don't get in the car with him. You don't go nowhere with him. I will come back and get you."

"Mikki—"

"You can think I am fucking around if you want to. I will call Daddy."

Monique's eyes widened so large that her eyelids disappeared. "Michelle!"

"No, I don't know this dude. Call me when it's over."

Monique recognized that Michelle was not Ricardo. Her manipulative games did not work on her big sister. "Okay." She climbed out of the car without saying goodbye, slammed the door, and headed inside.

Monique glanced over her shoulder and Michelle was still sitting here. "Leave!" Monique said, pointing out of the lot.

"I will be back here at four if you don't call," Michelle shouted through the open window. "And I will come inside looking for you."

Monique thought about the man with the leather gloves who had tried to snatch her years ago in the park. The memory sat with her like a shadow clinging to her mind. It stayed with all of them. Something about it felt unfinished, as if it would happen again one day, like the job was just waiting to be filled. Monique recognized the look on Michelle's face. She often forgot that Michelle had lived through that day too, until she saw this particular expression. It reminded her that Michelle had almost lost her once and didn't want to lose her again.

"Alright, Mikki. I will call as soon as it ends."

"Okay." Michelle met her eyes and years of unspoken communication flowed between them. Michelle was satisfied this time. She slowly pulled out of the parking lot.

CHAPTER TWENTY FOUR

Research

Armand sat in the parking lot, waiting and watching. He wanted to know more about this girl with the bright smile and sparkling almond shaped eyes. Chew wasn't giving up much information and Armand wasn't asking him. Pride wouldn't allow it. He and he alone knew everything there was to know about his woman, he wouldn't allow Chew the pleasure of thinking he had the manual to Monique's heart.

She went to Wilson. Her mother was a school teacher. They lived in the neat house on the hill. No one that he knew claimed to have had sex with her. Rumor was that she was still a virgin. Armand liked that most of all. She was fresh, still pure. Once he claimed her, she would be 100% percent his. No man had been there before.

Armand didn't talk to many people outside of his crew, and only a few of them were still in school, but the word from Raymond's people was that she was a simple good girl. Destined for college and great things. With no negative reputation. She was a keeper.

The engine of his car was off, but his music was on. Armand nodded his head up and down, counting the two knots of cash that Dut had delivered to him a couple of hours ago. He thought about the artillery that he and Dut needed to purchase; Titan had told him to grip up after the move on Kane. Armand bit his lip. He had no regrets. And Titan didn't give him a hard time about it. That was something he appreciated. Once the initial chaos had died down, Titan had his back. Titan was a true leader, Armand recognized that over and over again. One day, it would be him. And he would remember the feeling of following a true leader. Armand would be that type of leader.

A small tan car pulled into the parking lot. Armand noted the Malibu, saw two brown girls in the front seat. Irritation chafed his calm. Monique had brought a friend? Both girls were talking, heads adamantly shaking, hands flailing up and down in expression. The girl driving looked familiar. Armand could have sworn she was the point guard on the East High basketball team. The girl's team that had gone all the way to the championship.

Armand wondered how she and Monique could be connected. He watched as Monique jumped out the car, slammed the door and stared at the girl and then shouted at the car, pointing her arm out of the lot. The point guard was a true lesbian, it was well known that she didn't let boys anywhere near her. Was Monique a lesbian too? What other kind of quarrel would two girls have like this, that had Monique shouting and pointing, then standing there with her arms folded across her chest, anger pouring from her like steam from a pot.

Armand couldn't hear what they were saying. He started to roll down his window, but decided not to. He wanted to watch Monique and see the true her, see how she was when she didn't know she was being observed. Something about her made his heart skip and made him feel…happy. Happiness wasn't a welcome emotion. In fact, in his line of work, it was scary. If she had that ability, by just a few conversations, then she ultimately would have the power to hurt him. Armand wanted to make sure he knew the true person he was dealing with, the person beyond the "representative," before he fell hard for her.

Maybe no one could claim to have had sex with Monique because she was into girls, not guys. Or maybe she was bicurious. Armand shook his head. He could handle the curiosity, but he wasn't getting involved in a love triangle with two lesbians.

The Malibu pulled off, with the girl in the front seat turning up the volume. Monique took several deep breaths, her fingers pulling at her bouncy hair. She exhaled slowly. If Armand didn't know better, he would almost suspect she was counting. After a minute, she moved forward, walking into the planetarium and letting the heavy darkened glass doors close behind her.

Armand glanced in his overhead mirror and made sure he was neat and clean looking. Monique had his interest, that was for sure. Everything about her was covered and closed. He was going to have fun opening her up.

Armand exited his car ten minutes later and made his way into the planetarium. He had never been here before. He wondered how such a large building could exist on the East side of the city and he had never before noticed it. Maybe, back when he had Camilla, maybe he would have come to the planetarium then. Uncle Marshall might have taken him, just to show him something different. But those days were far behind him. And they were never returning.

Armand entered through the glass doors. The inside of the lobby was dark, with long ropes sectioning off an anticipated line. Monique was to the far right, purchasing tickets at the ticket booth. Her back was to him as she chatted back and forth with the attendant. A deep sloping hallway led up to what Armand assumed was the main theater. To the side was an exhibit, it almost looked like the museum display. Armand felt out of place. This wasn't a movie theater. It was dark and quiet. There were no concessions.

But everywhere Armand looked there were dynamic posters and pictures of the galaxy and other worlds.

Armand didn't want to walk up on Monique and surprise her. Instead, he floated to the ceiling high display, his eyes scanning from the floor to the ceiling. It was amazing because this wasn't fiction, it was someplace that actually existed. Another world.

"You made it." Monique stood next to him. The frustrated girl he had seen earlier was gone, instead she was cool and easy. He was glad he had seen her before, glad to know that she had levels to her that were hidden from him. For now.

"Yes, I made it. " He leaned in and gave her a hug. "Hi ma ma."

She smiled and closed her eyes, enjoying the hug. "Hi."

He noticed she didn't try to tag him with a stupid nickname. Another point for Monique.

She held up two tickets. "We have a few minutes before the show."

Armand looked at the tickets and wondered how much they had cost her. He tried to glance at the ticket prices. She quickly slid the tickets into her bag. "Stop trying to look at the price," she said with a grin. "It's my treat. I normally have to come alone. I'm glad you're here."

"Oh." Her wide open honesty surprised him. "No doubt."

"Let's go to the exhibit." She hitched her small Coach book bag over her shoulders. "It's over there."

Armand saw the dark hallway ahead. For all he knew, it could be a trap. The large atrium was empty. "Does anybody work here?"

"It always feels empty like this." She turned the corner to the exhibit. "I like it. I imagine this is how it feels in space."

"I guess." Armand was thinking about the guns that he left in the car. He would feel better if he had one on him now. Just in case.

Monique looped her thumbs under the shoulder straps. "Don't worry," she said with a knowing glance. "It's safe in here. First of all, no one comes in here except for people interested in this stuff. Second, there is nothing for anyone to take, if you really think about it."

Armand breathed. "Alright." He rarely went by someone's word. But he was willing to risk it just this once.

"Did you know the sun is really just a star?"

The question came out of nowhere. Armand looked at the glass in front of him, showing that the sun was the closest star to planet Earth. "That can't be right."

"It is." Monique had a far-away look in her eyes. "It's nothing more than a regular star to someone else on some other world. But it's everything to this planet. Everything to us."

Armand thought about that.

"So, since it's a star, it can die. It can consume itself and explode. Or implode. Or create a black hole. But, when a star falls apart, it scatters, forming new stars." Monique nodded. "I like that."

"But, if the sun dies out, we are all dead."

"Yep, just like that." Monique looked at Armand appreciatively. "That's why every minute counts," she said as she led him out of the exhibit and toward the theater. "That's why I come here, to remember that no day is promised. When you see space and how massive the solar system is, and understand that there are galaxies beyond us, then we seem so small. Just a tiny planet fueled by one star. It's all random. And it could all end in an instant."

"Like a meteor." Armand smiled.

"Or aliens." Monique's eyes got wider.

"Aliens? Now you're going too far." They both laughed.

"Either way, all the small stuff, all the hurt and stuff, it just doesn't seem so serious." Monique shrugged a little. "Not in the overall scheme of things."

He fought the urge to wrap his arms around her and tell her that he would always protect her. She was right. In the overall scheme of things, everything about life was random. Small. And it could all be taken away in seconds. Without explanation and with no measure of right or wrong. He didn't want to get deep and spill his pain onto her. Instead, he simply nodded his head.

Armand followed Monique into the theater which was shaped like a dome, with movie style seating in a circle around a pit in the middle of the room.

She sat in the last row. "I don't like people behind me that I can't see," she explained. "Especially since the theater never fills up."

A few others trickled in around them as they sat in the padded seats, which had speakers lined in the headrest.

The lights faded. Monique touched his hand by accident. It was just a brush. But she didn't move her fingers away. Armand wrapped her hand in his, his fingers interlocking hers. They glanced at each other. Neither smiled. They both felt the same thing. He knew it in that moment. Sound surrounded them, flowing from the speakers in their seats, and as it did a huge planetarium projector began to rise from the center of the room.

"What the hell…?" Armand whispered.

Monique smiled. "Just wait."

Within second the pictures on the dome change and it became the sky. Armand sat back and allowed himself to be absorbed in the experience of being surrounded by space, as they spun through galaxies and past stars and witnessed a star imploding and creating a black hole.

Armand forgot about everything in the 45 minutes, captivated by an entirely different world.

As the projector sunk back into the pit and the dim lights returned, Armand turned to Monique.

"So, what did you think?" Monique asked.

"I understand why you like it so much." Armand answered.

"Yeah, okay." Monique leaned forward, her sarcasm etched on her face. "Well, thank you for being kind about it."

"No really," Armand still held her hand. "I get it," he said, standing up. She stood up with him. They faced each other, in the narrow aisle between the rows of seats. "I definitely get it."

He hadn't meant to kiss her, but he couldn't help himself. His lips covered hers and his fingers landed in the mound of bouncy curls.

She didn't kiss back at first, but stood there absorbing him with her eyes closed. Then she relaxed, with a sigh, and kissed back. Armand felt his heart jump.

"Monique." The small voice ricocheted through the small theater. The basketball girl that had driven Monique to the theater stood at the entry way.

Monique looked furious. "Mikki, are you serious?"

Armand's fist got tight. He wasn't going to fight some crazy lover for her that was for sure. He took a step back.

Monique looked at him questioningly at first, then she seemed upset with him, too.

They faced each other with confusion mounting between the two of them like Biggie and Tupac. Armand could feel her anger at him, but he was angry, too. He didn't like games.

"I told you 4pm." She walked up to them and put her hands on her hip.

"Yeah, but you didn't have to come inside." Monique shrunk back from Armand, the slight move putting miles of distance between the two. Monique walked over to the girl. "I can't believe you."

"Who are you?" The girl looked at Armand with wide blinking eyes, a fake smile on her face. The smile said it all, that she would do Armand harm if she had to.

"Who are you?" Armand took a step back and looked directly into Monique's eyes. "I don't know what you got going on, ma ma, but I'm not for the games."

Monique's head jerked back as if Armand had slapped her. "Games…?"

Armand looked at Michelle, his eyes cold. He had to be careful dealing with females, especially lovers. If the little one jumped on him, he couldn't put his hands on her—there was no way he could justify handling someone so little. So that left him exposed. And he was in a planetarium, surrounded by white folks, so he was in a no-win situation.

A knowing look flashed across Monique's face. Monique started laughing. "Army, she's my sister. Not my…woman." She shook her head and laughed at him.

Army felt…stupid. He would have never thought they were related. Except for all the hair. But the little ones hair was wild, matching her wild eyes and her wild demeanor. She was capable of anything. She was either going to be Armand's friend or foe. She was clearly the type who didn't recognize a middle ground. Armand glanced back and forth between the two.

"I'm Michelle," the smaller one said, crossing her arms with a know-it-all look on her face. "I recognize you. You went to East?"

"No," Monique interrupted. "You are not about to stand here interrupting us. Why are you in here? I asked you to wait in the car."

Armand smiled, tension and confusion easing away as he realized what was going on. Her sister was all up in her business. This was probably one of the reasons Monique was so secretive—her sister was nosey.

"We are clearing out the theater for the next show," the attendant called out.

They moved out toward the exit, Michelle and Monique fussing back and forth.

"At least let him answer…" Michelle said.

"Yes, I went to East." Armand said. "You're the point guard, right? On the championship team."

Michelle lit up like someone had flipped a switch. "Yep, that's me." She pointedly looked at Monique. "How you know Mo?"

Armand just grinned at her. She was doing too much. He shrugged and stared directly at her. He wasn't afraid and he wasn't about to be bullied by an over assertive sister. "We are getting to know each other."

"Oh," Michelle stood there for a minute, smiling as her eyes roamed between the two of them.

"Mikki, please…" Monique put her hand over her face.

Michelle rolled her eyes. "Alright! I'll be in the car. It was nice meeting you, Army." She said his name with exaggeration, laughing as she made her way back outside.

"I'm so sorry," Monique whispered.

Armand shrugged. "No big deal. But, I would have given you a ride. You didn't have to have your sister come and get you."

Monique's hand still covered half her face. "I…it's not always easy for me to get away like that." She sighed. "Obviously."

Armand could tell she was really upset. It was cute. He must mean something, for her to be that angry. "Let it go, baby girl. She just loves you, that's all."

"Yeah, I guess." Monique looked like she was about to cry out of frustration.

Armand touched her cheek with the back of his hand, then kissed her on the lips, very gently. "Come on, I will walk you out."

He held his hand out and Monique took it.

"Thank you for coming," she said.

"You already thanked me," he smiled. "It's all good."

They walked across the lot. Michelle was waiting in front of the building. Of course. Armand shook his head a little. No wonder Monique was so distant. He walked her to the car and opened the door.

"Call me when you get home," he said to Monique.

She nodded.

Michelle turned down the volume of the music that was shaking the Malibu. She leaned over Monique, her hair dangling into Monique's lap. "Is that your Lexus? The one over there?"

"Gotdamn!" Armand wondered how she knew which ride belonged to him. She must have been watching him when he was watching her. She was savvy, more so than Monique. "Yeah, that's me."

"Nice ride." Michelle's eyebrow raised.

Armand felt like saying "*I know this.*" Instead he just nodded at Michelle and met eyes with Monique. "I will talk to you later."

"Okay."

He stepped away from the car and watched as they pulled out of the lot. Just like before, he saw arms flailing in the air and hair blowing wildly. Clearly, Monique was screaming at her sister.

Armand smiled to himself. Michelle knew what Armand knew—that Monique was worth protecting.

CHAPTER TWENTY FIVE
Hard Headed

"Listen, don't go to school today." Armand held the phone to his cheek as he reached for a bowl in his cabinet. "You haven't seen my place yet. Come chill over here."

"You want me to skip?" Monique asked, a smile in her voice.

Armand dropped the bowl on the table and searched the other cabinet for cereal. "It's not skipping when school is going to close early today. You already know it is. They are saying there is going to be a blizzard."

"Yeah, but I have to go to school. I have a report due."

Armand was silent as he opened his refrigerator and grabbed the milk. "You haven't seen my place yet," he finally said.

"I know." Monique's voice was quiet.

Armand didn't like this. He didn't like feeling like he was begging for her to spend time with him. Since when did he do this? It was very rare for him to bring anyone back to his home. Yet, he had offered it to Monique a few times and she always had an excuse.

It frustrated him that the one person he invited to come over, that he wanted to share his world with, was nonchalant about it.

"You know what," he said, his tone changing. "Don't worry about it."

Monique caught the change immediately. "Army, it's not like that. I just…I can't get caught skipping. You don't know my mom, she is not like most people. She will make me pay."

"I hear you." Armand poured the milk into the bowl and then searched for a clean spoon. He found a huge spoon and sunk it in the bowl. "Maybe this isn't a good look…right now." Armand didn't really mean to say that, but he was tired of trying to create time for them. She should be the one pressing, trying to find a way to fit into his schedule, not the other way around.

"What?" Monique's voice sounded far away. "Really?" She paused. "You know what, maybe your right."

"What!" Armand stopped moving and looked at his phone. She clearly didn't know who he was. He placed it back up to his ear. "What did you just say?"

"I'm saying, Army, you are getting mad at me for something I can't control. I can't just skip. I want to see you. I want to come over. I…I just have to do it when I can make it work."

There was a moment of silence.

"I thought you understood that," Monique continued.

"I do understand that, Mo, but I'm making time. You aren't. I'm out here grinding. You are just going to school. How is it I can get away and you can't?"

"Maybe this weekend?"

"No, the weekends don't work. I already told you that." Armand scooped a spoonful of cereal in his mouth. He sighed. "You know what, I don't want to start today off like this. Let's just forget it, alright?"

There was no answer on the line.

"Hello?" Armand said.

No answer.

A second later he heard a click. "I'm sorry, Army, that was Mikki."

"Wait, you had me on hold?"

"I said hold on. I thought you heard me."

Armand felt like he was going to explode. But he had to have patience. Monique didn't know any better. She clearly knew nothing about a hustler, about a hustler's life, about the type of man he was. He had to force himself to remember that. Had she been any other female, he would have barked on her. In fact, he wouldn't even be having this conversation with any other chick because he wouldn't go out of his way to invite them over. It was only because Monique was so innocent and unknowing that was he willing to tip toe this line with her. If she had any real knowledge of this life, or how to deal with a man like him, then she would truly understand that the invitation into his home was sacred. And she would feel lucky to be invited. And she would do anything to get there, before he recanted.

But Monique wasn't that person. She didn't know anything about the streets and a man like him. She was a school teacher's daughter with a wild little big sister. She was a nerd trying to get to college. She was a virgin. She was special and different and rare. And he was willing to wait for her. He was willing to move slower for her. He was willing to wait for her.

"Army, I'm sorry." Monique's voice sounded uncertain. "I just can't today. Please don't be mad."

"I'm not mad, ma ma." He scooped down some more cereal. They spoke every morning while she made her way to school. He had called earlier today, thinking that she could come over since school was going to be cancelled if it stormed. "I'm not."

They had only seen each other a few times since the planetarium. Michelle was always Monique's driver, escorting her like an annoying nanny and making sure she picked Monique up on time. Armand was sure that Monique's mother was strict, although he couldn't figure out why Michelle had so much freedom to be herself, while Monique was stuffing herself into a conservative shell.

Armand didn't understand it, but he really didn't care. He wanted time alone with Monique that wasn't confined to Michelle playing mommy duty. And, he wanted a chance to touch her—even if she wasn't ready to go far he couldn't still put his arm around her, or kiss her, or touch the back of her neck. Things that he didn't want to do in public. He wanted private time alone with her.

"Are you almost at school?" he said.

"Yeah, I'm here. My mom dropped me off."

"Okay, call me when school is over. I will come get you."

"Okay." Monique's voice sounded happier. "I will. Have a good day."

"You too, baby girl."

Armand disconnected the phone. He finished his cereal as he looked out of the window. They were calling for heavy snow and the sky was completely gray. There was going to be a blizzard. There were moves that needed to be made before he got shut inside, unable to drive and maneuver on the icy Rochester streets. He started making phone calls, intent on making arrangements to pick up money and check on the dissemination of product. Blizzards were good for business, the working folks bought extra supply to get them over the hump. He needed to make sure the crews contacted their working clients and supplied the demand.

TWENTY SIX

First

Armand looked up at Raymond, who was standing in front of the safe.

"I special ordered this one." Raymond looked at it appreciatively. "Can't no one break into this."

"Anything with a lock can be broken into, Raymond. It's the balance of things."

"Yo, I don't want to hear that ying yang shit." Raymond tapped the safe. "Hear what I am saying," he shouted, laughing. "Ain't no one getting in this motherfucker here!"

"Better not, for how much you spent on it. I don't see why we need it."

"What?" Raymond huffed, facing Armand indignantly like Armand had just spoken against him. "It's temporary safety. We got to stop relying on folks. This way, the cash or the product is locked down until we need it."

"Who has the combination?"

"Just me and you."

"How you know I trust you?"

"Well, if you don't by now, then it's your problem." Raymond pulled a blunt to his lips. "You smoking?"

Armand shook his head. "Naw, I'm good boy. I gotto make a run. Don't want to be on the streets dirty. Not with the weather like this. You stay off the streets, too. If you get locked up it may be a week before we can pull you out. You remember the last blizzard?"

"Yea, stupid ass Dut." Raymond shook his head. "It took two weeks to get before the judge."

They both glanced out the window. The snow was coming down in sheets, the thick snowflakes filling the air like dense powder.

"I'm about to get outta here, son." Armand stood up. "Once I get in the house I ain't coming back out. Not in this."

"Me either." Raymond looked at the ounce of marijuana siting in a gallon freezer bag. "I don't have nowhere to go. Patrice coming over in a minute. You know what's up." He laughed.

"Whatever." Armand stood up. "I'm out."

They gave each other a pound.

Armand jogged off the porch of the house and down to his car. It was already covered with snow. He dusted a little off with a gloved hand, then he sat inside, started the car, and let the warmth melt away at the sheet of snow covering the windows.

He glanced at his phone. There were no calls from Monique.

School had closed early. Armand had been waiting for her call. He wondered why she hadn't called. Maybe he should fade her back. When they were together, it was a perfect fit. He felt complete with her by his side. There wasn't a need for many words, it was like they already knew each other. But when she wasn't around and he was pressing to see her, it made him feel vulnerable. And he hated that feeling.

Armand knew that Monique normally walked the back streets, taking Aberdeen Street to Wellington Avenue, and winding her way through the 19th ward to get home. It didn't make sense to him that she walked that way home, it was at least 15 minutes longer than just walking straight down Genesee Street. But Monique had said that she loved the neighborhood and walking though it made her feel safe.

But on a day like today, in this intense cold and snow, he was sure Monique wasn't lazily making her way home. If Michelle or her mother hadn't gone to get her, she would be walking up Genesee St.

The snow was falling faster and heavier than he had originally realized. Everything was white everywhere he looked. And although his car was warm, the snow wasn't melting when it touched his windshield, because it was accumulating so fast. Armand turned the windshield wipers on high. It was stupid for him to drive down Genesee Street. There was no doubt that Monique was home or somewhere else, she was too smart to be caught out in this weather, like him.

Armand shook his head and exhaled loudly. He stared to turn right onto Brooks Avenue, to head back to his house, but decided to go straight. Something deep inside of him was gnawing at him, pressing him to stay on the street, to just see if he saw her. There were a few things about Monique that he was going to have to change. She wasn't calling when she was supposed to. He had made it clear that he expected her to call when he asked her to. Now he was out in the snow, with her on his mind, not sure whether or not she was safe. If she had called when she was supposed to he wouldn't have to take the unnecessary trip down the snow and ice covered street. If something happened to his car, like hitting an ice patch and sliding into a pole, he was going to be done with her.

The snow was getting thicker by the minute. He could barely see in front of the car. Armand thought about the truck parked in the yard over on Lyell Avenue, he should have had Dut deliver it to him. The roads were too bad to be floating around in the Lexus. Armand turned the wipers up to the highest level. He turned his bright lights on. The snow was completely consuming; Armand couldn't even make out the painted yellow line dividing the street. The car slid, just a little, when he padded the brake. Armand coasted into the slide then turned his wheel out of it. He moved the car farther to his left, driving down the center of the street.

"Fuck this," he said the second time the car pulled to the right as he tried to guide it straight. He was only doing 20 mph, at this slow pace it would take him an hour to make the ten minute drive home. Irritation danced around the fringes of his thoughts. As much as he was feeling Monique, he had placed himself in danger. And for what? He turned his blinker on to turn right.

That's when Armand spotted Monique.

Armand squinted. His soul knew it was her before his eyes confirmed it. Everything in him tried to fight the reality, not wanting to believe it was so, that she couldn't be walking down the street in a blizzard, a scarf tied around her face, a Styrofoam container in her hand. But his heart jumped, just like he did whenever she was near.

Armand checked the rearview mirror, but he couldn't see through the snow. He put on his hazard lights and padded the brakes. She was walking slowly, her head bowed low, each step slow and deliberate. He could tell that her chest was heaving up and down. Her mass of hair was completely covered in white, and her book bag was bobbing up and down, the wind blowing it to the side, which was pushing her body over. It looked like she was walking in slow motion, trying to push herself against the wind.

Armand felt himself cringe. The car stopped.

He opened the door, leaving the car running in the middle of the street, and jogged over to the sidewalk. He jumped over the curb took a few steps toward her. She almost walked directly into him.

When she raised her head, her face was covered in the strain of desperation. Tears were tumbling down her eyes, and patches of ice clung to her hair. It looked like she had been pummeled with snowballs. Armand fought the urge to scoop her up and carry her to the car.

"What are you doing out here?" He asked the only thing that came to mind.

She started crying, although Armand was sure that she probably didn't realize it. She was out of it. He quickly led her to his car, ignoring the couple of cars that took a wide route around them. She said something, but Armand didn't hear it. She could have died. He wondered whether she understood that. Whether she had paid attention to the dead bodies that were found after these unexpected blizzards, news that someone foolish enough to be out in the artic weather, improperly dressed, that didn't make it. Had she ever heard of frostbite? And where was her wild ass sister now? What about the mother he always heard of? How was it that they blocked him from having access to her, as if they gave a damn, but left her on her own to get home in a snow storm?

He pulled the Styrofoam container from her frozen hands. Her fingers were stuck, frozen around it. Armand shook it. Chicken? She bought chicken wings? He sighed and slammed the container onto the ground. Clearly she was going home alone to eat alone. There was something about her that he recognized, something that felt so familiar to him. Armand hadn't been able to put his finger on it until this very second. Abandoned. She was just as abandoned as him, all alone when it really mattered. Fending for herself, just when she really needed someone.

He would be there for her. He would protect her. Armand wasn't for the bullshit, for the sister always being in his face when she wanted to spend time with him, but no one thinking to pick her up from school during a storm.

Armand stood in front of her and brushed the snow off.

"Thank you," she whispered through chattering teeth. He wanted to wrap his arms around her and promise that everything would be alright.

"You don't ever have to thank me. One day, baby girl, you will understand that." Armand guided her into the seat.

He walked around to the driver side and jumped in.

She didn't say anything else, her eyes closed as she put her fingers to the heater.

Armand turned the heat all the way up. He pulled her seatbelt across her body and fastened it, then did the same for himself.

Monique started shaking her hands, the tears still tumbling down her face.

"Are your hands stinging, ma?" Fear crept into his mind.

Her fingers were completely white. At least they weren't blue. But he knew they were frozen and thawing them out was going to be painful.

She nodded her head yes, biting her lips to keep in the pain.

Armand snatched the wet scarf and through it in the back seat. "Take off your boots," he said. She kicked off the stylish string up boots. She didn't even have on winter gear. Armand fought the urge to fuss at her. What was she thinking?

By the time they got to his building, she had caught her breath, the indescribable look of panic was easing away from her face, and the pain seemed to be lessoning. He saw her finally look away from the heater, glancing around her.

He wondered if she would say anything in protest, if she was going to demand he take her home instead of to his place. Monique closed her eyes and sighed, relief covering her like a blanket.

***

They stepped off the elevator to the wide private hallway. Armand held her book bag, her boots and her coat. Monique walked in her socks, with her arms folded across her chest, glancing around the private foyer.

"This is yours?"

"Yep." Armand didn't look at her, but he felt his chest spread with pride. She was impressed. He liked that she liked it.

Armand unlocked the door and held it open for her. She stepped into the sunken living room and stared up at the cathedral ceiling.

"Wow," she said, and met his eyes with a smile just for him. "I love your space, Army."

"It's alright." He hung her coat in the closet by the door. Then he crossed the room and flipped a switch. The fireplace lit up. "Let's get you warmed up."

"Did you really just light the fireplace like that?" Her smile was worth a million dollars. She shook her head and smiled at him. "You did that like it was no big deal, huh?" She moved toward the fire, her eyes fixated on it. "It's so pretty."

"What? Fire?"

"Yeah," Monique answered. She stared at it.

He watched her staring at the fire, her eyes lost in the leaping flames in front of her. She didn't know much about him, but she knew enough to know that his home was an accomplishment. That he was proud of himself. And she was clearly proud of him.

"Your clothes are wet, ma," he said, deflecting the pride that she made him feel. "You have to get out of them so you don't catch cold."

She nodded but didn't look away from the fire. Monique moved slowly, inching her way closer to the couch. Armand went into his private bedroom to get a towel. Monique was still looking at the fire, her arms crossed in front of her, when he returned. Armand watched her watching the fire as he passed his kitchen. "Your captivated, ma, wake up." He laughed.

Monique looked away from the fire and met Armand's eyes. Her smile was devilish as she peeled off her sweater. Underneath she had on a tank top.

"You playing, huh?" He shook his head and smiled at her. Armand moved toward her with the towel in hand.

Monique laughed a little and began to slide out of her jeans. Armand stopped walking.

Her jeans were soaked and Monique struggled to get out of the wet denim. There was no sexy way to do it. She tugged and pushed, but they wouldn't slide down.

"Sit down," Armand said.

She leaned back on the couch. Armand grabbed the bottom of her jeans and pulled hard, the jeans released their suction grip, coming off her legs, but Monique also slid off the couch and hit the floor.

She shrieked. "I can't believe—"

"Are you okay?"

They met each other's eyes and cracked up laughing. Monique peeled off her socks and her tank top. "You think I should take off my underwear? It's wet, too."

"Uhm," Armand said. He didn't know what had happened to his player card, but she had just stunned him. He stood there feeling like he was fourteen again, peeking at curves that she had that he hadn't imagined.

Monique picked up the pile of wet clothes.

He stepped forward and took them from her. He touched her arm. She was still freezing.

"Want to take a warm shower?"

Monique bit her lip, her eyes locked on him, and nodded.

Armand kissed her eyelids, one at a time. "Are you alright?" he said.

"Yes." Monique met his eyes, holding them for a long time. "Finally."

"Come on." Armand led her to the bathroom inside of his bedroom.

Monique let out a sigh in surprise when she stepped into the huge room, the same size as his master bedroom, and glanced around. The tile encased shower stall stood in the center of the room, next to it was the Jacuzzi tub. The toilet and Bordeaux were in their own rooms, and a wall of marble and tile and glass and cabinets lined the other wall. Her eyes widened. "This is paradise."

"Yeah," he shrugged. "I like it."

"You like it." Monique pushed him. "You can't always be cool. Even you have to get excited over some things."

"Oh, I gets excited. Believe that."

"Whatever, Armand."

He walked into the shower stall with her and showed her how to turn on the showerheads. Then, he stepped out, not wanting her to strip down further and test his ability to say "*no*." Armand wanted her in the worst way, but he would wait as long as she needed. And, having just saved her life, it just didn't seem that this was the right time to press up on her. He felt lucky she was actually at his house and Michelle wasn't going to be popping in on them at the exact wrong moment.

Armand felt her eyes on him as he walked out, the warm water causing steam to seep into the room.

Armand put her clothes in the wash machine and turned it on. He wondered how long she would stay with him. He wasn't going out in the snow. Armand glanced out the window and was surprised by the mounds of snow. They were going to be stuck together for at least a full day. Armand wondered how she would handle it and whether or not she would be able to stay without getting on his nerves. He rarely had anyone in his space, sometimes he had to adjust. This was going to be make or break for whatever it was that they had.

Armand heated up some water and made cocoa for both he and Monique. That was something his mother used to do that always made him to feel better. It was something simple that he could give Monique, a gift from his mother that would warm her and make her feel good. He stuffed fresh marshmallows on top of the mug and moved them to the tray sitting on the coffee table.

Armand could hear the water stop. He waited a second and turned on the television. Monique was naked in his shower. He liked the thought of that. Armand heard the bathroom door open. A second later, Monique was standing in the doorway, wrapped in a large towel.

Armand jumped up. "Let me give you something to put on." He scrambled into his room, rummaging through his drawers. He didn't have anything to give her. He wanted to cover her, to distract himself from the thoughts that were rushing through his head. Armand wondered how she would sound when he pressed into her. How would she taste when he finally kissed her sweet spots?

Monique followed him, smiling, and stood in front of his closet. She pointed to one of the built in shelves that were stacked with t-shirts. "Can I put on a t-shirt?"

"Yeah, okay," he nodded.

She stood on her tip toes to get the shirt. Armand started to snatch the towel off her. He chuckled to himself. It would be funny, but then she might really get mad. It wasn't worth the risk. They were too new.

Monique pulled on one of his long t-shirts. He looked away while the towel fell. She picked up the Eucerin with oatmeal. "Can I use some lotion?"

"Anything you want." He watched as she put lotion on.

"I have to call my mom and Mikki. Just so they know where I am at." Monique looked sad for a moment.

"Yeah, uhm, here." He handed her his phone. She held it and looked at him.

It took a second to realize that she needed privacy. Armand moved out of the room and let her make the call in private. Twenty minutes later she joined him in the living room.

"Army, I can't believe you saved me today." She smiled and plopped down on the couch next to him.

"Why not?" Armand said. "You don't listen, though. I told you to call me."

"I know. I have no idea what happened to my phone."

"You know you really could have been in danger."

"I *was* in danger." Monique's voice sounded small. "I was really scared, Army. That's never happened to me before."

"Listen, Mo, you don't understand. I have lost the three women I loved most in this world. They are gone forever. My moms, grandma and my sister. In a fire. I don't really want to discuss it, but…I can't risk being with someone who isn't careful with herself. I can't lose someone over something stupid again."

Monique put her finger tips on his cheek.

"Yo, you scared me today."

"I'm sorry."

"Sorry doesn't change bad things when they happen. Don't be sorry. Be careful. Be more careful with yourself than that."

She nodded, looking like a child being scolded.

Armand looked away from her. He hadn't meant to get deep, hadn't meant to discuss his family and the pain that flowed like a constant river through his heart. He focused on the television, blocking her out until he could reign in his emotion.

She leaned on him, watching the television, her head laying on his chest.

Armand lowered his head and rested his lips against her forehead for a second, then exhaled.

"You're hard headed."

She laughed. "I heard that before."

"You going to have to learn some respect." He smiled.

"Whatever. From who?"

"Who you think?" Armand sat straight up.

"Many have tried to tame me and failed." She shook her head as she said that.

"Oh yea. They weren't me."

"No, they weren't."

She spotted the mugs on the edge of the coffee table. "You made cocoa?"

He shrugged.

"Damn." Monique whispered. "You are so kind to me."

Armand hadn't heard her curse before. He looked at her. Monique's eyes were sincere, moist and wide.

He shrugged again.

Her eyes sparkled at him. He pulled her closely and inhaled. She smelled fresh and sweet.

She kissed him, on the tip of his nose. Then his forehead. Then each of his cheeks.

"Monique…" he started.

She kissed him on the mouth, firm and sure. The kiss was slow at first, her lips resting against his. Both of their eyes were open. Armand watched her, wondering if she knew that she was playing with fire. Maybe he needed to stop her and explain that with her it was different, with her, he would lay claim. That unless she wanted to be his, she shouldn't play games.

But he couldn't make himself stop her. He didn't want her to stop.

His lips parted. He closed his eyes. Her tongue slid into his mouth. She was kissing him deeply, lovingly. Armand lifted her up by both arms and pulled her body into his. Monique straddled his lap and kissed him again.

Armand sighed and fought the desire burning in him. He opened his eyes and smiled at Monique. "What are you doing?"

"I want you."

"Don't do this if you aren't ready, Mo."

She picked up his hands and placed them on her hips, under her t-shirt. The softness of her skin surprised him and made him want her more. His hands ran down her hips and around her thighs, his thumbs tickling the edges of her private hair, then pressing against her raw skin pressing against him.

"Why?" Armand asked, vulnerability on his face. "Why do you want to do this?"

"I trust you." She kissed him again. "You make me feel safe. Safer than anyone ever has."

"I can't promise you anything, Monique. I don't want you to do this and think it's more than what I can—"

"I just want to be here with you right now. Together. This is what I have wanted since I met you."

Then she said the words that he wanted to hear: "I want you to be my first. So I will always remember."

Armand kissed her deeply, the restraint he was using finally broke like a dam. He stood up, with her straddling him and she wrapped her legs around his waist as Armand buried his head in her neck, kissing and biting her.

He carried her into his bedroom.

CHAPTER TWENTY SEVEN

Rescue

Monique, age 18
Armand, age 20

"My baby girl is graduating, you didn't think I would miss this did you?"

The gruff voice made Monique's face blush as her heart warmed. "Granddaddy!" Monique ran into the kitchen. Her grandparents were standing there with her Aunt Niecey their bags in a pile in the kitchen.

"Yay!" Monique clapped her hands, "You made it. I can't believe you made it!" Monique shouted and ran into her grandfather's arms.

"What's this child talking about, David? She thought we weren't going to get here?" Lensy winked at Monique.

Monique embraced her grandmother, tears running down her face. She hadn't seen them both in a couple of years.

Miriam laughed, "Ya'll you just made it. Monique has to be at the stadium in half an hour, we have be there in an hour if we are going to get seats."

"Yeah yeah...stop fussing." David dug around in his pocket. "Seems like someone left a little something in my pocket."

Monique squealed, feeling like she was five again, getting treats from her grandfather. He pulled out a necklace with a platinum cross lined with small diamonds.

"David, you carrying that thing around in your pocket? Are you crazy?"

Monique shouted, grabbed the necklace and held it up to the light. "It's beautiful."

"Thought you needed something to go with that Waters chain of yours." He pointed at the diamond TW2 chain Monique had worn since Pete decided that all his kids needed to be covered by his seal. "That ain't the only family you got, you know."

"I know, Granddaddy," Monique laughed at her territorial grandfather. "I know I got more than one family. You tell me all the time."

"Well, now I got something for you. Damn Pete and his shiny TW2 nonsense. Put that on instead."

Monique held it up, her grandmother undid the clasp and put it around her neck. She ran to the mirror. "It's so pretty. I love it."

"You can take that other one off now," David pressed, pointing his cane at her.

"I love you, Granddaddy." Monique laughed. The Waters family crest didn't come off her neck for anybody, and they all knew it. There was no need in even addressing his comment.

"What did you get her, Miriam?" Lensy dug into her purse for a peppermint.

Miriam glanced at Monique, then at her parents. Her smile faded a little.

Monique already knew the answer. She jumped in, not wanting to hear her mother actually say what she already knew was true. "Grandma, you know how Mommy is. I didn't ask her for nothing—"

"You didn't buy this baby girl a graduation gift, Miriam?"

"What?" David coughed into his handkerchief. "You didn't get the girl a gift? Ain't she got a scholarship to college? You don't have to pay college tuition and you didn't give her a gift for that alone?" David shook her head. "That's why the girl always over there with those Waters', acting like she ain't got no family."

"Please don't do this now," Monique pleaded. "It's alright…I'm okay." She started moving toward the door, wanting to escape before the drama started.

"I started to buy her something, but the day I went to order it she disrespected me with that mouth of hers. So she didn't get anything."

The silence that filled the room made Monique uncomfortable. Her grandparents stared at Miriam like she had just farted. Monique just wanted to escape. "Uhm, I'm going to grab my purse and stuff." No one was listening. They were all staring at Miriam, who was looking back at them indignantly.

There was no way Monique was going to ride in the car with Miriam to graduation now. She would have to pay for Miriam being embarrassed in front of her family. It would be a ride from hell.

She made the call.

Armand answered on the second ring. "Whatsup, baby girl?"

No matter what he was doing, no matter what was going on around him, if Monique called and Armand had his phone, he answered. That type of loyalty alone put Armand on another level. His voice made her shiver. She smiled and tried to get herself under control. She could hear noise in the background, voices and laughter sprinkling through the line. "Hi Army."

"Hey baby, it's almost time, right?"

"Yes. I…uhm…are you busy?"

The background noise disappeared. He had moved to another space. "No, talk to me. What's wrong?"

Her heart skipped. He was so attentive that he knew something was wrong with her even though she hadn't said a word. No one else was so in tune with her.

"Nothing, really." The truth was that everything was wrong. It was wrong that her mother actually hadn't bought her anything for graduation. It hurt. It was wrong that her grandparents had called Miriam on it, that now she would make Monique pay for being embarrassed in front of her parents. Monique wanted the lump in her throat to disappear. "I just was wondering—"

"Where are you?"

"Home."

"I'll be there in five minutes, okay?"

Monique sighed. "Okay." A quiet pause. "Thank you."

"No doubt."

Monique gathered her robe and hat and slid on her heels. Relief rinsed through her like ocean spray.

"Monique." Miriam appeared at her bedroom door. "I don't appreciate you putting me on the spot like that in front of my parents."

Monique stared at her mother. It was moments like this when she wondered whether Miriam was sane. "Mommy, I didn't do anything. Grandma asked you about that, not me."

"Still, I didn't appreciate it."

Monique dropped hairpins into her purse. "I'm sorry." She would say anything to make Miriam go away.

"I need your help with something. Come to my room."

Monique stalled…this was clearly a setup for something ridiculous. "Uhm, I got to get ready to go, can I do it later?"

"It will just take a second." Her voice was final. Monique grabbed her things and walked down the narrow hallway to her mother's room. Sitting on the dresser was a platinum bracelet with platinum roses encasing pink diamonds. It was breathtaking. It lay open in a plush baby blue case, a Tiffany's box sitting next to it, the bag right behind it.

Monique's mouth dropped open. She smiled, amazement flooding her mind along with relief. Maybe today wouldn't be ruined by Miriam after all. "Mommy—"

"I need help putting on my new bracelet. I can't quite get the clasp."

Monique stood still for a second. She was confused. "What?"

"I started to order something for you, but, as usual, your mouth ruined it for you. So, I got myself something instead." Miriam picked up the bracelet. "See, I had inscribed to me, Miriam Waters, see my name—I paid extra for diamond tipped script." Miriam turned the bracelet over for Monique to see the inscription. "Can you fix the clasp for me?" Miriam studied her face, craving to see a reaction.

Monique coughed and smiled. It was the first time she had allowed the feeling of hate to invade the special part of her heart reserved for her mother. Miriam was her enemy on so many insidious levels. Monique's need for a mother was so deep, the starvation so real, that she often forgot how Miriam enjoyed hurting her. She put it out of her mind, trying desperately to believe she had a mother who loved her like everyone else. But then Miriam would do something like this, so cold and manipulative, something so little that Monique couldn't tell anyone without seeming like a crybaby pouting over spilled milk, but so real that it hurt like an open knife wound to her heart.

"Yep." Monique fidgeted with the clasp. "It's very pretty," she said without emotion as she slid it into place. She would be damned if she gave Miriam the satisfaction of being hurt. Her phone buzzed.

"I know," Miriam smiled at her wrist. "I like it."

Monique walked out, carrying her robe, purse and phone. She kissed her grandparents goodbye and headed for the door. She forced back the tear that lingered just behind her lids.

Armand was standing just outside of it, looking at her through the glass of the screen door. Monique's heart skipped a beat again.

"Hi." Monique kissed him on the lips as she stepped out of the screen door.

"You ready?" Armand looked her up and down, his eyes taking in her hair, her face, her outfit. Every second of him observing her made her feel warm, like sunshine falling across her body.

"Yeah."

"Who's that at the door, Lensy?"

"How am I supposed to know David? I don't live here. Monique, who you got over there?"

"Oh shit." Monique mumbled under her breath.

Armand smiled. "What, you don't want me to meet your people?"

"You know it's not that." It was exactly that.

"Hmm, he is a handsome young man," Grandma Lensy piped in, all smiles and big eyes. "Who is this Monique?"

"Uhm, this is my, uhm…"

Armand stepped up the stairs and extended his hand. "I'm Armand. It's nice to meet you."

"Pleasure is all mine." Grandma Lensy put her hand on his back. Armand glanced at Monique with a smirk on his face.

"Where you taking my Grandbaby?" David pointed his cane at Armand.

"Wherever she wants me to take her, sir." Armand answered.

"Hmm, you got a slick tongue. Better watch this one here." David chuckled, a good sign.

Miriam turned the corner. "Hi Armand, I didn't know you were here?" She ignored Monique. "Are you going to take Monique to the graduation?"

"Yes, ma'am."

"Thank you, that is very helpful. This is my mother and father. I have to get us all there."

"It's not a problem. My pleasure."

"Better watch 'your pleasure'," David piped in.

"Let's go," Monique pushed Armand out the house.

He laughed. "You thought I couldn't handle your family."

"It's not that." Monique sighed. "I just needed to get away from them...from her." She shook her head.

"I got you ma ma, you know that." He backed his car out of the driveway and leaned over to give her a kiss. He didn't ask why her eyes were watery or what had happened that had her so frazzled. In the middle of the street, still in reverse, he kissed her. His actions were slow and gentle. On the lips, on her cheek, on her earlobe. On her neck. When they separated her eyes were still closed, facing him, wanting more. "Later, we can get back to that later. I got to deliver my princess to her big day."

"You make things better, you know. Just like that." Monique smiled, finally able to take a deep breath into her lungs.

He glanced at her. "You look nice today."

"Thank you," Monique brightened up, a full smile on her face. "I never thought this day would come. I'm actually here. This is actually happening."

"Of course it's happening. You deserve this and more. And this is just your beginning."

"I will be out of her house in one month. Just one more month."

"The life ahead of you is so much bigger than this, Mo. Arguing with your moms, that's going to seem like nothing when you look back. You got so much to accomplish, baby girl. We got things we can build together."

"We gonna build together, now?" Monique smiled. "I thought conquering the world was a solo thing for you."

"Nah, Imma have you right by my side, believe that."

Monique was speechless as Armand pulled in front of the University Auditorium. She was too fragile to be played with. She blinked and looked up at him. His words meant more than idle chit chat. "You mean that?" Her voice was barely above a whisper.

"No doubt." He kissed her. "It's going to always be me and you. Remember that."

In that moment, Monique gave up her heart to Armand. Always him and her—it was an oath and she would never forget.

CHAPTER TWENTY EIGHT

Covered

The after party was too much. Monique stood by the door, listening to the pounding of the bass line. She glanced at the dance floor, watching her graduating class jump up and down to the music, bodies gyrating in freedom and accomplishment. They had made it. With the exception of Carlton, who had been taking out of the graduation by a last minute fluke, they had all made it. And even he was one of them, one of the 133 graduates that started out together and were ending together.

Monique stared at them, knowing that she would never see all these people in one space together again. She was going to the University for a year, until she could transfer to Columbia in New York City. She always wanted to live in the City, always wanted to experience the grit of New York. Living in Rochester was a strange experience, a small city with a big city complex. Which meant that people tried to prove they were just as wild, as gutter, as ruthless as someone from the city. And, because they were overcompensating, they wound up being more lethal, crueler and causing more devastation over much smaller situations.

How many funerals had she already attended? Semaj stabbed when she was 12, Tyler shot over a craps game when she was 14. Letitia raped by four guys when they were 16, Marcus's father being found with a bullet through his head when she was 15. Michelle's little brother choking in his sleep the same year. On and on, over and over, it was useless and Monique was overwhelmed.

Escaping Rochester was her sole focus. Had she not met Armand, she wouldn't have even considered the University for a year. Instead she would have gone to any university out of the city that accepted her. She had to get away from the small city that danced around her like a picket fence, taunting her by giving her a glimpse of life on the other side, but keeping her entrapped. She had to get away from Miriam, from the duplicity of her cruelty, which only played out behind closed doors and in quiet moments, when Monique needed her most. She had to escape Pete, whose family legacy sometimes felt like a bound rope around her neck, covering her with expectations and obligations.

Her friends were jealous of her life with Pete, the freedom that she had, the money she spent. But they didn't know that failure was not an option, he had paid too heavy a price for her, success was the payback that she owed. They didn't know how distant and cold he could be, walking past without uttering a word for days at a time, blunts laced with marijuana hanging from his lips, his glare straight and direct. They didn't know how Monique didn't fit in to her own family, like a broken puzzle piece trying to squeeze in between Michelle, her little big sister that Pete adored and Ricardo, her big brother that Pete mentored. They didn't know that Monique was a stranger in her own family, the only child that Pete didn't assign responsibility to and didn't ask anything of, other than educational success. And that made her feel like an orphan stuck between two absent parents.

None of which she could tell anybody. Because then she would just seem like a whiny privileged kid.

But, for tonight, she didn't have to think about it. Red wine splashed on the floor in front of her. "Tina, be careful." Monique glanced down at her Christian Louboutin red bottoms, the crème linen toe splattered by the red liquor. She shook her head. "Damn girl," Monique wiped at the tip of her shoes. "You don't need to drink."

"We made it, Mo," Tina slurred, planting a kiss on Monique's forehead. "I love you, with your conceited self," Tina laughed.

"Whatever, I luv you back, whino."

Tina pushed her. Monique laughed.

"Mo Mo, there you are!" Michelle grabbed her.

Monique looked down, her tiny big sister was standing next to her with four other females. They were all sporting natural locks and half cut shirts, ripped up jeans, tattoos and piercings. Except for Michelle, who had on khakis and boat shoes, a t-shirt with a button down shirt on top of it, her sunglasses pushing her wild locks back.

Monique smiled, relief pouring through her like it always did when she saw Michelle. It was from a lifelong training that Pete had given them, that family was all that they had, all that mattered. Monique never felt quite right unless Michelle was near her. That was, until she met Armand. He made everything alright, but in a different way.

"Mikki, where the hell you been?"

"Mo, don't start talking shit—"

"At the graduation, you said you were going to meet me over here after you got some beer. Where's the beer? And it took you two hours?"

Monique looked at the three women standing behind Michelle, who were glancing around the party, swaying to the music. Monique stared at her sister, with a knowing look on her face. Michelle smiled.

"See, that's that bullshit, Mikki. That's what I'm talking about. You didn't bring it. And you come up in here with them—"

"Whatever Mo," Rika stood next to Michelle, her hand up in the air. "Don't even start with the complaining."

Monique laughed and put her hand up to Rika, talking over her. "So how am I supposed to fit in that tiny ass car of yours with all your homies, Mikki?"

Michelle was dancing, bopping around in front of her sister. "Mo Mo graduated high school. My baby sister did the damn thing."

"And what did you give me? Nothing!"

"You always want something." Michelle bopped her head to the music. "You got enough already."

"She's spoiled," Rika threw in, wrapping her arm around Monique. "You already know."

"But I got something for you." Michelle laughed, still dancing. She stuck both her middle fingers in the air. "That's all you, right there."

"I hate you, man," Monique laughed and pushed her sister back. She snatched Michelle's shades out of her hair. "Gimme back my damn sunglasses."

"Hell no," Michelle jumped and snatched them back. She put them on her face. "You see that, now I am invisible."

The small group around her laughed.

"Don't laugh at her stupid jokes." Monique smiled. "I'm glad you finally came, I'm ready to go."

"You ain't riding with me."

"Whatever," Monique looked around for Tina. "Tina, you got a ride?"

"I'm good," Tina called out, her arm around her boyfriend Preston.

"Cool," Monique started heading for the door, giving hugs as she walked through the crowd.

"I'm serious as a heart attack, Mo. You ain't riding with me."

Monique sighed. She stepped out into the cool night air glancing around for Michelle's Malibu.

Armand was standing against the tree, a few feet away. She smiled as a warm jolt spread through her body from head to toe.

Michelle followed Monique's stare. "Aw shit." Michelle walked between her and Armand. "Let me give this to you now, before you lose your mind out here with Army."

"Give me what?"

Michelle pulled keys out of her pocket. "Your graduation gift. Spoiled bitch."

Monique snatched the keys. "What? Are you serious? Where?"

Michelle smiled and shrugged. "Figure it out." She turned to Armand. "Look out for my baby sister. Don't have me looking for your ass."

"I got you." Armand smiled.

Monique ran to the parking lot, clicking the button. The crimson red Toyota Camry beeped. "Yes!"

Monique danced around in the parking lot. "I can't believe it." She really couldn't believe it. Pete rarely bought new cars, and definitely nothing that shined or stood out. That was one of his rules, to blend in as much as possible. Which is why a luxury car was never going to happen. She was lucky as hell that he had given her this. She ran over to Michelle, kissing her all over her face.

"Yuck, get off me."

Armand walked up to it. "I like it, ma, it fits you."

"Get in."

"Can you drive?" Armand looked doubtful. "Maybe you can just meet up with me later."

"Oh really?" Monique jumped in the car. "Fine, stay out here then."

She smiled. He climbed in with her. She ran her hand over the seat, up and down the console.

"It smells brand new," Armand inhaled deeply. "I love that smell."

Monique put the car in drive and hit the road, rolling the windows down to let the night air in. She circled the city, taking 390 to 590.

"Where are you taking me?" Armand watched her drive. She glanced at him and smiled.

"I got a spot."

"Hell no," Armand leaned back in his seat. "You got to tell me where you are taking me."

"You have to trust me. You know how to do that?"

"Do what?"

"Trust."

He shrugged, and turned on the radio. Two minutes of the 1980s groove from WDKX and he turned it back off. "You got to get your iPod in here, ma ma," as he yanked out his iPod to connect with the car.

Monique didn't answer. She enjoyed the cool night breeze through her hair. This night was perfect. She was with the one person in the world that she felt right with. Her heart jumped. She wondered about that feeling, about what made it love instead of like. It was that he was there for her, in every way. Reliable. As much as he could be. Unquestionable. His word was his bond. Most guys said it, none lived it. Except for the three men in her life—Pete, Ricardo and now Armand.

Monique was in love.

She swung off Henrietta Road onto the side street behind the airport and rode down the dark paved street.

"There are no street lights back here." Armand put his hand on her leg. "Slow down on the curves, Ma."

She lifted her foot from the pedal and paused, "I love you."

"What?" Armand sat up and smiled. "What you say?"

"You heard me." The wide open feeling that she had a second before shut down, regret filling her like crème stuffing a twinkie. There was a reason she was always so guarded, why she refused to let folks know how she really felt. Because the vulnerability, the fear of being laughed down, made the risk not worth it. "Never mind." Monique clenched her teeth. "I'm tripping."

"Pull over."

"No." *Fuck you.* Now she wanted to take his ass home. The night was over. She should have just kept her stupid emotions in check. She had ruined everything by being weak. But she could fix it. She could shut him out, deaden her heart to him, reset.

"Yo, pull the car over. Now." Armand's voice was steady and forceful.

Monique thought about it while she accelerated.

Armand snatched the wheel, making the car jerk. "Don't make me crash this damn car. Do what I said."

Monique knew he was crazy enough to do it. She pulled off the road and into the field. Armand jumped out the car before she had put it all the way into park. "Get out."

She sat there for a moment. He didn't get to order her around.

"Monique."

She climbed out of the car, her high heels sinking into the dirt.

Armand grinned, very subtle, the turn of his lips barely noticeable. She couldn't see the pupils of his black eyes in the dark of the night. But his stare pierced into her, like electric sparks jumping from him. He stood on her side of the car, near the front hood.

"Come here."

She had to fight the urge to cross her arms and stomp over to him. Acting like a baby sometimes came natural. Instead, she uneasily took a couple of steps toward him. He reached out his hand. She grabbed it. He pulled her into his tall frame, wrapping his arms around her.

"Say it again."

She shook her head "*no*."

"I want to hear it." Armand planted his lips on her forehead. She closed her eyes. He kissed her cheek bone. She sighed. He held her a little closer, his hips pressing into her. "Say it."

"I…I love you." She whispered quickly, the words running together into one rushed word.

"Yeah, I already know you do." He kissed her neck. "You think I don't know? Open your eyes."

She cracked her lids, looking past him into the dark night. Another plane passed overhead, its roar shaking the air around them, rumbling past like thunder.

He didn't bother to look up. He watched her as a tear slid from her eye, down her cheekbone. He kissed the tear. "Why are you scared?"

"I'm not."

"Look at me."

It was hard, like trying to force two magnets of the same charge to touch. She tried to look in his eyes, but her glance bounce all around from his forehead, to his chin, to his thick neck.

"Mo," the way he said her name made her smile. "Look at me, baby girl." He placed his hand on her throat, his fingertips stroking the space just below her earlobe.

The chill that travelled up her spine broke the silence. Monique met his eyes. He kissed her deeply, his tongue pushing into her mouth, tickling her tongue.

She melted into his body.

He pressed her against the hood of the car.

Monique lost her breath, so lost in the warmth of his kiss, his tongue circling hers, sucking hers, licking hers. She couldn't help the groans that spilled from her, his hips pressing his print deep into her. He lifted her up onto the hood, still kissing her. She wrapped her arms around his neck.

"Never be afraid to tell me how you feel." Armand's words tore through her fog. She almost wasn't aware that he was speaking. "You hear me?"

Monique nodded, pressing her mouth against him, not wanting him to stop.

"Monique, your mine, baby girl. You know that, right?"

She nodded, not paying his words much attention.

Her dress was up, the warmth flooding her body felt foreign to her, she had never been so turned on before. There was nothing she wanted in the world more than Armand. He pushed into her, her legs wrapped around him, her back leaning against the hood of the car. He held her as he pushed deep into her, his head buried in her chest, her lips planting kisses against the top of his head.

It took a few minutes before she heard him, over her own groaning, the quiet "I love you, Mo," that he said over and over again like a chant.

Monique gave herself over to him, sliding up and down until they both exploded.

A plane roared over their heads.

Neither of them moved for several minutes, her body curled around his, leaning against the car, her legs still wrapped around his waist.

She kissed his forehead again.

He looked up at her, this time she could see his black pupils, a look of vulnerability on his face, his heart wide open and laid out for her.

"I trust you, baby girl, you gotta trust me. I will never hurt you."

"I know, Army." He kissed her again as she slid off the hood of the car, back onto unsteady heels on the uneven dirt.

He stood right behind her and held her close in a hug, kissing the back of her neck. "You have a future Mo, a life with greatness. I see that. I know your worth and I am riding with you."

She nodded, her eyes closed, letting that promise seal up all the cracks in her heart.

"Let's go home," he said.

She handed him the keys. She was willing to give him anything he wanted.

Special Thanks

There is never enough space or time to name everyone who matters to me. For those still in my world, I adore you and am grateful for your encouragement. That said, I want to give a special thanks to:

~My children—with each passing day you morph into someone more incredible, more self-assured, more confident and more able. Not a day goes by that I don't breathe a sincere prayer of thanks for each and every aspect of your lives, your personalities, your past, present and your future. I hope I have said "I love you" enough for you to really understand that the word "love" is a finite expression for a feeling much deeper and more surreal. My love for you is limitless.

~My mother—for always being there and being so supportive. Having a praying mother changes things. I hope you know I see each and every sacrifice you made for me. Your love and prayers cover me.

~The readers—you are so true and genuine and you raise the bar for each story. You believe in love, despite it all, which is the real reason Armand and Monique have a chance. Thank you for your tremendous patience and incredible support. I appreciate you!

~Test and concept readers—L.A., Miss Queen, Ms. Ayala, Michelle James, Kesha Mays and Malicha. You are remarkable. Thank you for: Declaring it great or horrible, forcing me to reconstruct ideas, convincing me to let go of bad segments that I am irrationally attached to and demanding that I consider other points of views.

~Editors and Typesetting—Michelle James, Miss Queen and Ms. Ayala, another incredible job. I appreciate your grace in completing the most grueling of tasks under ridiculous time constraints. Thank you.

~Cover Design—Kellie of Dzine by Kellie, thank you again for your phenomenal patience and all your work. As always, you understood the vision and immediately captured the young Monique. I sincerely appreciate you.

~Guaranteed Paper Publications—thank you to the team that took a small dream and harvested it into such an incredible reality. You are irreplaceable.

~AAMBook Club—Tameka Newhouse, remember the beginning, years ago, discussing and planning? What an amazing thing to see this reality several years later. Thank you for all your help and unwavering support over the years.

~5Star Publications—Shawn and L.A., you have displayed incredible grace and support for this project. I sincerely thank you. Daughter of the Game III: Burning Waters is the finale and the culmination of all our hard work.

~Finally, and most importantly, I am grateful to God. Only God doesn't change. He is the only one who has never abandoned me, turned on me, or distorted love into something controlling, ugly and unwanted. With Him there are no lies, no broken promises. It is Him who holds me as I float through life's highs or stumble through my lowest valleys. From Him I have no secrets. Only in Him can I trust. Only in God is there unconditional love; unchanging love; unselfish love. True love. *Love never fails. 1 Corinthians 13:4-8*

Special Thanks

Rochester, New York

Thank you for tolerating the one sided view of Rochester in this story, knowing that there is so much more to the city than I could begin to capture in this series. Thank you for grooming me, preparing me to stretch beyond my wildest dreams and accomplish things so far from my world, but never quite impossible. My dreams were always limitless.

Thank you to all the families who adopted and raised me, all the friends who made me a cousin and a god-sister, and all the extended family who dropped bits of themselves into me daily.

Thanks to the Aenon Baptist Church Family, where my foundation was poured and solidified.

Here's To Old School Rochester: All Day Sunday breaker belts and nameplates; EBS's from Midtown Plaza; Bomber jackets from Archies; Nick Tahou's Garbage Plate; Fresh Fests at the War Memorial; fried chicken from Eddies Chicken Coop; Flashing lights at Skate Town; the JackRabbit at Seabreeze; my revolutionary brothers at the Mosque on Genesee St.; arcades and bowling at Olympics; Country Sweet Chicken; firecrackers downtown; house parties ALL OVER the city!!; splashing waters at Charlotte Beach; Abbott's custard and low flying airplanes; cookie club at Wegmans;

street parties on Jefferson and Genesee (yep, I'm really old school); hot summer days at Genesee pool; Chinese jump rope on Sawyer; Sal's Birdland; Arnett library; penny candy from the Westside corner stores; spicy beef patties on West Main; Mennezes Pizzeria; Kodak Park day at Darien Lake; grabbing a steak and cheese from G&G; winter time ice skeeting and running away before getting caught; 3on3 basketball tournaments on Main Street; the annual summer party on Terrace Park where ALL the ballers be; Campi's Bombers; East High v. Franklin – Wilson v. Edison; Crown Pop out of the warehouse; Zweigles franks, barbecued with beer; double dutching from sunup to sundown while the boys played football in the street-or tormented us, just because; and much love to the 19th Ward-my home forever!

KAI's PLAY LIST

1. **Trophies**, Drake—Drake was definitely my muse for this project. …*Can I tell you the truth? If I was doing this for you then I'd have nothing left to prove, Nah, this for me though, I'm just trying to stay alive and take care of my people. And they don't have no awards for that…*

2. **Try**, Pink—Pink's songs always capture a deep emotion. **Try** reminds me of Armand and Ricardo. They are the flame, struggling to keep moving forward. *Where there is desire, there is gonna be flame, where there is a flame someone's bound to get burned, but just because it burns doesn't mean you're gonna die, you gotta get up and try, try, try…*

3. **The Worst**, Jhene Aiko—This song captures so many emotions, the perfect expression of vulnerability wrapped in a hardened shell…*And don't take this personal, but you're the worst, you know what you've done to me, and although it hurts I know I just can't keep running away, but I don't need you…*

4. **God Has Not 4Got,** Tonex—A song of hope. This makes me think of Armand's Grandma Queen and that unyielding faith that her generation displayed, despite all evidence of defeat.

5. **Pills N Potion**, Nikki Minaj—The rap, more than the chorus, captures Miriam's struggle with loving Pete but having to leave him, a struggle Monique later has in life as well.

6. **Love More**, Chris Brown—What is there to say? Music from the quintessential bad boy makes writing Armand that much more enjoyable.

7. **Heard It All Before**, Sunshine Anderson—This reminds me of Rebe initially and, eventually, Miriam. When awareness and

maturity overtake the need to prove themselves to the man they love. Eventually they move on with their lives, Rebe moreso than Miriam.

8. **From Time**, Drake featuring Jhene Aiko—This song captures the idea behind Monique and Armand's relationship. It works because Monique doesn't need Armand for love. She is loved by her family. She is validated with or without Armand. Their love is not a needy thing, its finding comfort in each other, just as they are. For right now, they are each other's safe zone…*I love me, I love me enough for the both of us, that's why you trust me, I know you been through more than most of us…*

9. **Happy (So In Love With You)**, Tasha Cobbs—A beautiful song, this brings peace and calm in the midst of any storm. A pure love song to God. One of my favorite songs. Period.

10. **Butterflies**, Michael Jackson—Although Armand would never admit it, this is what Monique has done to him—she has given him butterflies. Her interest mixed with her stiff-arm made pursuing her an adventure and captured his heart.

11. **Fuckin' Problems**, A$AP Rocky—I can just listen to this song, dance and laugh. I admit it, I just like it. And when writing about Pete's recklessness in this book, this song was the perfect background vibe for Pete's wildness.

12. **Because of You**, Kelly Clarkson—This song is Monique's ode to Pete and Miriam. Both of them traumatized her in different ways, and her need to escape led her to find solitude in Armand.

13. **Wade in the Waters**, Mary Mary—This version of this song often overwhelms me, it is so powerful and captivating. It makes me think of the Waters family as a pool, which is

disrupted, violently waving as if caught in a storm, or perfectly still and deceptively silent. I play this song during long road trips and just think about the Waters family and what journey they are going to take me on.

14. **Started From the Bottom**, Drake—Armand, Raymond, Chew and Dut remind me of this song. All are from different backgrounds and are in the game for different reasons, but they are grinding from the bottom, intent on climbing to the top.

AAMBC Interview:

Get To Know KAI

How did you begin writing?

Like most authors, I have always been an avid writer and reader. But I began seriously pursuing a writing career after my twins were born. For some reason, their birth sparked a desire to create and use my imagination in a way that I hadn't before. I penned the first version of my fantasy fiction teen novel and, after receiving overwhelming feedback about it, I started to submit stories to various publishers. Initially, every story I submitted was accepted and published, resulting in an unexpected demand in a short period of time. Under different pen names, I have been published across many genres including Christian, Poetry, Science Fiction, Fantasy Fiction, Erotica and Urban Fiction. I am proudest of my contribution to Letters to Our Children, a compilation of love letters from authors to their children, published for the Capital Book Fest in Washington, DC.

What was the inspiration for Daughter of the Game?

As a book reviewer, I reviewed a number of urban fiction novels that dealt with the drug game and its players, and the women loving them or using them, but I hadn't read a story about the family structure—people closely related to drug dealers who aren't in the game. I wanted to explore that reality and, in my own way, humanize the main drug dealer to expose his weakness and vulnerability. That is why Ricardo feels fear in his heart, or Armand contemplates why his life seems to be predestined for disaster, or Pete loves Miriam but can't put it to words, and Monique worries about the generational curses her father's empire will have on her and her children. Although Monique is the main character, I explore the different men and their choices and decisions as well.

Who is your favorite character?

That is hard to say. I have a deep affinity for Ricardo, Monique's brother, and Chew, the man who loves Monique but knows he can never have her. I also enjoy Anji, Titan's girlfriend. Her spirit and creativity made her fun to write. Michelle, Monique's big sister, seems to be the favorite character among my readers. I have received many demands that she have a bigger role in the series. Michelle's relationship with Pete is touching and she is a fighter, possessing that wild "around the way girl" charm that everyone knows and loves. But my favorite character is Armand. I love his sexiness and his bad boy charisma. Armand is the type of man who can be dead wrong and it doesn't matter—you will love him anyway. Case in point: I have yet to meet one reader who dislikes him despite him leaving Monique alone in the trap so that he could hide the stash.

What is a question most asked by readers?

I am constantly asked to reveal Armand's true identity. This series is fiction. One of my biggest pet peeves is that people assume the story is about someone they know or someone in my life. I cannot tell you how many people have tried to guess who Armand really is in my circle. They will never get it right because Armand is a fictional character. I think that many of us know these personality types, so the characters feel very real to us. I study people, how they react to situations, how they express themselves, how they communicate and it is reflected in the characters I create. The closest person to Armand I ever met grew up in Rochester, New York with me, was my close friend and he still lives there. And even he is not Armand. I must admit, I am surprised by how deeply attached to Armand the readers are and the stories they share with me about men very similar to him. There is an affinity among women who have loved men like him, and only other women who have been in that situation can relate and understand. He is a magnetic character, flawed but genuine.

You place a lot of emphasis on love in both the Daughter of the Game series and in The Loudest Silence. Are these love stories?

The concept of love fascinates me, I must admit. When I think of love, I think of the fairy tales and the "love conquers all" theory. When we listen to music most songs are about love: craving it, needing it and doing anything for it. But what does it mean in real life. Should we really love unconditionally? How high is the price of love? What happens when you strip away your dignity in the name of love? Is that really love? Many of my works also challenge the concept of love being forever. I believe that love is demonstrated by action, such as being considerate or selfless. But what happens when a person truly loves you and has no idea how to show it? Or what happens when his expression doesn't fit your idea of what love should look like? Obviously, I don't have any answers. But playing with the different types of "love" tends to make my characters struggle in different ways.

Why the delay?

As with all things business related, sometimes it takes time to get things situated the way they should be. It wasn't initially intended for Daughter of the Game to be a series and the demand for more stories about these characters surprised us all. So we had to lay out a new plan for the Water's family and strategize how the series should move forward. And, to make up for the delay, we are releasing two Daughter of the Game's novels this year—Daughter of the Game Prequel: In the Shadows and Daughter of the Game III: Burning Waters. Also, I wanted to write stories that would make it worth the wait, my readers have high expectations and they are brutally honest with me, so I had to develop stories worth their time. That said, I am grateful for all the readers and your incredible support and I sincerely thank you for taking this journey with me.

For more AAMBC interviews with KAI, visit:

http://aambookclub.com/daughter-of-the-game-by-kai
http://aambookclub.com/the-loudest-silence-new-edition-by-kai

For KAI Web-Links:
http://www.guaranteedpaperpublishing.com
http://www.facebook.com/pages/Novels-by-Kai/
http://www.twitter.com/discoverkai
http://www.twitter.com/guaranteedpp
http://www.facebook.com/guaranteedpaper
Email Address: kai@guaranteedpaperpublishing.com

.

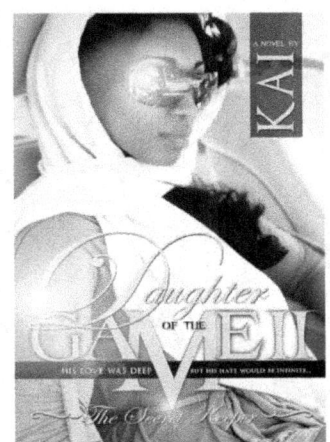

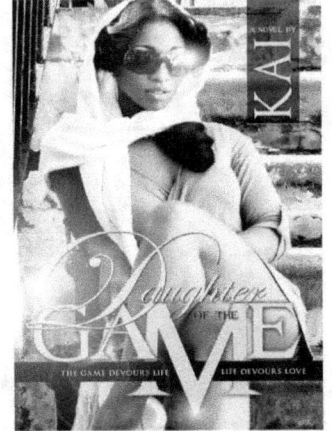

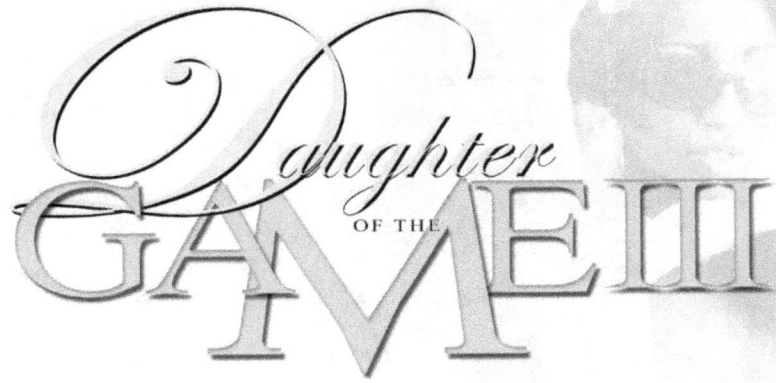

Taken For Granted

"I don't care what you say," Monique sighed, sitting in the chair opposite the bed. Armand was sprawled out across the king size bed in the hotel room. A fold up cot was near the door. "Ricardo isn't going to "your storage", whatever that is."

"Shut up." Armand covered his ears with his hands. "Turn the light off, it's blinding me."

"Where am I supposed to sleep?"

"I give a fuck?" Armand's voice escalated, then reduced to a whisper. "Monique, leave me alone."

Monique was past caring about Armand. "When do I see my father?"

"Yo, we're here. You know the city just like me, probably better. You can go."

"Really?" Monique stood up. "Fine." She headed for the door.

Armand groaned. If his head wasn't hurting so badly, he would scream at her again. "Don't make me get off this bed, Mo, I swear…if I get up."

"Hmph," Monique picked up her purse. As she opened the door, his arm came from behind her and slammed it closed.

Armand gripped her elbow, and banged his forehead against hers, pressing his head so tightly into hers that the pain made her eyes water. "Don't make me hurt you."

A deep fear echoed in her when she saw the look of hate in his eyes.

"Too much has already been lost because of you." Armand stood back. Monique held her head, trying to lessen the pain. "Take your ass and sit in the chair. I changed my mind, that's where you sleep—you can't have the cot."

Monique didn't dare disobey. Not right now. Not in his face. She turned around and headed back to the uncomfortable chair. Monique watched him carefully as he stripped off the layers of clothes he was wearing.

She saw the bruises along his back. "Oh my God."

"What—?"

"Your side, Army, it's bruised up. So is your back."

Armand shrugged.

Monique knew she wasn't getting an explanation. He lay across the bed again.

She sat there quietly. "Can I ask a question?" she finally said.

"No."

"Why are we here?"

He stared at her.

"Not why we are in Rochester. I mean, why are we at a hotel?"

"Because I haven't slept. We'll leave after I get some sleep."

"How do you know I will be here when you wake up?"

"I don't. But you better remember me, since you seem so brand new. Think on it and decide if it's worth the price you are going to pay once I have to come find you."

Quiet was Monique's response.

A few minutes later, when his snores were very light, Monique interrupted his snooze. "Question."

Armand sighed. "No."

"Can I take a shower?"

Army was quiet for a second. "Yes. And don't say another word to me."

Monique stood up and headed for the bathroom. Just before she closed the door she said, "Okay."

"And you wonder why I don't fuck with you anymore," Armand said, his voice loud enough to seep through the door.

Despite her attempt to not care, that comment struck her heart like an arrow hitting bulls eye. She looked at herself in the mirror, horrified by the sight that looked back at her. She looked worse than she had at Troy's place.

Monique stripped off her clothes and took a long hot shower. Her body was aching. She washed off the stench of the last couple of days, hoping the memories of Troy could go down the drain with the water.

Hoping the latest memories of her and Armand would follow down the drain, too.

Monique leaned her head against the wall of the shower. The warm water felt like a massage, pulsing against her back. She sighed. She wanted to see her father, her sister and her brother. She needed to be with the circle that had surrounded her life. They felt fragmented right now, so disjointed. Until now, Monique thought she had excelled in school and life because she was smart and groomed by Miriam to do so. She had underestimated the security blanket around her, the strength that being a Waters gave her. It manifested in her courage and fearlessness. She could take risks others couldn't, she could soar as high as she wanted, because as a Water she had a safety net when she fell or stumbled.

Even being with Armand had been possible because of who she was, who her family was. The same things that terrified others made her comfortable, because she had Uncle John and Uncle Jimmy to create and break the mold, she had Pete and Ricardo to uphold and protect the legacy. And she had Michelle to constantly pull her back in, remind her of who she really was, and be there for her no matter how awful she behaved.

With the exception of Armand, Monique never needed anyone else, not even a girlfriend. She dealt with her home girls when she wanted to, faded away when she wasn't interested. She had everything she needed because she was a Waters. It had made her exactly who she was. And she needed to return to the circle as soon as possible, to reunite it and keep it strong.

The door to the bathroom opened. She could hear Armand walk in and use the toilet. The never ending sound of him peeing made her aware that they were both naked in the bathroom.

"I'm about to flush." His voice was raspy and tired. It was considerate of him to warn her about the flush, as hard as she had tried to aggravate him, anyone else would have just flushed and let her suffer the change in temperature.

She turned the water off. "Go ahead."

He flushed and stumbled out of the bathroom.

Monique stepped from the tub. She took her time putting lotion on her skin with the thin hotel lotion, conditioned her wet hair and brushed it back into a tight ponytail.

She wrapped the large white towel around her body.

Armand's naked frame covered the entire bed.

Monique dug in the bag Armand had brought from a convenience store and fished out one of his wife beater t-shirts and his boxer briefs. She curled up on the chair and watched Armand sleep.

When he slept, he looked like the man she loved. His face was blank, no anger and no disgust. He was completely relaxed, his thick eyebrows shifting slightly to something in the dream. She remembered how cozy his love had felt, another barrier against the world, like a tight embrace. She remembered all of the nights that she normally tried to forget, laying in the bed while he rubbed her scalp or watching a movie together. Or her massaging away one of his muscle spasms, listening to music and laughing at each other's corny jokes.

Being together had been so easy then. Now that safe place seemed so far away.

Armand was right, they needed rest. Once she was with her family, who knew when they would sleep again. Things were about to get bad. Monique had lived through family wars before, and sleep was a luxury that no one got while fearing for their lives and praying for their family.

She was grateful for her chair. She curled up, watching Armand, until she faded to sleep.

***

Her phone vibrated. It was her study alarm. She glanced around the room. The sun was fading. Armand was still knocked out sleep.

Monique looked at his body. He had two new tattoos. He had turned on his side, and the silhouette of his mother, grandmother and sister, were still there.

She moved closer, noticing that he had another new tattoo on his back. It was a roaring wave, crashing into the sea line like an explosion. Waters. It was a monument to being a Waters.

Armand was part of the circle, too. He was also part of her strength and protection.

She leaned in closer, careful not to touch him, her eyes following the intricate detail of the waters exploding on his back. Suddenly, he shouted in his sleep and the sound was deep and painful. Monique jumped back, expecting him to yell at her for being so close. He didn't wake up. She watched as he coughed and clenched his fists. Monique had forgotten about his nightmares, about how vivid they were, so much so that he would start fighting and she would have to jump out of the bed to keep from being pummeled. She had been accidentally elbowed more than once.

Monique started to return to her chair when he shouted again, this time screaming out in agony. The sound made her spin around and look at him, wondering what he was reliving that was so awful. Tears ran down his face. Armand didn't cry awake. In fact, his eyes were always dry. But, in his sleep, he flinched, shouted and cried. Crying meant the nightmare was an emotional one, not a survival one. He wouldn't throw blows tonight. But he would shake, clench, moan and be in turmoil. The fighting ones were better for her to endure, at least they didn't show how much pain Armand was really in, deep down within him.

The tears on his cheeks made her feel so sad. Whatever he was dreaming, Monique didn't want to ever experience it. Whatever made his eyebrows twitch, his lips curl and his jaw clench was something she knew she couldn't handle.

He flinched again, clenching his fist, and shouted, "No…please, no!"

Monique grabbed him, laying down next to him and wrapping her arms around him. "It's okay, Army. I'm here. It's okay."

After a couple of minutes he relaxed. She held on to him, rubbing his back.

Monique couldn't help herself. She kissed his cheek, the taste of his tears on her lips. His eyes opened and met hers, but they were blank. His mind wasn't there, it was still in the dream world. She wiped his face and kissed his forehead. She rubbed his arm. "It's okay, Army. I'm here," she repeated.

He focused on her. She could tell when reality came back to him and his black pupils actually registered her. For an awful second,

Monique thought that he was going to send her back to the chair. He flinched. A second later, he relaxed. As her lips brushed his cheek, he sighed. He shook his head, as if he wanted to stop himself, but then he let go. She felt his entire body relax against her. Armand lifted her up, slowly and gently, and wrapped her in his arms, holding her tight. He tucked her body into his, pressed his lips against her neck, and fell back to sleep.

This time his breathing was steady, no ragged, jarring snores. This time his eyebrows were relaxed instead of furrowed, his jaw was slack instead of gritted.

This time his sleep was peaceful.

Monique lay awake as long as she could and swore to remember each and every second of feeling his heartbeat against hers. Being with Armand was more than a notion, it was a privilege. When someone so guarded and protected actually allowed a glimpse through the window to their soul, it was an honor. Monique had taken that lightly, so used to being around warriors with steel cages walled around their emotions. But, she realized in the split second when he looked at her and let her kiss him, let her rub him, and allowed himself to yield to her, that loving him was a gift that she would never again undervalue.

AVAILABLE NOW FROM ~KAI~

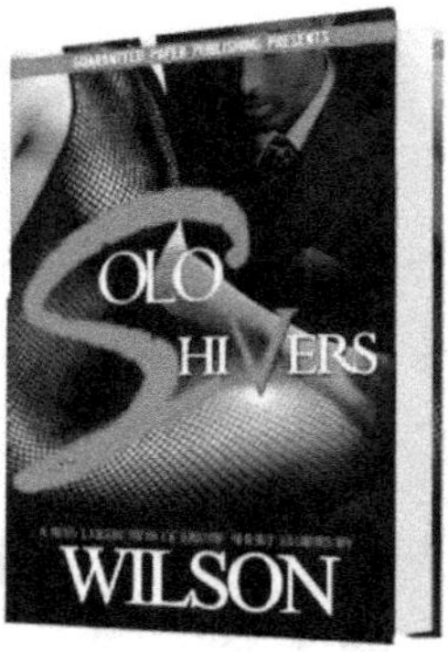

It's the middle of the night. Again. Zuri is laying next to her man. Unsatisfied. Again. While his snores bounce around the room, her mind plays out scenes from her last lover, the one who made her scream with a single touch, a perfectly placed kiss. Zuri doesn't want to make the phone call-cheating isn't an option. Which leaves her with only her imagination and creativity to fill the void...

But every thing done in the dark, hidden by his closed eyes and deep snores, will certainly come to light. Is satisfaction worth the risk?

When Rena hooked up with Omar, she thought she had the upper hand. He was a bad boy, but she was a little older and a lot wiser. Until his touch turned into her addiction. She simply can't say no. When Omar's sexual challenges take her on a dark and twisted path, Rena does everything in her power to resist him. But who can say no to a bad boy with that good grind?

www.ingramcontent.com/pod-product-compliance
Lightning Source LLC
Chambersburg PA
CBHW071202250626
47159CB00001B/173
9780979177538